CREEP SHADOW CREEP

CREEP SHADOW CREEP

Shadows which whisper, seductive shadows, shadows weaving a shroud; shadows with nothing visible to cast them . . .

Could shadows have driven four men to their deaths—amid the skyscrapers and neon-lights of modern New York? And what part did the woman play, the beautiful Dahut de Keradel? According to ancient legend, there had once been another Dahut, a mistress of shadows in the drowned city of Ys. She rode by the sea on a black horse with the shadow-pack behind her.

The modern Dahut had a father, who owned a house behind high walls on a lonely island. Nobody knew what went on behind those walls, but it was rumoured that strange hounds hunted there at night.

Three men determine to challenge de Keradel and his daughter, because they know that witchcraft is real. They know about Madame Mandalip, the doll-maker (whose terrifying story was told in *Burn Witch Burn*), and that she had a lover whose powers matched or exceeded her own. They suspect that de Keradel was that lover, but even they cannot guess the monstrous power which he is trying to invoke— the "Gatherer" who comes at the moment of sacrifice amid the standing stones.

Dr. Alan Caranac has a special part to play in that ritual, for he remembers—or thinks he remembers— Ys and Dahut and the fate that overcame them. So now he must go alone to de Keradel's island and destroy the evil if he can.

Creep Shadow Creep is one of the weirdest and most compelling stories of modern witchcraft ever written.

*   *   *

Also available in this edition:
A. Merritt's *Burn Witch Burn*

CREEP SHADOW CREEP

by

A. Merritt

TOM STACEY

First published in Great Britain 1935

This edition published 1972 by
Tom Stacey Reprints Ltd
28–29 Maiden Lane, London WC2E 7JP
England

ISBN 0 85468 225 2

Printed in Great Britain by
C. Tinling & Co. Ltd, Prescot and London

CONTENTS

A*

CHAPTER I

FOUR SUICIDES

I UNPACKED my bags at the Explorers' Club gloomily enough. The singularly unpleasant depression with which I had awakened in my berth the night before had refused to be shaken off. It was like the echo of some nightmare whose details I had forgotten, but which still lurked just over the threshold of consciousness.

Joined to it was another irritation. Naturally, I had not expected any mayor's committee to welcome me home. But that neither Bennett nor Ralston had met me began to assume the aspect of a major tragedy of neglect. I had written to both before sailing, and I had looked for one to be on the dock to meet me.

They were the closest friends I had, and the queer current of hostility between them had often amused me. They thoroughly liked, yet as thoroughly disapproved of, each other. I had the idea that underneath they were closer to each other than to me; that they might have been Damon and Pythias if each hadn't so disliked the other's attitude towards life; and maybe were Damon and Pythias despite it.

Old Aesop formulated their discordance centuries ago in his fable of the Ant and the Cricket. Bill Bennett was the Ant. The serious-minded, hard-working son of

Dr. Lionel Bennett, until recently one of the modern, civilized world's five outstanding experts upon brain pathology. I make the distinction of modern and civilized because I have had proof that what we are pleased to call the uncivilized world has many more such experts; and I have good reason to believe that the ancient world had others much farther advanced than those of the modern world, civilized or uncivilized.

Bennett, the elder, had been one of the few specialists whose mind turned upon his work rather than his bank account. Distinguished but poor. Bennett, the younger, was about thirty-five, my own age. I knew that his father had rested heavily upon him. I suspected that along some lines, and especially in the realm of the sub-conscious, the son had outstripped the sire; his mind more flexible, more open. He had written me a year ago that his father had died, and that he had associated himself with Dr. Austin Lowell, taking the place of Dr. David Braile, who had been killed by a falling chandelier in Dr. Lowell's private hospital.[1]

Ralston was the Cricket. He was heir to a fortune so solid that even the teeth of the depression could only scratch it. Very much the traditional rich man's son of the better sort, but seeing no honour, use, joy or any other virtue in labour. Happy-go-lucky, clever, generous—but decidedly a first-class idler.

I was the compromise—the bridge on which they could meet. I had my medical degree, but also I had enough money to save me from the grind of practice. Enough to allow me to do as I pleased—which was drifting round the world on ethnological research.

[1] See *Burn Witch Burn*.

Especially in those fields which my medical and allied scientific brethren call superstition—native sorceries, witchcraft, voodoo and the like. In that research I was as earnest as Bill in his. And he knew it.

Dick, on the other hand, attributed my wanderings to an itching foot inherited from one of my old Breton forebears, a pirate who had sailed out of St. Malo and carved himself a gory reputation in the New World, and ultimately was hanged for it. The peculiar bent of my mind he likewise attributed to the fact that two of my ancestors had been burned as witches in Brittany.

I was perfectly understandable to him.

Bill's industry was not so understandable.

I reflected, morosely, that even if I had been away for three years it was too short a time to be forgotten. I managed to shake off my gloom and to laugh at myself. After all, they might not have received my letters; or they might have had engagements they couldn't break.

There was an afternoon paper on the bed. I noticed that it was of the day before. My eye fell upon some headlines. They ran:

$5,000,000 COPPER HEIR
KILLS HIMSELF

RICHARD J. RALSTON, Jr., PUTS
BULLET THROUGH HEAD

No Reason Known for Act—Fourth New York Man
of Wealth to Take His Life Without
Apparent Cause in Last Three
Months—Police Hint
Suicide Club

3

I read the story:

'Richard J. Ralston, Jr., who inherited some $5,000,000 when his father, rich mine owner, died two years ago, was found dead in his bed this morning in his apartments at 35,642 Park Avenue. He had shot himself through the head, dying instantly. The pistol with which he had killed himself was lying on the floor where it had fallen from his hand. The Detective Bureau identified the finger-marks on it as his own.

'Discovery was made by his butler, John Simpson, who said that he had gone into the room about eight o'clock, following his usual custom. From the condition of the body, Dr. Peabody, of the coroner's office, estimated that Ralston must have shot himself about three o'clock, or approximately five hours before Simpson found him.'

Three o'clock? I felt a little prickling along my spine. Allowing for the difference between ship time and New York time, that was precisely when I had awakened with that strange depression. I read on:

'If Simpson's story is true—and the police see no reason to doubt it—the suicide could not have been premeditated and must have been the result of some sudden overmastering impulse. This seems to be further indicated by the discovery of a letter Ralston had started to write, and torn up without finishing. The scraps of it were found under a desk in the bedroom where he had tossed them. The letter read:

'DEAR BILL,—Sorry I couldn't stay any longer. I wish you would think of the matter as objective and not subjective, no matter how incredible such a thing may seem. If Alan were only here. He knows more——'

4

'At this point Ralston had evidently changed his mind and torn up the letter. The police would like to know who "Alan" is and have him explain what it is that he "knows more" about. They also hope that the "Bill" to whom it was to have been sent will identify himself. There is not the slightest doubt as to the case being one of suicide, but it is possible that whatever it was that was "objective and not subjective, no matter how incredible" may throw some light on the motive.

'At present absolutely no reason appears to exist to explain why Mr. Ralston should have taken his life. His attorneys, the well-known firm of Winston, Smith & White, have assured the police that his estate is in perfect order, and that there were no "complications" in their client's life. It is a fact that, unlike so many sons of rich men, no scandal has ever been attached to Ralston's name.

'This is the fourth suicide within three months of men of wealth of approximately Ralston's age, and of comparatively the same habits of life. Indeed, in each of the four cases the circumstances are so similar that the police are seriously contemplating the possibility of a suicide club.

'The first of the four deaths occurred on July 15, when John Marston, internationally known polo-player, shot himself through the head in his bedroom in his country house at Locust Valley, Long Island. No cause for his suicide has ever come to light. Like Ralston, he was unmarried. On August 6, the body of Walter St. Clair Calhoun was found in his roadster near Riverhead, Long Island. Calhoun had driven his car off the main road, here heavily shaded by trees, into the middle of an open field. There he had put a bullet through his brains. No one ever discovered why. He had been divorced for three years. On August 21, Richard

Stanton, millionaire yachtsman and globe-trotter, shot himself through the head while on the deck of his ocean-going yacht *Trinculo*. This happened the night before he was about to set out on a cruise to South America.'

I read on and on . . . the speculations as to the suicide pact, supposedly entered into because of boredom and morbid thrill-hunger . . . the histories of Marston, Calhoun and Stanton . . . Dick's obituary.

I read, only half understanding what it was I read.

I kept thinking that it couldn't be true.

There was no reason why Dick should kill himself. In all the world there was no man less likely to kill himself. The theory of the suicide club was absurdly fantastic; at least so far as he was concerned. I was the 'Alan' of the letter, of course. And Bennett was the 'Bill'. But what was it I knew that had made Dick wish I had been with him?

The telephone buzzed, and the operator said: 'Dr. Bennett to see you.'

I said: 'Send him up.'

Bill came in. He was white and drawn, and more like a man still in the midst of a stiff ordeal than one who has passed through it. His eyes held a puzzled horror, as though he were looking less at me than within his mind at whatever was the source of that horror. He held a hand out, absently, and all he said was:

'I'm glad you're back, Alan.'

I had the newspaper in my other hand. He took it and looked at the date. He said:

'Yesterday's. Well, it's all there. All that the police know, anyway.' He said it rather oddly.

I asked: 'Do you mean you know something that the police don't?'

He answered, evasively I thought: 'Oh, they've got their facts all straight. Dick put the bullet through his brain. They're right in linking up those other three deaths——'

I repeated: 'What do you know that the police don't know, Bill?'

He said: 'That Dick was murdered!'

I looked at him, bewildered.

'But if he put the bullet through his own brain——'

He said: 'Dick killed himself. That's certain. I *know* just as certainly that he was murdered.'

He sat down upon the bed.

'I need a drink.'

I brought out the bottle of Scotch the Club steward had thoughtfully placed in my room for home-coming welcome. He poured himself a stiff one. He said:

'I'm glad you're back! We've got a tough job ahead of us.'

I asked: 'Finding Dick's murderer?'

He answered: 'More than that. To stop more murders.'

I poured him and myself another drink. I said: 'Stop beating about the bush. Tell me what it's all about.'

He looked at me, thoughtfully.

'Not yet.'

He put down his glass.

'Suppose you had discovered a new bug, an unknown germ—or thought you had. And had studied it and noted its peculiarities. Suppose you wanted some one to check up. What would you do—give him all your

7

supposed observations first, and then ask him to look into the microscope to verify them? Or simply give him an outline, and tell him to look into the microscope and find out for himself? '

' Outline—and find out for himself, of course.'

' Exactly. Well, maybe I've found such a new bug— or a very old one, although it has nothing whatever to do with germs. I'm not going to tell you any more about it until I put your eye to the microscope. I want your opinion uncoloured by mine. Send out for a late paper, will you? '

I called the office and told them to get me the latest editions. When they came, Bill took one. He glanced over the first page, then turned the sheets until he came to what he was looking for. He read it, and nodded, and passed the paper to me.

' Dick's reduced from page one to page five,' he said. ' Read the first few paragraphs—all the rest is rehash and idle conjecture. Very idle.'

I read:

' Dr. William Bennett, the eminent brain specialist and associate of Dr. Austin Lowell, the distinguished psychiatrist, visited Police Headquarters this morning and identified himself as the " Bill " of the unfinished letter found in the bedroom of Richard J. Ralston, Jr., after the latter's suicide yesterday morning.

' Dr. Bennett said that undoubtedly the letter had been meant for him, that Mr. Ralston had been one of his oldest friends and had recently consulted him for what he might describe roughly as insomnia and bad dreams. Mr. Ralston had, in fact, been his guest at dinner the night before. He had wanted Mr. Ralston to spend the night with him, but after consenting, he had changed his mind and gone home to sleep. That was what he had referred to in the opening sentence of his letter. Professional etiquette prevented Dr. Bennett from going into further description of Mr. Ralston's symptoms. Asked whether the mental condition of Mr. Ralston might explain why he had killed himself, Dr. Bennett guardedly replied that suicide was always the result of some mental condition.'

In spite of my perplexity and sorrow, I couldn't help smiling at that.

'The "Alan" referred to in the letter, Dr. Bennett said, is Dr. Alan Caranac, who was also an old friend of Mr. Ralston, and who is due in New York to-day on the *Augustus* after three years in Northern Africa. Dr. Caranac is well known in scientific circles for his ethnological researches. Dr. Bennett said that Mr. Ralston had thought that some of his symptoms might be explained by Dr. Caranac because of the latter's study of certain obscure mental aberrations among primitive peoples."

'Now for the kicker,' said Bill, and pointed to the next paragraph.

'Dr. Bennett talked freely with the reporters after his statement to the police, but could add no essential facts beyond those he had given them. He did say that Mr. Ralston had withdrawn large sums in cash from his accounts during the two weeks before his death, and that there was no evidence of what had become of them. He seemed immediately to regret that he had given this information, saying that the circumstance could have no bearing upon Mr. Ralston's suicide. He reluctantly admitted, however, that the sum might be well over $100,000, and that the police were investigating.'

9

I said: 'That looks like blackmail—if it's true.'

He said: 'I haven't the slightest proof that it is true. But it's what I told the police and the reporters.'

He read the paragraph over and got up.

'The reporters will soon be here, Alan,' he said. 'And the police. I'm going. You haven't seen me. You haven't the slightest idea of what it's all about. You haven't heard from Ralston for a year. Tell them after you get in touch with me you may have something more to say. But now—you don't know anything. And that's true—you don't. That's your story, and you stick to it.'

He walked to the door.

I said: 'Wait a minute, Bill. What's the idea behind that bunch of words I've just read?'

'It's a nicely baited hook.'

I said: 'What do you expect to hook?'

He said: 'Dick's murderer.'

He turned at the door.

'And something else that's right down your alley.'

'What's that?' I asked.

'A witch,' he said.

He shut the door behind him.

CHAPTER II

THE DEMOISELLE DAHUT

NOT long after Bill had gone, a man from the Detective Bureau visited me. It was evident that he regarded the call as a waste of time, just a part of the routine. His questions were perfunctory, nor did he ask me if I had seen Bennett. I produced the Scotch and he mellowed. He said:

'Hell, if it ain't one thing it's another. If you ain't got money you wear yourself out tryin' to get it. If you got it, then somebody's tryin' all the time to rob you. Or else you go nuts like this poor guy, and then what good is your money? This Ralston wasn't so bad at that, I hear.'

I agreed. He took another drink and left.

Three reporters came; one from the *City News* and the others from afternoon papers. They asked few questions about Dick, but showed flattering interest in my travels. I was so relieved that I sent for a second bottle of Scotch and told them a few stories about the mirror magic of the Riff women—who believe that at certain times and under certain conditions they can catch the reflections of those they love or hate in their mirrors, and have power thereafter over their souls.

The *City News* man said that if he could get the Riff women to teach him that trick, he could lift all the mirror-makers in America out of the depression and get rich doing it. The other two morosely agreed that they knew some editors whose reflections they'd like to catch. I laughed and said it would be easier to bring over a good old-fashioned Bulgarian mason or two. Then all they need do was to get the mason a job, decoy the editor to the place where he was working, and have the mason measure his shadow with a string. After that, the mason would put the string in a box and build the box into the wall. In forty days the editor would be dead and his soul be sitting in the box beside the string.

One of the afternoon men glumly said that forty days would be too long to wait for those he had in mind. The other asked, with disarming *naïveté*, whether I believed such a thing possible. I answered that if a man were strongly enough convinced he would die on a certain day, he would die on that day. Not because his shadow had been measured and the string buried, but because he believed that this was going to kill him. It was purely a matter of suggestion—of auto-hypnosis. Like the praying to death practised by the *kahunas*, the warlocks, of the South Seas, of the results of which there was no doubt whatever. Always providing, of course, that the victim knew the *kahuna* was praying for his death—and also knew the exact time his death was to occur.

I ought to have known better. The morning papers carried only a few lines to the effect that I had talked to the police and had been unable to throw any light on the Ralston suicide. But the early editions of the naïve reporter's paper featured a special article.

12

WANT TO GET RID OF YOUR ENEMIES?
GET A RIFF GAL'S MAGIC MIRROR—
OR BRING IN A BULGARIAN MASON

DR. ALAN CARANAC, NOTED EXPLORER, TELLS HOW TO
SEPARATE YOURSELF SAFELY FROM THOSE YOU
DON'T WANT AROUND—BUT THE CATCH
IS THAT FIRST YOU HAVE TO MAKE
'EM BELIEVE YOU CAN DO IT

It was a good story, even if it did make me swear in spots. After all, I'd brought it on myself.

The 'phone rang, and Bill was on the line. He asked: ' What put it in your head to talk to that reporter about shadows? '

He sounded jumpy.

I said, surprised: 'Nothing. Why shouldn't I have talked to him about shadows? '

' Nothing happened to direct your mind to that subject? Nobody suggested it? '

' You're getting curiouser and curiouser, as Alice puts it. But no, Bill, I brought the matter up all by myself. And no shadow fell upon me whispering in my ear—— '

He interrupted, harshly: 'Don't talk like that! '

And now I was truly surprised, for there was panic in Bill's voice, and that wasn't like him at all.

' There really wasn't any reason. It just happened,' I repeated. 'What's it all about, Bill? '

' Never mind now.' He swiftly changed the subject. ' Dick's funeral is to-morrow. I'll see you there.'

Now the one thing I won't be coerced or persuaded into doing is to go to the funeral of a friend. Unless

13

there are interesting and unfamiliar rites connected with it, it's senseless. There lies a piece of cold meat for the worms, grotesquely embellished by the undertaker's cosmetic arts. Sunken eyes that never more will dwell upon the beauty of the clouds, the sea, the forest. Ears shut for ever, and all the memories of life rotting away within the decaying brain. Painted and powdered symbol of life's futility. I want to remember friends as they were—alive, alert, capable, eager. The coffin picture superimposes itself, and I lose my friends. The animals order things much better, to my way of thinking. They hide themselves and die.

I said: 'You'll not see *me* there.' To shut off any discussion, I asked: 'Had any nibble at your witch bait?'

'Yes and no. Not the real strike I'm hoping for, but attention from unexpected quarters. Dick's lawyers called me up after I'd left you and asked what he had told me about those cash withdrawals. They said they'd been trying to find out what he had done with the money, but couldn't. They wouldn't believe me, of course, when I said I knew absolutely nothing; that I had only vague suspicions and had tried a shot in the dark. I don't blame them. Stanton's executor called me up this morning to ask the same thing. Said Stanton had drawn substantial amounts of cash just before he died, and they hadn't been able to trace them.'

'That's queer. How about Calhoun and Marston? If they did the same, it smells damned fishy.'

'I'm trying to find out,' he said. 'Good-bye——'

'Wait a minute, Bill,' I said. 'I'm a good waiter, and all of that. But I'm getting mighty curious. When

14

do I see you, and what do you want me to do in the meantime?'

'Sit tight, until I can lay the cards before you. I'll tell you one thing, though. That interview of yours is another hook—and I'm not sure it isn't baited even better than mine.'

That was on Tuesday.

Obviously I was puzzled and curious to a degree. So much so that if it had been anybody but Bill who had sat me down in my little corner chair and told me to be quiet, I would have been exceedingly angry. But Bill knew what he was about—I was sure of that. So I stayed put.

On Wednesday, Dick was buried. I went over my notes and started the first chapter of my book on Moroccan sorceries. Thursday night, Bill called up.

'There's a small dinner-party at Dr. Lowell's to-morrow night,' he said. 'A Dr. de Keradel and his daughter. I want you to come. I'll promise you'll be interested.'

De Keradel? The name was familiar.

'Who is he?' I asked.

'Rene de Keradel, the French psychiatrist. You must have read some of his——'

'Yes, of course,' I interrupted. 'He took up Charcot's hypnotic experiments at the Salpêtrière, didn't he? Carried them on from the point where Charcot had stopped. Left the Salpêtrière under a cloud some years ago. Subjects died, or he was too unorthodox in his conclusions, or something?'

'That's the chap.'

I said: 'I'll be there. I'd like to meet him.'

'Good,' said Bill. 'Dinner's at seven-thirty. Wear your dinner jacket. And come an hour ahead of time. There's a girl who wants to talk to you before the company comes, as we used to say.'

'A girl?' I asked, astonished.

'Helen,' said Bill with a chuckle. 'And don't you disappoint her. You're her hero.'

He hung up.

Helen was Bill's sister. About ten years younger than I. I hadn't seen her for fifteen years. An impish sort of kid, I recalled. Eyes sort of slanting and yellow brown. Hair a red torch. Gawky when I saw her last and inclined to be fat. Used to follow me round when I was visiting Bill during college vacations, and sit and stare at me without speaking until it made me so nervous I stuttered. Never could tell whether it was silent adoration or sheer devilment. That was when she was about twelve. Nor could I forget how she had led me, apparently innocently, to sit on a subterranean nest of hornets; nor the time when, going to bed, I had found it shared by a family of garter snakes. The first might have been an accident, although I had my doubts; but the second wasn't. I had dumped the snakes out of the window and never by word, look or gesture referred to them, having my reward in the child's bafflement at my reticence, and avid but necessarily mute curiosity. I knew she had gone through college, and had been studying art in Florence. I wondered what she had grown to be.

I read over some of de Keradel's papers at the Academy of Medicine Library next day. He was a queer bird without doubt, with some extraordinarily arresting theories. I didn't wonder that the Salpêtrière had eased him out. Stripped of their scientific verbiage, the framework of his main idea was startlingly like that expounded to me by the Many-Times-Born Abbot of the Lamasery at Gyang-tse, in Tibet. A holy man and an accomplished wonder-worker, a seeker of knowledge along strange paths; what would be loosely called by the superstitious—a sorcerer. Also by a Greek priest near Delphi, whose Christian cloak covered a pure case of pagan atavism. He offered to demonstrate his hypothesis, and did. He nearly convinced me. Indeed, visualizing again what he had made me see, I was not sure that he hadn't convinced me.

I began to feel a strong interest in Dr. de Keradel. The name was Breton, like my own, and as unusual. Another recollection flitted through my mind. There was a reference to the de Keradels in the chronicles of the de Carnacs, as we were once named. I looked it up. There had been no love lost between the two families, to put it mildly. Altogether, what I read blew my desire to meet Dr. de Keradel up to fever point.

I was half an hour late getting to Dr. Lowell's. The butler showed me into the library. A girl got up from a big chair and came towards me with hand outstretched.

'Hello, Alan,' she said.

I blinked at her. She wasn't so tall, but her body had all the lovely contours the sculptors of Athens' Golden Age gave their dancing girls. The dress of filmy black she wore hid none of them. Her hair was burnished copper and helmeted her small head. The heavy chignon at the nape of her neck showed she had resisted the bob. Her eyes were golden amber, and tilted delicately.

Her nose was small and straight and her chin rounded. Her skin was not the creamy white that so often goes with red heads, but a delicate golden. It was a head and face that might have served as the model for one of Alexander's finest golden coins. Faintly archaic, touched with the antique beauty. I blinked again. I blurted:

'You're never—Helen!'

Her eyes sparkled, the impishness that my experience with the hornets had set indelibly in my memory danced over her face. She took my hands, and swayed close to me; she sighed.

'The same, Alan! The same! And you—oh, let me look at you! Yes, still the hero of my girlhood! The same keen, dark face—like—like—I used to call you Lancelot of the Lake, Alan—to myself, of course. The same lithe, tall and slender body—I used to call you the Black Panther, too, Alan. And do you remember how like a panther you leaped when the hornets stung you——'

She bent her head, her rounded shoulders shaking.

I said: 'You little devil! I always knew you did that deliberately.'

She said, muffled: 'I'm not laughing, Alan. I'm sobbing.'

She looked up at me, and her eyes were indeed wet, but not, I was sure, with any tears of regret. She said:

'Alan, for long, long years I've waited to know something. Waited to hear you tell me something. Not to tell me that you love me, darling. No, no! I always knew that you were going to do that, sooner or later. This is something else——'

I was laughing, but I had a queer, mixed feeling too.

18

I said: 'I'll tell you anything. Even that I love you—and maybe mean it.'

She said: '*Did* you find those snakes in your bed? Or did they crawl out before you got in?'

I said again: 'You little devil!'

She said: 'But were they *there*?'

'Yes, they were.'

She sighed contentedly.

'Well, there's one complex gone for ever. Now I know! You were so damned superior at times I just couldn't help it.'

She held her face up to me.

'Since you're going to love me, Alan, you might as well kiss me.'

I kissed her, properly. She might have been fooling with me about having been her girlhood's hero, but there was no fooling about my kiss—nor the way she responded to it. She shivered and laid her head on my shoulder. She said, dreamily:

'And there's another complex gone. Where am I going to stop?'

Somebody coughed at the doorway. Somebody else murmured, apologetically: 'Ah, but we intrude.'

Helen dropped her arms from round my neck, and we turned. In a way, I realized that the butler and another man were standing at the door. But all I could focus my eyes upon was the girl—or woman.

You know how it is when you're riding in the subway, or at the theatre, or at a race track and suddenly one face, for some reason or no reason, thrusts itself out from the crowd, and it's as though your mental spotlight was turned on it and every other face gets misty and recedes into the background. That often happens to me. Something in the face that stirs some old forgotten memory, no doubt. Or stirs the memory of our ancestors whose ghosts are always peering through our eyes. Seeing this girl was like that, only far more so. I couldn't see anything else—not even Helen.

She had the bluest eyes I'd ever beheld. They were a curious deep violet, and big and unusually wide apart, with long curling black lashes and slimly pencilled black eyebrows that almost met above her high-arched, delicately modelled nose. You felt, rather than saw, the colour of her eyes. Her forehead was broad, but whether it was low I could not tell, for it was coifed with braids of palest gold, and there were little ends of hair that curled up all over her head, and they were so fine and silken that the light in the hall shining through them made a queer silver-gilt aureole round her head. Her mouth was a bit large, but beautifully formed and daintily sensuous. Her skin was a miracle, white, but vital—as though moon fires shone behind it.

She was tall almost as I, exquisitely curved, deep bosomed. Her breasts echoed the betrayal of her lips. Her head and face and shoulders came like a lily out of the calyx of a shimmering sea-green gown.

She was exquisite—but I had swift understanding that there was nothing heavenly about the blue of her eyes. And nothing saintly about the aureole round her head.

She was perfection—and I felt a swift hatred against her, understanding, as the pulse of it passed, how one could slash a painting that was a masterpiece of beauty, or take a hammer and destroy a statue that was another such masterpiece—if it evoked such hatred as that which I, for that fleeting moment, felt.

Then I thought: *Do I hate you—or do I fear you?* It was all, mind you, in a breath.

Helen was moving past me, hand outstretched. There was no confusion about Helen. Our embrace that had been interrupted might have been a simple handshake. She said, smiling and gracious:

'I am Helen Bennett. Dr. Lowell asked me to receive you. You are Dr. de Keradel, aren't you?'

I looked at the man who was bending over her hand, kissing it. He straightened, and I felt a queer shock of bewilderment. Bill had said I was to meet Dr. de Keradel and his daughter. But this man looked no older than the girl—if she was his daughter. True, the silver in the gold of his hair was a little paler; true, the blue of his eyes had not the violet-purple of hers. . . .

I thought: *But neither of them has any age!* And on top of that I thought: *What the hell's the matter with me anyway?*

The man said: 'I am Dr. de Keradel. And this is my daughter.'

The girl—or woman—seemed now to be regarding both Helen and me with faint amusement. Dr. de Keradel said with curious precision:

'The Demoiselle Dahut de Keradel—' he hesitated, then finished, 'd'Ys.'

Helen said: 'And this is Dr. Alan Caranac.'

The name of Dahut d'Ys fingered half-forgotten chords of memory.

As Helen named me, I saw the violet eyes dilate,

become enormous, the straight brows contract until they met above the nose in a slender bar. I felt the glance of her eyes strike and encompass me. She seemed to be seeing me for the first time. And in her eyes was something threatening—possessive. Her body tensed. She said, as though to herself:

'Alain de Carnac. . . .'

She glanced from me to Helen. There was calculation in that glance, appraisal. Contemptuous indifference, too—if I read it aright. A queen might so have looked upon some serving wench who had dared to lift eyes to her lover.

Whether I read the glance aright or not, Helen evidently got something of the same thought. She turned to me and said sweetly:

'Darling, I'm ashamed of you. Wake up!'

With the side of her little high-heeled slipper she gave me a surreptitious and vigorous kick on the shin.

Just then Bill came in, and with him a dignified, white-haired gentleman I knew must be Dr. Lowell.

I don't know when I had ever been so glad to see Bill.

CHAPTER III

THEORIES OF DR. DE KERADEL

I GAVE Bill the old fraternity high-sign of distress, and after introductions he bore me away, leaving the Demoiselle Dahut to Helen, and de Keradel with Dr. Lowell. I felt an urgent need for a drink, and said so. Bill passed me the brandy and soda without comment. I drank a stiff brandy neat.

Helen had bowled me off my feet, but that had been a pleasant upset, nothing that called for any alcoholic lever to right me. The Demoiselle Dahut had been an entirely different matter. She was damned disconcerting. It occurred to me that if you compared yourself to a ship bowling along under full sail, through charted seas, with your mind as a capable navigator, Helen was a squall that fitted normally into the picture—but the Demoiselle was a blow from a new quarter entirely, heading the ship into totally strange waters. What you knew of navigation wouldn't help you a bit.

I said: 'Helen could blow you into Port o' Paradise but the other could blow you into Port o' Hell.'

Bill didn't say anything, only watched me. I poured out a second brandy. Bill said, mildly:

'There'll be cocktails and wine at dinner.'

I said: 'Fine,' and drank the brandy.

I thought: *It's not her infernal beauty that's got me going. But why the hell did I hate her so when I first saw her?*

I didn't hate her now. All I felt was a burning curiosity. But why did I have that vague sense of having long known her? And that not so vague idea that she knew me better than I did her? I muttered:

'She makes you think of the sea, at that.'

Bill said: 'Who?'

I said: 'The Demoiselle d'Ys.'

He stepped back; he said, as though something was strangling him: 'Who's the Demoiselle d'Ys?'

I looked at him suspiciously. I said: 'Don't you know the names of your guests? That girl down there—the Demoiselle Dahut de Keradel d'Ys?'

Bill said, rather stupidly: 'No, I didn't know that. All Lowell introduced her by was the de Keradel part of it.'

After a minute, he said: 'Probably another drink won't hurt you. I'll join you.'

We drank.

He said casually: 'Never met them till to-night. De Keradel called on Lowell yesterday morning—as one eminent psychiatrist upon another. Lowell was interested, and invited him and his daughter to dinner. The old boy is fond of Helen, and ever since she came back to town she's been hostess at his parties. She's very fond of him, too.'

He drank his brandy and set down the glass. He said, still casually: 'I understand de Keradel has been here for a year or more. Apparently, though, he never got around to visiting us until those interviews of mine and yours appeared.'

I jumped as the implication of that struck me. I said: 'You mean——'

24

'I don't mean anything. I simply point out the coincidence.'

'But if they had anything to do with Dick's death, why would they risk coming here?'

'To find out how much we know—if anything.' He hesitated. 'It may mean nothing. But—it's precisely the sort of thing I thought might happen when I baited my hook. And de Keradel and his daughter don't exactly disqualify as the sort of fish I expected to catch —and especially now I know about the d'Ys part. Yes— especially.'

He came round the table and put his hands on my shoulders.

'Alan, what I'm thinking wouldn't seem as insane to you, maybe, as it does to me. It's not Alice in Wonderland, but Alice in Devil-land. I want you to-night to say anything that comes into your head. Just that. Don't be held back by politeness, or courtesy, or conventions or anything else. If what you want to say is insulting—let it be so. Don't bother about what Helen may think. Forget Lowell. Say whatever comes into your mind. If de Keradel makes any assertions with which you don't agree, don't listen politely—challenge him. If it makes him lose his temper, all the better. Be just drunk enough to slip out of any inhibitions of courtesy. You talk. I listen. Do you get it?'

I laughed and said: '*In vino veritas*. But your idea is to make my *vino* bring out the *veritas* in the other party. Sound psychology. All right, Bill, I'll take another small one.'

He said: 'You know your limit. But watch your step.'

We went down to dinner. I was feeling interested,

amused and devil-may-care. The image I had of the Demoiselle was simplified to a mist of silver-gold hair over two splotches of purple-blue in a white face. On the other hand, Helen's was still the sharp-cut, antique coin. We sat down at table. Dr. Lowell was at the head, at his left de Keradel, and at his right the Demoiselle Dahut. Helen sat beside de Keradel and I beside the Demoiselle. Bill sat between me and Helen. It was a nicely arranged table, with tall candles instead of electric lights. The butler brought cocktails and they were excellent. I lifted mine to Helen and said:

'You are a lovely antique coin, Helen. Alexander the Great minted you. Some day I will put you in my pocket.'

Dr. Lowell looked a bit startled. But Helen clinked glasses and murmured:

'You will never lose me, will you, darling?'

I said: 'No, sweetheart, nor will I give you away, nor let anybody steal you, my lovely antique coin.'

There was the pressure of a soft shoulder against me. I looked away from Helen and straight into the eyes of the Demoiselle. They weren't just purple-blue splotches now. They were the damnedest eyes—big, and clear as a tropic shoal, and little orchid sparks darted through them like the play of the sun through a tropic shoal when you turn over and look up through the clear water.

I said: 'Demoiselle Dahut—why do you make me think of the sea? I have seen the Mediterranean the exact colour of your eyes. And the crests of the waves were as white as your skin. And there was seaweed like your hair. Your fragrance is the fragrance of the sea, and you walk like a wave——'

Helen drawled: 'How poetic you are, darling. Perhaps you'd better eat your soup before you take another cocktail.'

I said: 'Sweetheart, you are my antique coin. But you are not yet in my pocket. Nor am I in yours. I will have another cocktail before I eat my soup.'

She flushed at that. I felt badly about saying it. But I caught a glance from Bill that heartened me. And the Demoiselle's eyes would have repaid me for any remorse—if I hadn't just then felt stir that inexplicable hot hatred, and knew quite definitely now that fear did lurk within it. She laid her hand lightly on mine. It had a curious tingling warmth. At the touch, the strange repulsion vanished. I realized her beauty with an almost painful acuteness. She said:

'You love—the old things. It is because you are of the ancient blood—the blood of Armorica. Do you remember——'

My cocktail went splashing to the floor. Bill said: 'Oh, I beg your pardon, Alan. That was awkward of me. Briggs, bring Dr. Caranac another.'

I said: 'That's all right, Bill.'

I hoped I said it easily, because deep in me was anger, wondering how long it had been between that 'remember' of the Demoiselle's and the overturning of my glass. When she had said it, the tingling warmth of her hand had seemed to concentrate itself into a point of fire, a spark that shot up my arm into my brain. Instead of the pleasant candle-lighted room, I saw a vast plain covered with huge stones arranged in ordered aisles all marching to a central circle of monoliths within which was a gigantic cairn. I knew it to be Carnac, that place

27

of mystery of the Druids and before them of a forgotten people, from which my family had derived its name, changed only by the addition of a syllable during the centuries. But it was not the Carnac I had known when in Brittany. This place was younger; its standing stones upright, in place; not yet gnawed by the teeth of untold centuries. There were people, hundreds of them, marching along the avenues to the monolithed circle. Although I knew that it was daylight, a blackness seemed to hover over the crypt that was the circle's heart. Nor could I see the ocean. Where it should have been, and far away, were tall towers of grey and red stone, misty outlines of walls, as of a great city. And as I stood there, long and long it seemed to me, slowly the fear crept up my heart like a rising tide. With it crept, side by side, cold, implacable hatred and rage.

I had heard Bill speaking—and was back in the room. The fear was gone. The wrath remained.

I looked into the face of the Demoiselle Dahut. I thought I read triumph there, and a subtle amusement. I was quite sure of what had happened, and that there was no need of answering her interrupted question—if it had been interrupted. She knew. It was hypnotism of sorts, suggestion raised to the nth degree. I thought that if Bill were right in his suspicions, the Demoiselle Dahut had not been very wise to play a card like this so soon—either that, or damned sure of herself. I closed my mind quickly to that thought.

Bill, Lowell and de Keradel were talking, Helen listening and watching me out of the corners of her eyes.

I whispered to the Demoiselle: 'I knew a witch-doctor down in Zululand who could do that same thing,

Demoiselle de Keradel. He called the trick "sending out the soul". He was not so beautiful as you are; perhaps that is why he had to take so much more time to do it.'

I was about to add that she had been as swift as the striking of a deadly snake, but held that back.

She did not trouble to deny. She asked: 'Is that all you think—Alain de Carnac?'

'No, I think that your voice is also of the sea.'

And so it was; the softest, sweetest contralto I've ever heard; low and murmurous and lulling, like the whisper of waves on a long smooth beach.

She said: 'But is that a compliment then? Many times you have compared me to the sea to-night. Is not the sea—treacherous?'

'Yes,' I said.

The dinner went on with talk of this and that. It was a good dinner, and so was the wine. The butler kept my glass filled so faithfully that I wondered whether Bill had given him orders. The Demoiselle was cosmopolitan in her points of view, witty, undeniably charming—to use that much misused word. She had the gift of being able to be what her conversation implied she was. There was nothing exotic, nothing mysterious about her now. She was a modern, well-informed, cultivated young woman of extraordinary beauty. Helen was delightful. There wasn't a single thing for me to grow unpleasantly argumentative about, nor discourteous, nor insulting. I thought Bill was looking a bit puzzled; disconcerted—like a prophet who has foretold some happening which shows not the slightest sign of materializing. If de Keradel were interested in Dick's death, there was nothing to show it. For some time Lowell and he had been absorbed in low-toned discussion to the exclusion of the rest of us. Suddenly I heard Lowell say:

'But surely you do not believe in the objective reality of such beings?'

The question brought me sharply to attention. I remembered Dick's torn note—he had wanted Bill to consider something as objective instead of subjective; I saw that Bill was listening intently. The Demoiselle's eyes were upon Lowell, faint amusement in them.

De Keradel answered: 'I *know* they are objective.'

Dr. Lowell asked, incredulously: 'You believe that these creatures, these demons—actually existed?'

'And still exist,' said de Keradel. 'Reproduce the exact conditions under which those who had the ancient wisdom evoked these beings—forces, presences, powers, call them what you will—and the doors shall open and They come through. That Bright One the Egyptians named Isis will stand before us as of old, challenging us to lift Her veil. And that Dark Power stronger than her, whom the Egyptians named Set and Typhon, but who had another name in the shrines of an older and wiser race—It will make Itself manifest. Yes, Dr. Lowell, and others will come through the opened doors to teach us, to counsel us, to aid and obey us——'

'Or to command us, my father,' said the Demoiselle, almost tenderly.

'Or to command us,' echoed de Keradel, mechanically. Some of the colour had drained from his face, and I thought there was fear in the glance he gave his daughter.

30

I raised my wine and squinted through it at de Keradel. I said: 'Dr. de Keradel is a true showman. If one provides the right theatre, the right scenery, the right supporting cast, the right music and script and cues—the right demons or what not bounce out from the wings as the stars of the show. Well, I have seen some rather creditable illusions produced under such conditions. Real enough to deceive most amateurs——'

De Keradel's eyes dilated; he half rose from his chair; he whispered: 'Amateur! Do you imply that I am an amateur?'

I said, urbanely, looking at my glass: 'Not at all. I said you were a showman.'

He mastered his anger with difficulty; he said to Lowell: 'They are not illusions, Dr. Lowell. There is a pattern, a formula, to be observed. Is there anything more rigid than that formula by which the Catholic Church establishes communion with *its* God? The chanting, the prayers, the gestures—even the intonation of the prayers—all are fixed. Is not every ritual— Mohammedan, Buddhist, Shintoist, every act of worship throughout the world, in all religions—as rigidly prescribed? The mind of man recognizes that only by exact formula can it touch the minds that are—not human. It is memory of an ancient wisdom, Dr. Caranac—but of that no more now. *I* tell you again that what comes upon my stage is not—illusion.'

I asked: 'How do you know?'

He answered: 'I *do* know.'

Dr. Lowell said, placatingly: 'Extremely strange, extremely realistic visions can be induced by combinations of sounds, odours, movements and colours. There even seem to be combinations which can create in different subjects approximately the same visions—establish similar emotional rhythms. But I have never had evidence that these visions were anything but subjective——' He paused, and I saw his hands clench, the knuckles whiten. He said, slowly: 'Except—once.'

De Keradel was watching him; the clenched hands could not have escaped his notice. He asked:

'And that once?'

Lowell answered, with a curious harshness: 'I have no evidence.'[1]

De Keradel went on: 'But there is another element in this evocation which is not of the stage—nor of the showman, Dr. Caranac. It is, to use a chemical term, a catalyst. The necessary element to bring about a required result—itself remaining untouched and unchanged. It is a human element—a woman or man or child—who is *en rapport* with the Being evoked. Of such was the Pythoness at Delphi, who upon her tripod threw herself open to the God and spoke with his voice. Of such were the Priestesses of Isis of the Egyptians, and of Ishtar of the Babylonians—themselves the one and the same. Of such was the Priestess of Hecate, Goddess of Hell, whose secret rites were lost until I rediscovered them. Of such was the warrior-king who was Priest of tentacled Khalk-ru, the Kraken God of the Uighurs, and of such was that strange priest at whose summoning came the Black God of the Scyths, in the form of a monstrous frog——'

Bill broke in: 'But these worships are of the far distant past. Surely, none has believed in them for

[1] See *Burn Witch Burn*.

32

many a century. Therefore the line of priests and priestesses must long ago have died out. How to-day could one be found?'

I thought the Demoiselle shot de Keradel a warning look, and was about to speak. He ignored her, swept away by this idea that ruled him, forced to expound, to justify it. He said:

'But you are wrong. They *do* live. They live in the brains of those who sprang from them. They sleep in the brains of their descendants. They sleep until one comes who knows how to awaken them. And to that awakener—what reward! Not the golden, glittering trash in the tomb of some Tut-ankh-Amen, not the sterile loot of Genghis Khan, or of Attila . . . shining pebbles and worthless metal . . . playthings. But storehouses of memories, hives of knowledge—knowledge that sets its possessor so high above all other men that he is as a god.'

I said, politely: 'I'd like to be a god for a time. Where can I find such storehouses? Or open such hives? It would be worth a few stings to become a god.'

The veins throbbed in his temples; he said: 'You mock! Nevertheless, I will give you a hint. Once Dr. Charcot hypnotized a girl who had long been a subject of his experiments. He sent her deeper into the hypnotic sleep than ever before he had dared to do with any subject. Suddenly he heard another voice than hers coming from her throat. It was a man's voice, the rough voice of a French peasant. He questioned that voice. It told him many things—things the girl could not possibly have known. The voice spoke of incidents of the Jacquerie. And the Jacquerie was six hundred years away. Dr. Charcot took down what that voice told him. Later, he investigated, minutely. He verified. He traced the girl's parentage. She had come straight down from a leader of that peasant uprising. He tried again. He pushed past that voice to another. And this voice, a woman's, told him of things that had happened a thousand years ago. Told them in intimate detail, as one who had been a spectator of those happenings. And again he investigated. And again he found that what the voice had told him was true.'

I asked, even more politely: ' And have we now arrived at transmigration of souls? '

He answered violently: 'You dare to mock! What Charcot did was to pierce through veil upon veil of memory for a thousand years. I have gone further than that. I have gone back through the veils of memory not one thousand years. I have gone back ten thousand. I, de Keradel, tell you so.'

Lowell said: ' But, Dr. de Keradel—memory is not carried by the germ plasm. Physical characteristics, weaknesses, predilections, coloration, shape and so on —yes. The son of a violinist can inherit his father's hands, his talent, his ear—but not the memory of the notes that his father played. Not his father's— memories.'

De Keradel said: ' You are wrong. Those memories *can* be carried. I do not say that every one inherits these memories of their ancestors. Brains are not standardized. Nature is not a uniform workman. In some, the cells that carry these memories seem to be lacking. In others, they are incomplete, blurred, having many hiatuses. But in others, a few, they are complete, the records clear, to be read like a printed book if the needle of consciousness, the eye of consciousness, can be turned upon them.'

He ignored me; to Lowell he said with intense earnestness: 'I tell you, Dr. Lowell, that this *is* so—in spite of all that has been written of the germ plasm, the chromosomes, the genes—the little carriers of heredity. I tell you that I have *proved* it to be so. And I tell you that there *are* minds in which memories go back and back to a time when man was not yet man. Back to the memories of his ape-like forefathers. Back further even than that—to the first amphibians who crawled out of the sea and began the long climb up the ladder of evolution to become what we are to-day.'

I had no desire now to interrupt, no desire to anger —the man's intensity of belief was too strong. He said:

'Dr. Caranac has spoken contemptuously of the transmigration of souls. I say that man can imagine nothing that cannot be, and that he who speaks contemptuously of any belief is, therefore, an ignorant man. I say that it is this inheritance of memories which is at the bottom of the belief in reincarnation—perhaps the belief in immortality. Let me take an illustration from one of your modern toys—the phonograph. What we call consciousness is a needle that, running along the dimension of time, records upon certain cells its experiences. Quite as the recording needle of a phonograph does upon the master discs. It can run back over these cells after they have been stored away, turning the graphs upon them into—memories. Hearing again, seeing again, living again, the experiences recorded on them. Not always can the consciousness find one of these discs it seeks. Then we say that we have for-gotten. Sometimes the graphs are not deep-cut enough, the discs blurred—and then we say memory is hazy, incomplete.

'The ancestral memories, the ancient discs, are stored in another part of the brain, away from those that carry the memories of this life. Obviously this must be so, else there would be confusion, and the human animal would be hampered by intrusion of memories having no relation to his present environment. In the ancient days, when life was simpler and the environment not so complex, the two sets of memories were closer. That is why we say that ancient man relied more upon his "intuitions" and less upon reasoning. That is why primitive men to-day do the same. But as time went on, and life grew more complex, those who depended less upon the ancestral memories than those which dealt with the problems of their own time—those were the ones with the better chance to survive. Once the cleav-age had begun, it must perforce have continued rapidly —like all such evolutionary processes.

'Nature does not like to lose entirely anything it has once created. Therefore it is that at a certain stage of its development the human embryo has the gills of the fish, and at a later stage the hair of the ape. And, therefore, it is that in certain men and women to-day, these storehouses of ancient memories are fully stocked —to be opened, Dr. Caranac, and having been opened, to be read.'

I smiled and drank another glass of wine.

Lowell said: 'That is all strongly suggestive, Dr. de Keradel. If your theory is correct, then these inherited memories would without doubt appear as former lives to those who could recall them. They could be a basis of the doctrine of transmigration of souls, of reincarnation. How else *could* the primitive mind account for them?'

De Keradel said: 'They explain many things—the thought of the Chinese that unless a man have a son, he dies indeed. The folk saying, "A man lives in his children——"'

Lowell said: 'The new-born bee knows precisely the law and duties of the hive. It does not have to be taught to fan, to clean, to mix the pollen and the nectar into the jellies that produce the queen and the drone, the different jelly that is placed in the cell of the worker. None teaches it the complex duties of the hive. The knowledge, the memory, is in the egg, the wriggler, the nymph. It is true, too, of the ants, and of many insects. But it is not true of man, nor of any other mammal.'

De Keradel said: 'It is true also of—*man.*'

CHAPTER IV

THE LOST CITY OF YS

THERE was a devil of a lot of truth in what de Keradel had said. I had come across manifestations of that same ancestral memory in odd corners of the earth. I had been burning to corroborate him, despite his excusable dig at my ignorance. I would have liked to talk to him as one investigator to a far better informed one.

Instead, I drained my glass and said severely: 'Briggs —I have not had a drink for five minutes.' And then to the table in general: 'Just a moment. Let us be logical. Anything so important as the soul and its travels deserves the fullest consideration. Dr. de Keradel began this discussion by asserting the objective existence of what the showman produced. That is correct, Dr. de Keradel?'

He answered, stiffly: 'Yes.'

I said: 'Dr. de Keradel then adduced certain experiments of Dr. Charcot in hypnotism. Those cases are not convincing to me. In the South Seas, in Africa, in Kamchatka, I have heard the most arrant fakirs speak not in two or three but in half a dozen voices. It is a well-known fact that a hypnotized subject will sometimes speak in different voices. It is quite as well known that a schizoid, a case of multiple personality, will speak in voices ranging from high soprano to bass. And all this without ancestral memories being involved. It is a symptom of their condition. Nothing more. Am I right, Dr. Lowell?'

Lowell said: 'You are.'

I said: 'As for what Charcot's subjects told him—who knows what they had heard their grandmothers say? Stories passed down by the family—heard when children, treasured by the subconsciousness. Built up, improvements suggested, by Charcot himself. Charcot finds two or three points true, naturally. There is none so incredulous as he who seeks evidence to support his *idée fixe*, his pet theory. So these few points become all. Well, I am not so credulous as Charcot, Dr. de Keradel.'

He said: 'I read your interviews in the newspaper. I seemed to detect a certain amount of credulity there, Dr. Caranac.'

So he *had* read the interviews. I felt Bill press my foot. I said:

'I tried to make plain to the reporters that belief in the hokum was necessary to make the hokum effective. I admit that to the victim of his belief it doesn't make much difference whether it is hokum or reality. But that doesn't mean that the hokum is real or can affect anybody else. And I tried to make plain that the defence against the hokum is very simple. It is—don't believe it.'

The veins on his forehead began to twitch again. He said: 'By hokum you mean, I assume, nonsense.'

'More than that,' I said, cheerfully. 'Bunk!'

Dr. Lowell looked pained. I drank my wine, and smiled at the Demoiselle.

Helen said: 'Your manners aren't so good to-night, darling.'

I said: 'Manners—hell! What're manners in a discussion of goblins, incarnation, ancestral memories and Isis, Set and the Black God of the Scyths who looked like a frog? Now I'm going to tell you something, Dr. de Keradel. I've been in a lot of out-of-the-way corners of this globe. I went there hunting for goblins and demons. And in all my travels I've never seen one thing that couldn't be explained on the basis of hypnotism, mass suggestion, or trickery. Get that. Not one thing. And I've seen a lot.'

That was a lie—but I wanted to see the effect on him. I saw it. The veins in his temples were twitching more than ever, his lips were white. I said:

'Years ago I had a brilliant idea which puts the whole problem in its simplest form. The brilliant idea was based on the fact that hearing is probably the last sense to die; that after the heart stops the brain continues to function as long as it has enough oxygen; and that while the brain does function, although every sense is dead, it can have experiences that seem to last for days and weeks, although the actual dream lasts but a fraction of a second.

'"Heaven and Hell, Inc." That was my idea. "Insure yourself an immortality of joy!" "Give your enemy an immortality of torment!" To be done by expert hypnotists, masters of suggestion, sitting at the bedside of the dying and whispering into his ear that which the brain was to dramatize, after hearing and every other sense was dead. . . .'

The Demoiselle drew a sharp breath. De Keradel was staring at me with a strange intentness.

'Well, there it was,' I went on. 'For a sufficient sum you could promise, and actually give, your client the immortality he desired. Any kind he wanted—from the houri-haunted Paradise of Mahomet to the angel choirs of Paradise. And if the sum were sufficient, and you could gain access, you could whisper into the ear of your employer's enemy the Hell he was going into for aeon after aeon. And I'll bet he'd go into it. That was my "Heaven and Hell, Inc."'

'A sweet idea, darling,' murmured Helen.

'A sweet idea, yes,' I said, bitterly. 'Let me tell you what it did for me. It happens that it's entirely practical. Very well—consider me, the inventor. If there is a delectable life after death shall I enjoy it? Not at all. I'll be thinking—*This is just a vision in the dying cells of my brain. It has no objective reality.* Nothing that could happen to me in that future existence, assuming it to be real, could be real to me. I would think—*Oh yes, very ingenious of me to create such ideas, but after all, they're only in the dying cells of my brain.*

'Of course,' I said, 'there is a compensation. If I happened to land in one of the traditional hells, I wouldn't take it any more seriously. And all the miracles of magic, or of sorcery, I have seen were no more real than those dying visions would be.'

The Demoiselle whispered, so faintly that none except me could hear: '*I* could make them real to you, Alain de Carnac—Heaven or Hell.'

I said: 'In life or in death, your theories cannot be proven, Dr. de Keradel. At least, not to me.'

He did not answer, staring at me, fingers tapping the table.

I went on: 'Suppose, for example, you desired to know

41

what it was that they worshipped among the stones of Carnac. You might reproduce every rite. Might have your descendant of priestess with the ancient ghost wide awake in her brain. But how could you *know* that what came to the great cairn within the circle of monoliths—The Gatherer within the Cairn, the Blackness in the Alkar-Az—was real?'

De Keradel asked, incredulously, in a curiously still voice, as though exercising some strong restraint:

'What can you know of the Alkar-Az—or of the Gatherer within the Cairn?'

I was wondering about that, too. I couldn't remember ever having heard those names. Yet they had sprung to my lips as though long known. I looked at the Demoiselle. She dropped her eyes, but not before I had seen in them that same half-amused triumph as when, under the touch of her hand, I had beheld ancient Carnac. I answered de Keradel:

'Ask your daughter.'

His eyes were no longer blue, they had no colour at all. They were like little spheres of pale fire. He did not speak—but his eyes demanded answer from her. The Demoiselle met them indifferently. She shrugged a white shoulder. She said:

'I did not tell him.' She added, with a distinct touch of malice: 'Perhaps, my father—he remembered.'

I leaned towards her, and touched her glass with mine; I was feeling pretty good again. I said:

'I remember—I remember——'

Helen said, tartly: 'If you drink much more of that wine, you're going to remember a swell headache, darling.'

42

The Demoiselle murmured: 'What do you remember, Alain de Carnac?'

I sang the old Breton song—to the English words:

'Fisher! Fisher! Have you seen
White Dahut, the Shadows' Queen,
Riding on her stallion black,
At her heels her shadow pack?
Have you seen Dahut ride by,
Swift as cloudy shadows fly
O'er the moon in stormy sky,
On her stallion black as night—
Shadows' Queen—Dahut the White?'

There was a queer silence. Then I noticed that de Keradel was oddly rigid and looking at me with that same expression he had worn when I had spoken of the Alkar-Az and the Gatherer in the Cairn. Also that Bill's face had bleached. I looked at the Demoiselle and there were little dancing orchid sparks in her eyes. I hadn't the slightest idea why the old song should have had such an effect.

Helen said: 'That's a weird melody, Alan. Who was Dahut the White?'

'A witch, angel,' I told her. 'A wicked, beautiful witch. Not a torch-tressed witch like you, but a blonde one. She lived twenty centuries or more ago in a city named Ys. Nobody knows quite where Ys was, but probably its towers rose where now the sea flows between Quiberon and Belle Isle. Certainly, there was once land there. Ys was a wicked city, filled with witches and sorcerers, but wickedest of all was Dahut the White, the daughter of the King. She picked her lovers where she would. They pleased her for a night, two nights—seldom three. Then she cast them from her . . . into the sea, some say. Or, say others, she made them into shadows——'

43

Bill interrupted : 'What do you mean by that?'

His face was whiter than before. De Keradel was looking sharply at him. I said:

'I mean—shadows. Didn't I sing to you that Dahut was Queen of Shadows? She was a witch—and could make shadows do her bidding. All sorts of shadows— shadows of the lovers she'd killed; demon shadows; Incubi and Succubi nightmares—a specialist in shadows was the White Dahut, according to the legend.

'At last the Gods determined to take a hand. Don't ask me what Gods. Pagan, if all this was before the introduction of Christianity—Christian, if after. Which- ever they were, they must have believed that who lives by the sword must die by the sword and all of that, because they sent to Ys a youthful hero with whom Dahut fell instantly, completely and madly in love. He was the first man she had ever really loved, despite her former affairs. But he was coy—aloof. He could forgive her previous philandering, but before he would accept her favours he must be convinced she truly loved him. How could she convince him? Quite easily. Ys, it appears, was below sea-level and protected by walls which kept out the tides. There was one gate which would let in the sea. Why was there such a gate? I don't know. Probably for use in case of invasion, revolution or something of the sort. At any rate, the legend says, there was such a gate. The keys to it hung always about the neck of the King of Ys, Dahut's father.

'"Bring me the keys—and I'll know you love me," said the hero. Dahut crept down to her sleeping father, and stole the keys from his neck. She gave them to

44

her lover. He opened the sea-gates. The sea poured
in. Finish—for wicked Ys. Finish—for wicked Dahut
the White.'

'She was drowned?' asked Helen.

'That's the curious detail of the legend. The story
is that Dahut had a rush of filial devotion, awakened
the father she had betrayed, took her big black stallion
and mounted it, drew the King up behind her and tried
to beat the waves to higher ground. There must have
been something good in her, after all. But—another
extraordinary detail—her shadows rebelled. They got
behind the waves and pushed them on higher and faster.
So the waves overtook the stallion and Dahut and her
papa—and that was indeed their finish. But still they
ride along the shores of Quiberon " on her stallion black,
at her heels her shadow pack——" ' I stopped, abruptly.

My left arm had been raised, the glass of wine in my
hand. By a freak of the light, the candles threw its
shadow sharply upon the white tablecloth, directly in
front of the Demoiselle.

And the Demoiselle's white hands were busy with the
shadow of my wrist, as though measuring it, as though
passing something under and around it.

I dropped my hand and caught hers. Swiftly she
slipped them beneath the edge of the table. As swiftly
I dropped my right hand and took from her fingers
what they held. It was a long hair, and as I raised it,
I saw that it was one of her own.

I thrust it into the candle flame and held it while it
writhed and shrivelled. . . .

The Demoiselle laughed, sweet, mocking laughter. I
heard de Keradel's chuckle echo hers. The disconcert-

ing thing was that his amusement seemed not only frank but friendly. The Demoiselle said:

'First he compares me to the sea—the treacherous sea. Then darkly, by inference, to wicked Dahut, the Shadow Queen. And then he thinks me a witch—and burns my hair. And yet—he says he is not credulous—that he does not believe!'

Again she laughed—and again de Keradel echoed her.

I felt foolish, damned foolish. I was *touché* for the Demoiselle, beyond any doubt. I glared at Bill. Why the devil had he led me into such a trap?

But Bill was not laughing. He was looking at the Demoiselle with a face peculiarly stony. Nor was Helen smiling. She was looking at the Demoiselle too, and with that expression which women wear when they intensely desire to call another by one of those beautifully descriptive old English words which the Oxford Dictionary says are 'not now in decent use'.

I grinned, and said to Helen: 'It appears that another lady has put me on a hornets' nest.'

Helen gave me a long, comforting look. It said: '*I can do that, but God help any other woman who tries it.*'

There was a short and awkward silence. De Keradel broke it.

'I do not quite know why, but I am reminded of a question I wished to ask you, Dr. Bennett. I was much interested in the account of the suicide of Mr. Ralston, who, I gathered from your interview in the newspapers, was not only a patient but a close friend.'

I saw Bill blink in the old way when he had come to some unshakable conviction. He answered smoothly, in his best professional manner:

46

'Yes, indeed, Dr. de Keradel, as friend and patient I probably knew him as well as any one.'

De Keradel said: 'It is not so much his death that interests me. It is that in the account of it three other men were mentioned. His death linked to theirs, in fact, as though the same cause were behind all.'

Bill said: 'Quite so.'

I had the idea that the Demoiselle was watching Bill intently from the corners of her lovely eyes. De Keradel took up his glass, twirled it slowly, and said:

'I am really much interested, Dr. Bennett. We are all of us physicians here. Your sister . . . my daughter . . . are of course in our confidence. They will not talk. Do *you* think that these four deaths had anything in common?'

'Without doubt,' answered Bill.

'What?' asked de Keradel.

'A shadow,' said Bill.

CHAPTER V

THE WHISPERING SHADOW

I BLINKED at Bill. I remembered his anxiety over my mention of shadows to the reporters, and his tenseness when I had told of the Shadows of Dahut the White. And here we were back to shadows again. There must be some link, but what was it?

De Keradel exclaimed: 'Shadows! Do you mean all suffered from identical hallucinations?'

'The Shadow—yes,' said Bill. 'Hallucinations—I'm not sure.'

De Keradel repeated, thoughtfully: 'You are not sure.' Then asked: 'Were these—shadows—what your friend and patient desired you to regard as objective rather than subjective? I read the newspaper reports with great interest, Dr. Bennett.'

'I'm sure you did, Dr. de Keradel,' said Bill, and there was an edge of irony to his voice. 'Yes—it was the shadow which he desired me to regard as real, not imaginary. The shadow—not shadows. There was only one——' He paused, then added with faint but deliberate emphasis: 'Only *one* shadow for each . . . *you know.*'

I thought I understood Bill's plan of battle. He was playing a hunch; bluffing; pretending to have knowledge of this shadowy decoy of death, whatever the thing might be, exactly as he had pretended to have knowledge of a common cause for the four suicides. He had used that bait to lure his fish within range of the hook. Now

48

that he thought he had them there, he was dangling the same bait. I thought he was dangerously underestimating the de Keradels. That last thrust had been a bit obvious.

De Keradel was saying, placidly: 'One shadow or many, what difference, Dr. Bennett? Hallucinatory shapes may appear singly—as tradition says the shade of Julius Caesar appeared to the remorseful Brutus. Or be multiplied by the thousands which the dying brain of Tiberius pictured thronging about his death-bed, menacing him who had slain them. There are organic disturbances which create such hallucinations. Ocular irregularities produce them. Drugs and alcohol spawn them. They are born of abnormalities of brain and nerves. They are children of auto-intoxication. Progeny of fever, and of high blood pressure. They are also products of conscience. Am I to understand that you reject all these rational explanations?'

Bill said, stolidly: 'No. Say, rather, that I do not yet accept any of them.'

Dr. Lowell said, abruptly: 'There is still another explanation. Suggestion. Post-hypnotic suggestion. If Ralston and the others had come under the influence of some one who knew how to control minds by such methods . . . then I can well understand how they might have been driven to kill themselves. I, myself——'

His fingers clenched around the stem of the wineglass. The stem snapped, cutting him. He wrapped a napkin round the bleeding hand. He said:

'It is no matter. I wish the memory that caused it went no deeper.'

The Demoiselle's eyes were on him, and there was a tiny smile at the corners of her mouth. I was sure de Keradel had missed nothing. He asked:

'Do you accept Dr. Lowell's explanation?'

Bill answered, hesitantly: 'No—not entirely. . . . I don't know.'

The Breton paused, studying him with a curious intentness. He said: 'Orthodox science tells us that a shadow is only a diminution of light within a certain area caused by the interposition of a material body between a source of light and some surface. It is insubstantial, an airy nothing. So orthodox science tells us. What and where was the material body that cast this shadow upon the four—if it was no hallucination?'

Dr. Lowell said: 'A thought placed cunningly in a man's mind might cast such shadow.'

De Keradel replied, blandly: 'But Dr. Bennett does not accept that theory.'

Bill said nothing.

De Keradel went on: 'If Dr. Bennett believes that a shadow caused the deaths, and if he will not admit that it was hallucination, nor that it was cast and directed by a material body—then inevitably the conclusion must be that he admits a shadow may have the attributes of a material body. This shadow came necessarily from somewhere; it attaches itself to some one, follows, and finally compels that some one to kill himself. All this implies volition, cognition, purpose—will and emotion. These in a—shadow? They are attributes of material things only—phenomena of the consciousness housed in the brain. The brain is material and lives in an indubitably material skull. But a shadow is not material, and

50

therefore can have no skull to house a brain; and therefore can have no brain, and therefore no consciousness. And, still again, therefore, can have no volition, cognition, will or emotion. And lastly, therefore, could not possibly urge, lure, drive, frighten or coerce a material living being to self-destruction. And if you do not agree with that, my dear Dr. Bennett, what you are admitting is—witchcraft.'

Bill answered, quietly: 'If so, why do *you* laugh at me? What are those theories of ritual you have been expounding to us but witchcraft? Perhaps you have converted me, Dr. de Keradel.'

The Breton stopped laughing, abruptly; he said: 'So?' and again, slowly: '*So!* . . . But they are not theories, Dr. Bennett. They are discoveries. Or, rather, rediscoveries of, let us say—unorthodox science.' The veins in his forehead were twitching; he added, with an indefinable menace: 'If it is truly I who have opened your eyes—I hope to make your conversion complete.'

I saw that Lowell was looking at de Keradel with a strange intentness. The Demoiselle was looking at Bill, the little devilish lights flickering in her eyes; and I thought that there were both menace and calculation in her faint smile. There was an odd tension about the table—as of something unseen, crouching and ready to strike.

Helen broke it, quoting dreamily:

> ' Some there be that shadows kiss,
> Such have but a shadow's bliss——'

The Demoiselle was laughing; laughter that was more like the laughter of little waves than anything else. But there were undertones to it that I liked even less than the subtle menace in her smile—something inhuman, as though the little waves were laughing at dead men who lay under them.

De Keradel spoke rapidly, in a tongue that I felt I ought to recognize, but did not. The Demoiselle became demure. She said, sweetly:

'Your pardon, Mademoiselle Helen. It was not at you that I laughed. It was that suddenly I am reminded of something infinitely amusing. Some day I shall tell you—and you too will laugh——'

De Keradel interrupted her, urbane as before: 'And I ask your pardon, Dr. Bennett. You must excuse the rudeness of an enthusiast, and also his persistency. Because I now ask if you could, without too great violation of confidence between physician and patient, inform me as to the symptoms of Mr. Ralston. The behaviour of this—this shadow, if you will call it so. I am greatly curious—professionally.'

Bill said: 'There's nothing I'd like better. You, with your unique experience, may recognize some point of significance that I have missed. To satisfy professional ethics, let us call it a consultation, even though it is a post-mortem one.'

I had the fleeting thought that Bill was pleased; that he had scored some point towards which he had been manœuvring. I pushed my chair back a little so that I could see both the Demoiselle and her father.

Bill said: 'I'll start from the beginning. If there is anything you want me to amplify, don't hesitate to interrupt. Ralston called me up and said he wanted me to look him over. I had neither seen nor heard from him for a couple of months; had thought, indeed, that he

52

was on one of his trips abroad. He began abruptly:
"Something's wrong with me, Bill. I see a shadow."
I laughed, but he didn't. He repeated: "I see a shadow,
Bill. And I'm afraid!" I said, still laughing: "If you
couldn't see a shadow you certainly would have something wrong with you." He answered like a frightened
child:

'"But, Bill—there's nothing to make this shadow!"

'He leaned towards me, and now I realized that he
was holding himself together by truly extraordinary
effort. He asked: "Does that mean I'm going crazy?
Is seeing a shadow a common symptom when you are
going insane? Tell me, Bill—is it?"

'I told him that the notion was nonsense; that in all
probability some little thing was wrong with his eyes
or his liver. He said: "But this shadow—whispers!"

'I said: "You need a drink," and I gave him a stiff
one. I said: "Tell me exactly what it is you think you
see, and, if you can, precisely when you first thought
you saw it."

'He answered: "Four nights ago. I was in the
library, writing——" Let me explain, Dr. de Keradel,
that he lived in the old Ralston house on 78th Street;
alone except for Simpson, the butler, who was a heritage
from his father, and half a dozen servants. He went
on: "I thought I saw some one or something slip
along the wall into the curtains that cover the window.
The window was at my back and I was intent upon my
letter, but the impression was so vivid that I jumped up
and went over to the curtains. There was nothing
there. I returned to my desk—but I couldn't get rid
of the feeling that some one or something was in the

53

room." He said: "I was so disturbed that I made a note of the time." '

'A mental echo of the visual hallucination,' said de Keradel. 'An obvious concomitant.'

'Perhaps,' said Bill. 'At any rate, a little later he had the same experience. Only this time the movement was from right to left, the reverse of the first. In the next half-hour it was repeated six times, always in the opposite direction—I mean, from left to right, then right to left and so on. He laid emphasis upon this, as though he thought it in some way significant. He said: "It was as though it were weaving." I asked what " it " was like. He said: "It had no shape. It was just— movement. No, it had no shape—*then*." The feeling of not being alone in the room increased to such an uncomfortable pitch that shortly after midnight he went from the library, leaving the lights burning, and turned in. There was no recurrence of the—the symptoms in his bedroom. He slept soundly. Nor was he troubled the next night. By the day following he had almost forgotten the matter.

'That night he dined out and came home about eleven o'clock. He went into the library to go over his mail. He told me: "Suddenly I had the strongest feeling that some one was watching me from the curtains. I turned my head, slowly. I distinctly saw a shadow upon the curtains. Or, rather, as though it were inter- mingled with them—like a shadow cast by something behind." It was, he said, about the size and shape of a man. He jumped to the curtains and tore them away. Nothing was behind them nor was there anything beyond the window to cast a shadow. He sat down again at the table, but still he felt eyes upon him. "Unwinking eyes," he said. "Eyes that never left me. Eyes of some one or something that kept always just past the edge of my field of vision. If I turned quickly, it slipped behind me, and was watching me from my other side. If I moved slowly, just as slowly did it move."

'Sometimes he caught a flickering movement, a shadowy flitting, as he pursued—the eyes. Sometimes he thought he had caught the shadow. But always it faded, was gone, before he could focus it. And then instantly he felt its gaze upon him from another quarter.

'"From right to left it went," he said. "From left to right . . . and back again . . . and back again and again . . . weaving . . . weaving . . ."

'"Weaving what?" I asked, impatiently.

'He answered, quite simply: "My shroud. . . ."

'He sat there, fighting until he could fight no more. Then he sought refuge in his bedroom. He did not sleep well, for he thought the shadow was lurking on the threshold; had pressed itself against the other side of the door, listening. If so, it did not enter.

'Dawn came, and after that he slept soundly. He rose late, spent the afternoon at golf, dined out, went with a party to the theatre and then to a night-club. For hours he had given no thought to the experience of the night before. He said: "If I thought of it at all, it was to laugh at it as childish foolishness." He reached home about three o'clock. He let himself in. As he closed the door he heard a whisper—"You are late!"

'"It was quite plain," he said, as though the whisperer stood close beside him——'

De Keradel interrupted: 'Progressive hallucination. First the idea of movement; then the sharpening into shape; then sound. Hallucination progressing from the visual field to the auditory.'

Bill went on, as though he had not heard: 'He said the voice had some quality which—I quote him—"made you feel the same loathing as when you put your hand on a slimy slug in a garden at night, and at the same time an unholy desire to have it go on whispering for ever." He said: "It was horror and ecstasy in one."

'Simpson had left the lights burning. The hall was well lighted. He could see no one. He stood for a few moments fighting for control. Then he walked in, took off hat and top-coat, and started for the stairs. He said: "I happened to look down, and *over the top of my eyes* I saw a shadow gliding along about six feet ahead of me. I raised my eyes—and it vanished. I went slowly up the stairs. If I looked down at the steps I could see the shadow flitting ahead of me. Always at the same distance. When I looked up—there was nothing. The shadow was sharper than it had been the night before. I thought it was the shadow of a woman. And suddenly I realized that the whispering voice had been that of a woman."

'He went straight to his room. He passed the door. He looked down and saw the shadow still those two paces before him. He stepped swiftly back and into the room, closing the door and locking it. He switched on the lights and stood with his ear against the door. He said: "I heard some one, something, laughing. The same voice that had whispered." And then he heard it whisper: "I will watch outside your door to-night

56

. . . to-night . . . *to-night.* . . ." He listened with that same mixture of horror and desire. He lusted to throw open the door, but the loathing held back his hand.

'He said: "I kept the lights on. But the thing did what it had promised. It watched all night at my door. It wasn't quiet though. It danced. . . . I couldn't see it, but I know it danced . . . out there in the hall. It danced and weaved . . . right to left . . . left to right and back again and again . . . danced and weaved till dawn outside my door . . . weaving . . . my shroud, Bill. . . ."

'I reasoned with him, much along your lines, Dr. de Keradel. I went over him thoroughly. I could find, superficially, nothing wrong. I took specimens for the various tests. He said: "I hope to God you *do* find something wrong, Bill. If you don't—it means the shadow is real. I think I'd rather know I was going crazy than that. After all, craziness can be cured."

'I said: "You're not going back to your house. You're going to live at the Club until I've got my reports. Then, no matter what they show, you're going to hop on a boat and take a long trip."

'He shook his head: "I've *got* to go back to the house, Bill."

'I asked: "Why, for God's sake?"

'He hesitated, puzzled distress on his face; he said: "I don't know. But I've got to."

'I said, firmly: "You stay here with me to-night, and to-morrow you hop on a boat. To anywhere. I'll let you know about the tests and do my prescribing by radio."

'He replied, still with that same puzzled look: "I

57

can't go away now. The fact is "—he hesitated—"the fact is, Bill . . . I've met a girl . . . a woman . . . I can't leave her."

'I gaped at him. I said: "You're going to marry her? Who is she?"

'He looked at me, helplessly: "I can't tell you, Bill. I can't tell you anything about her."

'I asked: "Why not?"

'He answered, with the same puzzled hesitation: "I don't know why I can't. But I can't. It seems to be a part of—of the other in some way. But I can't tell you." And to every question that touched upon this girl he had the same answer.'

Dr. Lowell said, sharply: 'You told me nothing of this, Dr. Bennett. He said nothing more to you than that? That he could not tell you anything about this woman? That he did not know why—but he could not?'

Bill said: 'That—and no more.'

Helen said coldly: 'What amuses you so, Demoiselle? I do not find anything in all this that is humorous.'

I looked at the Demoiselle. The little orchid sparks were alive in her eyes, her red lips smiling—and cruel.

CHAPTER VI

KISS OF THE SHADOW

I SAID: 'The Demoiselle is a true artist.'

There was a small, tense silence round the table. De Keradel broke it, sharply:

'Exactly what do you mean by that, Dr. Caranac?'

I smiled.

'All true artists are pleased when art attains excellence. Story-telling is an art. Dr. Bennett was telling his perfectly. Therefore, your daughter, a true artist, was pleased. Is it not true, Demoiselle?'

She answered, quietly: 'You have said it.'

But she was no longer smiling, and her eyes said something else. So did de Keradel's. Before he could speak, I said:

'Only a tribute from one artist to another, Helen. Go on, Bill.'

Bill went on quickly: 'I sat and reasoned with him. From time to time I gave him several stiff drinks. I related some famous cases of hallucination—Paganini, the great violinist, who at times thought he saw a shadowy woman in white standing beside him playing her violin while he played his. Leonardo da Vinci, who thought he saw and spoke with the shade of Chiron, wisest of all the Centaurs, who tutored the youthful Aesculapius—dozens of similar instances. I told him he had become a companion of men of genius and that it was probably a sign of something like that breaking out on him. After a while he was laughing.

59

'He said: "All right, Bill. I'm convinced. But the thing for me to do is not to run away. The thing for me to do is meet it and knock it out." I said: "If you feel you can, that is the one thing to do. It's only an obsession, sheer imagination. Try it to-night, anyway. If it gets a bit too thick, call me up on the 'phone. I'll be right here. And take plenty of good liquor."

'When he left me he was quite his old self.

'He didn't call me up until next afternoon, and then asked what I had heard about the specimens. I replied that what reports I had received showed him perfectly healthy. He said, quietly: "I thought they would." I asked what kind of a night he had had. He laughed, and said: "A very interesting one, Bill. Oh, very. I followed your advice and drank plenty of liquor." His voice was quite normal, even cheerful. I was relieved, yet felt a vague uneasiness. I asked: "How about your shadow?" "Plenty of shadow," he said. "I told you, didn't I, that I thought it was a woman's? Well, it is."

'I said: "You *are* better. Was your woman shadow nice to you?" He said: "Scandalously. And promises to be even scandalouser. That's what made the night so interesting." He laughed again, and hung up.

'I thought: "Well, if Dick can joke like that about something that had him terrorized to the liver a day ago, he's getting over it." It was, I said to myself, good advice I gave him.

'Still I felt the vague uneasiness. It grew. A little later I rang him up, but Simpson said he had gone out to play golf. That seemed normal enough. Yes—the whole trouble had been only a queer evanescent quirk that was righting itself. Yes—my advice had been good.

What'—Bill broke out suddenly—'what God-damned fools we doctors can be.'

I stole a look at the Demoiselle. Her great eyes were wide and tender, but deep within them something mocked.

Bill said: 'The next day I had more reports, all equally good. I called Dick up and told him so. I forgot to say I had also instructed him to go to Buchanan. Buchanan '—Bill turned to de Keradel—' is the best eye man in New York. He had found nothing wrong, and that eliminated many possibilities of cause for the hallucination—if it was that. I told Dick. He said, cheerfully: " Medicine is a grand science of elimination, isn't it, Bill? But if after all the elimination you get down to something you don't know anything about —then what do you do about it, Bill? "

'That was a queer remark. I said: " What do you mean? "

'He said: " I am only a thirsty seeker of knowledge."

'I asked, suspiciously: " Did you drink much last night? "

'He said: " Not too much."

'I asked: " How about the shadow? "

'He said: " Even more interesting."

'I said: " Dick, I want you to come right down and let me see you."

'He promised, but he didn't come. I had a case that kept me late at the hospital. I got in about midnight and called him up. Simpson answered, saying he had gone to bed early and had given orders not to be disturbed. I asked Simpson how he seemed. He answered that Mr. Dick had seemed quite all right, unusually cheerful, in fact. Nevertheless, I could not rid myself of the uneasiness. I instructed Simpson to tell Mr. Ralston that if he didn't come in to see me by five o'clock next day I would come after him.

'At exactly five o'clock he arrived. I felt a sharp increase of my doubt. His face had thinned, his eyes were curiously bright. There was a lurking amusement in them, and a subtle terror. I did not betray the shock his appearance gave me. I told him that I had got the last of the reports, and that they were negative. He said: " So I have a clean bill of health? Nothing wrong with me anywhere? " I answered: " So far as these tests show. But I want you to go to the hospital for a few days' observation." He laughed, and said: " No. I'm perfectly healthy, Bill."

'He sat looking at me for a few moments silently, the secret amusement competing with the terror in his over-bright eyes—as though he felt himself ages beyond me in knowledge of some sort and at the same time bitterly in fear of it. He said: " My shadow's name is Brittis. She told me so last night."

'That made me jump. I said: " What the hell are you talking about? "

'He answered with malicious patience: " My shadow. Her name is Brittis. She told me so last night while she lay in my bed beside me, whispering. A woman shadow. Naked."

'I stared at him, and he laughed: " What do you know about the Succubi, Bill? Nothing, I at once perceive. I wish Alan were back—he'd know. Balzac had a great story about one, I remember—but Brittis says she really isn't one. I went up to the library this

morning and looked them up. Ploughed through the
Malleus Maleficarum——"

'I asked: "What the hell is that?"

'"*The Hammer Against Witches*. The old book of
the Inquisition that tells what Succubi and Incubi are,
and what they can do, and how to recognize witches and
what to do against them and all of that. Very interesting. It says that a demon can become a shadow, and
becoming one may fasten itself upon a living person
and become corporeal—or corporeal enough to beget,
as the Bible quaintly puts it. The lady demons are the
Succubi. When one of them lusts for a man she beguiles
him in this fashion or another until—well, until she
succeeds. Whereupon he gives her his vital spark and,
quite naturally, dies. But Brittis says that wouldn't be
the end of me, and that she never was a demon. She
says she was——"

'"Dick," I interrupted him, "what's all this nonsense?"

'He repeated, irritably: "I wish to God you wouldn't
keep on thinking this thing is hallucination. If I'm as
healthy as you say, it can't be——" He hesitated.
"But even if you did believe it real, what could you do?
You don't know what those who sent the shadow to me
know. That's why I wish Alan were here. He'd know
what to do——" He hesitated again, then said slowly:
"But . . . whether I'd take his advice . . . I'm not
sure . . . now. . . ."

'I asked: "What do you mean?"

'He said: "I'll begin from the time we agreed I'd
better go home and fight. I went to the theatre. I
purposely stayed out late. There was no unseen whis-

perer at the door when I let myself in. I saw nothing as I went upstairs to the library. I mixed a stiff highball, sat down and began to read. I had turned on every light in the room. It was two o'clock.

' " The clock struck the half-hour. It roused me from the book. I smelled a curious fragrance, unfamiliar, evocative of strange images—it made me think of an unknown lily, opening in the night, under moon rays, in a secret pool, among age-old ruins encircled by a desert. I looked up and around seeking its source.

' " I saw the shadow.

' " It was no longer as though cast against curtains or walls. It stood plain, a dozen feet from me. Sharp-cut in the room. It was in profile. It stood motionless. Its face was a girl's, delicate, exquisite. I could see its hair, coiled around the little head and two braids of deeper shadow falling between the round, tip-tilted breasts. It was the shadow of a tall girl, a lithe girl, small-hipped, slender-footed. It moved. It began to dance. It was neither black nor grey as I had thought when first. I saw it. It was faintly rosy—a rose-pearl shadow. Beautiful, seductive—in a sense no living woman could be. It danced, and trembled—and vanished. I heard a whisper: ' I am here.' It was behind me—dancing—dancing . . . dimly I could see the room through it.

' " Dancing," he said, " weaving — weaving my shroud." He laughed. " But a highly embroidered one, Bill."

' He said he felt a stirring of desire such as he had never felt for any woman. And with it a fear, a horror such as he had never known. He said it was as though a door had opened, over whose threshold he might pass

64

into some undreamed-of hell. The desire won. He leaped for that dancing, rosy shadow. And shadow and fragrance were gone—snuffed out. He sat again with his book, waiting. Nothing happened. The clock struck three—the half-hour—four. He went to his room. He undressed, and lay upon the bed.

'He said: "Slowly, like a rhythm, the fragrance began. It pulsed—quicker and quicker. I sat up. The rosy shadow was sitting at the foot of my bed. I strained towards it. I could not move. I thought I heard it whisper—'Not yet . . . not yet . . .' "'

'Progressive hallucination,' de Keradel said. 'From sight to hearing, from hearing to smell. And then the colour centres of the brain become involved. All this is obvious. Yes?'

Bill paid no attention; continued: 'He went to sleep, abruptly. He awakened next morning with a curious exaltation of spirit and an equally curious determination to evade me. He had but one desire—that the day should end so that he could meet the shadow. I asked, somewhat sarcastically: "But how about the other girl, Dick?"'

'He answered, plainly puzzled: "What other girl, Bill?"'

'I said: "That other girl you were so much in love with. The one whose name you couldn't tell me."'

'He said, wonderingly: "I don't remember any other girl."'

I stole a swift glance at the Demoiselle. She was looking demurely down at her plate. But the little orchid sparks were dancing in her eyes.

Dr. Lowell asked: 'First, he could not tell you her

65

name because of some compulsion? Second, he told you he remembered nothing of her?'

Bill said: 'That's what he told me, sir.'

I saw the colour drain from Lowell's face once more, and saw again a lightning glance pass between the Demoiselle and her father.

De Keradel said: 'A previous hallucination negatived by a stronger one.'

Bill said: 'Maybe. At any rate, he passed the day in a mood of mingled expectancy and dread, " as though ", he told me, " I waited for the prelude of some exquisite event, and at the same time as though for the opening of a door to a cell of the condemned." But he was even more resolved not to see me, yet he could not be easy until he knew whether I had or had not found something that might account for his experiences. After he had talked to me he had gone out, not for golf as he had told Simpson, but to a place where I could not reach him.

' He went home to dinner. He thought that during dinner he detected fugitive flittings from side to side, furtive stirrings of the shadow. He felt that his every movement was being watched. He had almost panic impulse to run out of the house—" while there was still time ", as he put it. Against that impulse was a stronger urge to stay, something that kept whispering of strange delights, unknown joys. He said—"As though I had two souls, one filled with loathing and hatred for the shadow and crying out against slavery to it. And the other not caring—if only first it might taste of those joys it promised."

' He went to the library——

' And the shadow came as it had come the night

before. It came close to him, but not so close that he could touch it. The shadow began to sing, and he had no desire to touch it; no desire except to sit listening for ever to that singing. He told me: "It was the shadow of song, as the singer was shadow of woman. It was as though it came through some unseen curtain . . . out of some other space. It was sweet as the fragrance. It was one with the fragrance, honey sweet . . . and each shadowy note dripped evil." He said: "If there were words to the song, I did not know them, did not hear them. I heard only the melody . . . promising . . . promising . . ."

'I asked: "Promising what?"

'He said: "I don't know . . . delights that no living man had ever known . . . that would be mine—if . . ."

'I asked: "If what?"

'He answered: "I did not know . . . not then. But there was something I must do to attain them . . . but what it was I did not know . . . not then."

'The singing died and shadow and fragrance were gone. He waited awhile, then went to his bedroom. The shadow did not reappear, although he thought it was there, watching him. He sank again into that quick, deep and dreamless sleep. He awakened with a numbness of mind, an unaccustomed lethargy. Fragments of the shadow's song kept whispering through his mind. He said: "They seemed to make a web between reality and unreality. I had only one clear normal thought, and that was keen impatience to get the last of your reports. When you gave me them, that which hated and feared the shadow wept, but that which desired its embrace rejoiced."

67

'Night came—the third night. At dinner, he had no perception of the lurking watcher. Nor in the library. He felt a vast disappointment and as vast a relief. He went to his bedroom. Nothing there. An hour or so later he turned in. It was a warm night, so he covered himself only with the sheet.

'He told me: "I do not think I had been asleep. I am sure I was not asleep. But suddenly I felt the fragrance creep to me—and I heard a whisper close to my ear. I sat up——

' "The shadow lay beside me.

' "It was sharply outlined, pale rose upon the sheet. It was leaning towards me, one arm upon the pillow, cupped hand supporting its head. I could see the pointed nails of that hand; thought I could see the gleam of shadowy eyes. I summoned all my strength and laid my hand on it. I felt only the cold sheet.

' "The shadow leaned closer . . . whispering . . . whispering . . . and now I understood it . . . and then it was she told me her name . . . and other things . . . and what I must do to win those delights she had been promising me. But I must not do this thing until she had done thus and so, and I must do it at the moment she kissed me—when I could feel her lips on mine——"

'I asked, sharply: "What were you to do?"

'He answered: "Kill myself." '

Dr. Lowell pushed back his chair, stood trembling.

'Good God! And he did kill himself! Dr. Bennett, I do not see why you did not inform me of all this. Knowing what I told you of——'[1]

Bill interrupted: 'Precisely because of that, sir. I

---

[1] See *Burn Witch Burn.*

had my reasons for wishing to handle the case alone. Reasons which I am prepared to defend before you.'

Before Lowell could answer, he went on swiftly: 'I told him: "It's nothing but hallucination, Dick; phantom of the imagination. Nevertheless, it has reached a stage I don't like. You must take dinner with me, and stay here for the night at least. If you won't consent, frankly I'm going to use force to make you."

'He looked at me for a moment with the subtle amusement in his eyes intensified. He said, quietly: "But if it's only hallucination, Bill, what good will that do? I'll still have my imagination with me, won't I? What's to keep it from conjuring up Brittis here just as well as at home?"

'I said: "All that be damned. Here you stay."

'He said: "It goes. I'd like to try the experiment."

'We had dinner. I wouldn't let him speak again of the shadow. I slipped a strong sleepmaker into a drink. In fact, I doped him. In a little while he began to get heavy-eyed. I put him to bed. I said to myself: "Fellow, if you come out of that in less than ten hours, then I'm a horse doctor."

'I had to go out. It was a little after midnight when I returned. I listened at Dick's door, debating whether to run the risk of disturbing him by going in. I decided I wouldn't. At nine o'clock the next morning, I went up to look at him. The room was empty. I asked the servants when Mr. Ralston had gone. None knew. When I called up his house, the body had already been taken away. There was nothing I could do, and I wanted time to think. Time, unhampered by the police, to make some investigations of my own, in the light of certain other things which Ralston had told me and which I have not related since they are not directly related to the symptoms exhibited. The symptoms '— Bill turned to de Keradel—' were the only matters in which you were interested—professionally? '

De Keradel said: ' Yes. But I still see nothing in your recital to warrant any diagnosis but hallucination. Perhaps in those details you have withheld I might——'

I had been thinking, and interrupted him rudely enough : ' Just a moment. A little while back, Bill, you said this Brittis, shadow or illusion, or what not, told him that she was no demon—no Succubus. You started to quote Dick—" She said she was——" then stopped. What did she say she was? '

Bill seemed to hesitate, then said slowly : ' She said she had been a girl, a Bretonne, until she had been changed into—a shadow of Ys.'

The Demoiselle threw back her head, laughing unrestrainedly. She put a hand on my arm.

' A shadow of that wicked Dahut the White! Alain de Carnac—one of *my* shadows! '

De Keradel's face was imperturbable. He said : ' So? Now do I see. So! Well, Dr. Bennett, if I accept your theory of witchcraft, what was the purpose behind it? '

Bill answered : ' Money, I think. I'm hoping to be sure soon.'

De Keradel leaned back, regarding Lowell almost benevolently. He said : ' Not necessarily money. To quote Dr. Caranac, it could perhaps be only art for art's sake. The expression of a true artist. Pride. I once knew—well, a woman whom without doubt the superstitious would have called a witch. She had that pride

70

of workmanship. This will interest you, Dr. Lowell. It was in Prague——'

I saw Lowell start violently; de Keradel went blandly on: 'A true artist, who used her wisdom—or, if you prefer, Dr. Bennett, practised her witchcraft—solely for the satisfaction it gave her as an artist. Among other things, so it was whispered, she could imprison something of one she had killed within little dolls made in that one's image, animating them; and then make them do her will——' He leaned towards Lowell, solicitously: 'Are you ill, Dr. Lowell?'

Lowell was paper-white; his eyes fixed on de Keradel and filled with incredulous recognition. He recovered himself; said in a firm voice:

'A pang I sometimes suffer. It is nothing. Go on.'

De Keradel said: 'A truly great—ah, witch, Dr. Bennett. Although *I* would not call her witch but mistress of ancient secrets, lost wisdom. She went from Prague to this city. Arriving, I tried to find her. I learned where she had lived, but, alas! She and her niece had been burned to death with her dolls, their home destroyed. A most mysterious fire. *I* was rather relieved. Frankly, I was glad, for I had been a little afraid of the doll-maker. I hold no grudge against those who encompassed her destruction—if it were deliberate. In fact—this may sound callous, but you, my dear Dr. Lowell, will understand, I am sure—in fact, I feel a certain gratitude to them—if *they are.*'

He glanced at his watch, then spoke to the Demoiselle: 'My daughter, we must be going. We are already late. The time has passed so pleasantly, so quickly——' He paused, then said with emphasis, slowly: 'Had I the

71

powers she had at her command—for powers she did have, else I, de Keradel, would have felt no fear of her —I say, had I those powers, none who threatened me, none even who hampered me in what I had determined to do, would live long enough to become a serious menace. I am sure '—he looked sharply at Lowell, at Helen and Bill, let his pale eyes dwell for a moment on mine—'I am sure that even gratitude could not save them—nor those dear to them.'

There was an odd silence. Bill broke it. He said, sombrely: 'Fair enough, de Keradel.'

The Demoiselle arose, smiling. Helen led her to the hall. No one would have thought they hated each other. While de Keradel bade courteous farewell to Lowell, the Demoiselle drew close to me. She whispered:

'I will be awaiting you to-morrow night, Alain de Carnac. At eight. We have much to say to each other. Do not fail me.'

She slipped something in my hand.

De Keradel said: 'Soon I shall be ready for my greatest experiment. I look for you to witness it, Dr. Lowell. You, too, Dr. Caranac . . . *you* . . . it will especially interest. Till then—adieu.'

He kissed Helen's hand; bowed to Bill. I wondered with vague misgivings why he had not included them in the invitation.

At the door the Demoiselle turned, touched Helen lightly on the cheek. She said:

'Some there be that shadows kiss——'

Her laughter rippled like little waves as she swept down the steps after her father and into the waiting automobile.

CHAPTER VII

THE DOLL-MAKER'S LOVER

BRIGGS closed the door and walked away. We four stood in the hall, silent. Suddenly Helen stamped a foot. She said, furiously:

'Damn her! She tried to make me feel like a slave girl. As if I were one of your lesser concubines, Alan, whom it amused your Queen to notice.'

I grinned, for it was almost exactly what I had thought.

She said, viciously: 'I saw her whispering to you. I suppose she was asking you to come up'n see her some time.' She gave a Mae West wriggle.

I opened my hand and looked at what the Demoiselle had slipped into it. It was a thin silver bracelet, a half-inch band almost as flexible as heavy silk. Set in it was a polished, roughly oval black pebble. Incised upon its smoothed outer face, then filled in with some red material, was the symbol of the power of the ancient god of the Ocean, who had many names long centuries before the Greeks named him Poseidon; the three-tined fork; his trident with which he governed his waters. It was one of those mysterious talismans of the swarthy little Azilian-Tardenois people who some seventeen thousand years ago wiped out the tall, big-brained, fair-haired and blue-eyed Cro-Magnons, who, like them, came from none knows where into Western Europe. Along the silver band, its jaws holding the pebble, was cut a winged serpent.

73

Yes, I knew what that pebble was, right enough. But what puzzled me was the conviction that I also knew this particular stone and bracelet. That I had seen them many times before . . . could even speak the ancient name of the symbol . . . if I could force remembrance. . . .

Perhaps if I put it round my wrist I would remember——

Helen struck the bracelet from my hand. She put her heel on it and ground it into the rug. She said:

'That's the second time to-night that she-devil has tried to snap her manacles on you.'

I bent down to pick up the bracelet, and she kicked it away.

Bill stooped and retrieved it. He handed it to me and I dropped it in my pocket. Bill said, sharply:

'Pipe down, Helen! He has to go through with it. He's probably safer than you and I are, at that.'

Helen said, passionately: 'Let her try to get him!' She looked at me. 'But I don't exactly—trust you with the Demoiselle, Alan. Something rotten in Denmark there . . . something queer between you. I wouldn't hunger after that white fleshpot of Egypt if I were you. There've been a lot of misguided moths sipping at that flower.'

I flushed.

'Your frankness, darling, is of your generation, and your metaphors as mixed as its morals. Nevertheless, you need not be jealous of the Demoiselle.'

That was a lie, of course. I felt the vague, inexplicable fear of her, suspicion, and a lurking, inexorable hatred—yet there was something else. She was very

74

beautiful. Never could I love her in the way I could Helen. Still, she had something that Helen had not. Something which without doubt was evil, but an evil that it seemed to me I had drunk of long and long and long ago—and must drink of again—and I knew a deep thirst that could be quenched only by it.

Helen said: 'I could not be jealous of her. I am afraid of her—not for myself but for you.'

Dr. Lowell seemed to awaken. It was plain that, sunk in his thoughts, he had heard none of our talk. He said:

'Let us go back to the table. I have something to say.'

He walked to the stairs, and he walked like a man grown suddenly old. As we followed, Bill said to me:

'Well, de Keradel was fair enough. He gave us warning.'

I asked: 'Warning of what?'

Bill answered: 'Didn't you get it? Warning not to pursue the matter of Dick's death. They didn't find out all they hoped to. But they found out enough. I wanted them to. And I *did* find out what I wanted.'

I asked: 'What was that?'

'That they killed Dick,' he answered.

Before I could ask any more questions we were seated at the table. Dr. Lowell rang for coffee, then dismissed the butler. He tipped a full glass of brandy into his coffee, and drank it. He said:

'I am shaken. Undeniably I am shaken. An experience, a dreadful experience, which I had thought ended for ever, has been reopened. I have told Helen of that experience. She has a strong soul, a clear brain; she is a bright spirit. Am I to understand '—he addressed Bill—' that Helen was also in your confidence this evening; that she knew in advance the facts that so strongly surprised me?'

Bill answered: 'Partly, sir. She knew about the shadow, but she didn't know that the Demoiselle de Keradel had an Ys pinned on her name. No more did I. Nor had I any cogent reason to suspect the de Keradels when they accepted your invitation. Before that, I did not go into the details of the Ralston case with you because, from the very first, I had the feeling that they would revive painful memories. And obviously, until de Keradel himself revealed it, I could have had no suspicion that he was so closely connected with the dark centre of those memories.'

Lowell asked: 'Did Dr. Caranac know?'

'No. I had determined, whether or not my suspicions seemed to be warranted, to spread Dick's story before de Keradel. I had persuaded Dr. Caranac to anger him. I wanted to watch the reactions of himself and his daughter. I wanted to watch the reactions of Dr. Caranac and yourself. I hold myself entirely justified. I wanted de Keradel to show his hand. If I had laid my own hand before you, never would he have done so. You would have been on your guard, and de Keradel would have known it. He, also, would have been on his guard. It was your palpable ignorance of my investigation, your involuntary betrayal of the horror you felt over some similar experience, that prompted him, contemptuous now of you, to reveal his association with the doll-maker and to deliver his threat and challenge. Of course, there is no doubt that some way, somehow, he

76

had discovered the part you took in the matter of the doll-maker. He believes you are terrified to the core . . . that through fear of what may happen to Helen and me, you will force me to drop the Ralston matter. Unless he believed that, never would he have risked forearming us by forewarning.'

Lowell nodded.

'He is right. I am frightened. We are, the three of us, in unique peril. But, also, he is wrong. We must go on——'

Helen said, sharply: 'The three of us? I think Alan is in worse danger than any of us. The Demoiselle has her brand all ready to add him to her herd.'

I said: 'Try not to be so vulgar, darling.'

I spoke to Lowell: 'I am still in the dark, sir. Bill's exposition of the Ralston case was luminously clear. But I know nothing of this doll-maker, and therefore cannot grasp the significance of de Keradel's references to her. If I am to enlist in this cause, manifestly I should be in possession of all the facts to be truly effective—also, for my own protection.'

Bill said, grimly: 'You're not only enlisted, you're conscripted.'

Dr. Lowell said: 'I will sketch them for you, briefly. Later, William, you will put Dr. Caranac in possession of every detail, and answer all his questions. I encountered the doll-maker, a Madame Mandilip, through a puzzling hospital case; the strange illness and subsequent stranger death of a lieutenant of a then notorious underworld leader, named Ricori. Whether this woman was what is popularly known as a witch, or whether she had knowledge of natural laws which

77

to us, solely because of ignorance, seem supernatural, or whether she was simply a most extraordinary hypnotist—I am still not certain. She was, however, a murderess. Among the many deaths for which she was responsible were those of Dr. Braile, my associate, and a nurse with whom he was in love. This Madame Mandilip was an extraordinary artist—whatever else she might be. She made dolls of astonishing beauty and naturalness. She kept a doll-shop, where she selected her victims from those who came to buy. She killed by means of a poisonous salve, which she found means to use after winning the confidence of her victims. She made effigies—dolls—of these, in their faithful image, in faithful likeness to them. These dolls she then sent out on her errands of murder—animated, or at least so she implied, by something of the vital or, if you will, spiritual essence of those whose bodies they counterfeited; something that was wholly evil . . . little demons with slender stilettos . . . who went forth under care of a white-faced, terror-stricken girl whom she called her niece, subject so long to her hypnotic control that she had become, literally, another self of the doll-maker. But whether illusion or reality, of one thing there was no doubt—the dolls killed.

'Ricori was one of her victims, but recovered under my care in this house. He was superstitious, believed Madame Mandilip a witch, and vowed her—execution. He kidnapped the niece, and in this house I placed her under my own hypnotic control to draw from her the secrets of the doll-maker. She died in this hypnosis, crying out that the doll-maker's hands were round her heart—strangling it. . . .'

He paused, eyes haunted as though seeing again some dreadful picture, then went steadily on:

'But before she died, she told us that Madame Mandilip had possessed a lover in Prague to whom she had taught the secret of the living dolls. And that same night Ricori and some of his men went forth to —execute—the doll-maker. She was executed—by fire. I, though against my will, was a witness of that incredible scene—incredible still to me although I saw it. . . .'

He paused, then lifted his glass with a steady hand.

'Well, it seems that de Keradel was that lover. It seems that beside the secret of the dolls, he knows the secret of the shadows—or is it the Demoiselle who knows that, I wonder? And what else of the dark wisdom—who knows? Well, that is that—and now all is to be done again. But this will be more difficult——'

He said, musingly: 'I wish Ricori were here to help us. But he is in Italy. Nor could I reach him in time. But his ablest man, one who passed through the whole experience with us, who was there at the—execution, he is here. McCann! I'll get McCann!'

He arose.

'Dr. Caranac, you will excuse me? William—I leave things in your hands. I'm going to my study and then to bed. I am—shaken. Helen, my dear, take care of Dr. Caranac.'

He bowed and withdrew.

Bill began: 'Now, about the doll-maker——'

It was close to midnight when he had finished that story, and I had found no more questions to ask. As I was going out, he said:

'You bowled de Keradel almost clean out when you spoke of—what was it—the Alkar-Az and the Gatherer within the Cairn, Alan. What the hell were they?'

I answered: 'Bill, I don't know. The words seemed to come to my lips without volition. Maybe they did come from the Demoiselle—as I told her father.'

But deep within me I knew that wasn't true—that I did know, had known, the Alkar-Az and its dread Gatherer—and that some day I would . . . remember.

Helen said: 'Bill, turn your head.'

She threw her arms around my neck, and pressed her lips to mine, savagely. She whispered:

'It makes my heart sing that you are here—and it breaks my heart that you are here. I'm afraid—I'm so afraid for you, Alan.' She leaned back, laughing a little. 'I suppose you're thinking this is the precipitancy of my generation, and its morals—and maybe vulgar, too. But it really isn't as sudden as it seems, darling. Remember—I've loved you since the hornets and snakes.'

I gave her back her kiss. The revelation that had begun when I had met her had come to a complete and affirmative conclusion.

As I made my way to the Club, all that was in my mind was the face of Helen, the burnished copper helmet of her hair and her eyes of golden amber. The face of the Demoiselle, if I saw it at all, was nothing but a mist of silver-gilt over two purple splotches in a featureless white mask. I was happy.

I started to undress, whistling, Helen's face still clear-cut before me. I put my hand in my pocket and drew out the silver bracelet with the black stone. The face of Helen faded abruptly. In its place, as clearly cut, even more alive, was the face of the Demoiselle with her great eyes tender, her lips smiling——

I threw the bracelet from me, as though it had been a snake.

But when I went to sleep it was still the face of the Demoiselle and not the face of Helen that was behind my eyes.

CHAPTER VIII

IN DAHUT'S TOWER—NEW YORK

I WOKE up next morning with a headache. Also, out of a dream which began with dolls holding foot-long needles in one hand dancing with pink shadows round circles of enormous standing stones, and with Helen and the Demoiselle alternately and rapidly embracing and kissing me. I mean that Helen would embrace and kiss me, and then she would fade into the Demoiselle; and then the Demoiselle would do the same and as quickly fade into Helen, and so on and so on.

I remember thinking in that dream that this was quite like what occurred at a very unusual place of entertainment in Algiers named the 'House of the Heart's Desire'. It's run by a Frenchman, a hashish eater and also a truly astonishing philosopher. He and I were great friends. I won his regard, I think, by unfolding to him that same scheme for 'Heaven and Hell, Inc.', which had so interested the Demoiselle and de Keradel. He had quoted Omar:

> ' I sent my Soul out through the Invisible,
>   Some letter of that After-life to spell:
> And after many days my Soul returned
>   And said, " Behold, Myself am Heav'n and Hell." '

Then he had said my idea wasn't so original; it was really a combination of that quatrain and what made his place so profitable. He had a couple of renegade Senussi in his house. The Senussi are truly astonishing magicians, masters of illusion. He had a dozen girls, physically the most beautiful I've ever seen, and they were white and yellow and black and brown and intermediate shades. When one wanted to embrace 'The Heart's Desire', and that was a most expensive undertaking, these twelve girls would stand in a circle, naked; a big, wide circle in a big room, hands clasped in each other's with their arms out at full length. The Senussi squatted in the centre of the circle with their drums, while the aspirant for the 'World's Desire' stood beside them. The Senussi drummed and chanted and did this and that. The girls danced, intertwining. Ever faster and faster. Until at last white, brown, black and yellow and intermediate seemed to coalesce into one supernal damsel—the girl of his dreams, as the old sentimental songs so quaintly put it, with trimmings of Aphrodite, Cleopatra, Phryne,. and what not—at any rate, the girl he had always wanted, whether he had realized it or not. So he took her.

'Was she what he thought her? How do I know?' shrugged this Frenchman. 'To me—looking on—there were always eleven girls left. But if he thought so—then, yes.'

Helen and the Demoiselle melting so rapidly into each other made me wish that they would coalesce. Then I'd have no bother. The Demoiselle seemed to stay a moment or two longer. She kept her lips on mine . . . and suddenly I felt as though I had both water and fire in my brain, and the fire was a stake upon which a man was bound, and the flames rushed up and covered him like a garment before I could see his face.

And the water was a surging sea . . . and out upon it,

pale gold hair adrift, wave-washed, was Dahut . . . eyes staring up to a sky less blue than they . . . and dead.

It was then I woke up.

After a cold shower I felt a lot better. While I ate breakfast, I marshalled the events of the night before into coherent order. First, Lowell's experience with the doll-maker. I knew much about the magic of the animate doll, which is far ahead of the simple idea of the effigy into which one sticks pins, or roasts at a fire or what not. Nor was I so sure that the hypothesis of hypnotism could account for a belief of such ancient and widespread popularity. But more ancient still, and much more sinister, was the shadow magic that had slain Dick. The Germans might give it the more or less humorous twist of Peter Schliemel who sold his shadow to the Devil, and Barrie give it his own laboured whimsicality of Peter Pan whose shadow was caught in a drawer and got torn—yet the fact remained that of all beliefs this of the sharing of his shadow in a man's life, personality, soul—whatever one may term it —was, perhaps, the most ancient of all. And the sacrifices and rites connected with propitiation or safety of shadows could parallel any for downright devilishness. I determined to go up to the library and look up shadow lore. I went to my room and called up Helen.

I said: 'Darling, do you know that I love you desperately?'

She said: 'I know that if you don't you're going to.'

I said: 'I'm going to be tied up this afternoon—but there is to-night.'

Helen said: 'I'll be waiting for you, darling. But you're not going to see that white devil to-day, are you?'

I answered: 'I am not. I've even forgotten what she looks like.'

Helen laughed. My foot touched something and I looked down. It was the bracelet I had thrown away.

Helen said: 'To-night then.'

I picked up the bracelet and dropped it in my pocket. I answered, mechanically: 'To-night.'

Instead of looking up shadow lore, I spent the afternoon at two unusual private libraries to which I have access, delving into old books and manuscripts upon ancient Brittany—or Armorica as it was called before the coming of the Romans and for five centuries thereafter. What I was looking for were references to Ys, and what I hoped for was to find some mention of the Alkar-Az and the Gatherer in the Cairn. Obviously, I must have read or heard those names somewhere, at some time. The only other reasonable explanation was that the Demoiselle had suggested them to me, and recalling the vividness of that vision of Carnac under the touch of her hand, I was not inclined to reject that. On the other hand she had denied it, and I was as strongly disinclined to reject her denial. It had sounded like truth to me. Of the Alkar-Az I found no mention whatsoever. In a palimpsest of the seventh century, one torn leaf, there were a few sentences that might or might not refer to the Gatherer. It read, translating freely the monkish Latin:

'. . . is said that it was not because this people of Armorica took part in the Gaulish insurrection that the Romans treated them with such severity but because of certain cruel and wicked rites unparalleled in their evil by any tribe or people with whom the Romans had come in contact. There was one—[several words illegible]—the place of the standing stones called—[two whole lines illegible]—beating in their breasts first slowly—[another lapse]—until breast and even the heart were crushed and then when within the crypt of the centre temple the Blackness began . . .'

Here the fragment ended. Could this 'place of the standing stones' have been Carnac, and the 'Blackness' that began 'within the crypt of the centre temple' have been the Gatherer within the Cairn? It well might be. I knew, of course, that the Romans had practically exterminated the primitive population of Armorica after that insurrection of A.D. 52, and that the survivors had fled from their wrath, leaving the country unpopulated until the fifth century, when numbers of Celtic inhabitants of Britain, driven out by the Angles and Saxons, emigrated to Armorica and repopulated a great part of the peninsula. The Romans, taken all in all, were a broad-minded lot with the widest tolerance for the gods of those they conquered. Nor was it their custom to deal thus savagely with the conquered. What could have been these 'cruel and wicked rites unparalleled in their evil' which had so shocked them that they had so ruthlessly stamped out those who practised them?

Of references to a great city which had sunk beneath the sea I found many. In some it was named Ys, in others nameless. The accounts which placed its destruction within Christian times were clearly apocryphal. The city, whatever it was, belonged to prehistoric times. In almost all the references accent was put upon its wickedness; its prostitution to evil spirits; to sorcery.

Largely, the legend clung closely to the résumé I had
given the night before. But there was one variant
which interested me mightily. This said it was a Lord
of Carnac who had brought about the fall of Ys. That
he had 'beguiled Dahut the White, daughter of the
King, even as she had beguiled many men to their
destruction'. It went on to say that 'so great was the
beauty of this sorceress that not for long could the
Lord of Carnac summon resolution to destroy her and
evil Ys; and she had a child, a daughter; and when he
had opened the sea-gates he had fled with this child,
while the shadows of Ys thrust him on to safety even
as they thrust on the waves to overwhelm Dahut and
her father who pursued him'.

That, in the light of de Keradel's theory of ancestral
memories, rather startled me. For one thing, it gave
me a clearer angle upon the Demoiselle's remarks about
my 'remembering'. And it gave another explanation,
though seemingly a preposterous one, why I had spoken
those two names. If this Dahut came straight down
from that Dahut, maybe I came straight down from the
Lord of Carnac who had so 'beguiled' her. In that
event, contact might have started one of the de Keradel
discs in my brain to action. I thought that the Alkar-
Az and the Gatherer must have made a very strong
impression upon the ancient Lord of Carnac, my
ancestor, to cause the particular disc which registered
them to be the first to become articulate. I grinned at
the idea, and thought of Helen. Whatever the other
memories, I remembered I had a date with Helen that
night, and I was damned glad. I had a date with
Dahut, too, but what of it?

I looked at my watch. It was five o'clock. I pulled out my handkerchief and something fell tinkling to the floor. It was the bracelet, and it lay with the black talisman staring up at me like an eye. I stared back at it with that uncanny feeling of recognition of its symbol growing stronger and stronger.

I went to the Club to dress. I had ascertained where the de Keradels were staying. I sent Helen a telegram:

'Sorry. Unexpectedly called out of town. No time to telephone. Call you up to-morrow. Love and kisses.—ALAN.'

At eight I was sending my card in to the Demoiselle.

It was one of those towering apartment houses over-looking the East River; sybaritic; their eastward and most desirable windows looking down upon Blackwell's Island where the outcasts, the lesser fry of criminals, those not worthy of Sing Sing's social life, Dannemora's austerity or the honour of occupancy in similar fortresses of civilization, are penned; a catch basin for the dregs. The apartment houses were the Zenith complacently contemplating the Nadir.

The elevator went up and up. When it stopped, its operator signalled, and after a second or two a massive door in the shaft slid aside. I stepped out into a hall that was like the ante-room of a medieval chamber. I heard the door whisper its closing, and turned. Tapestries which had been held aside by two men were dropping into place, hiding it. I took swift note of the tapestry's design, solely through force of habit—an adventurer's habit of studying landmarks along the

88

path in event of forced retreat. It portrayed the sea-woman, the fay Melusine, being surprised by Raymond of Poitiers, her husband, during her weekly bath of purification. It was very ancient.

The men were Bretons, swarthy, stocky, but clothed as I had never seen men in Brittany. They wore loose tunics of green, tight belted, and on their right breasts, in black, the red symbol of the bracelet's pebble. Their leg coverings were fawn-colour, baggy, tapering below the knee and tied tightly at the ankle, like those of the Scythians and the old Celts. Their feet were sandalled. As they took my coat and hat I gave them pleasant greeting in the Breton tongue—a noble's customary greeting to a peasant. They responded humbly, and in kind, and I saw a furtive, puzzled glance pass between them.

They drew aside another tapestry, one pressing his hand against the wall as he did so. A door slid open. I passed through into a surprisingly large, high-ceilinged room panelled with ancient dark oak. It was dimly lit, but I glimpsed carven chests here and there, an astrolabe, and a great table strewn with leathern and vellum-covered books. I turned just in time to see the door slip back in place, leaving the panelling apparently unbroken. Nevertheless, I thought I could find it again in case of need.

The two men led me across the room towards its right-hand corner. Again they drew a tapestry aside, and a mellow golden glow bathed me. They bowed, and I passed into the glow.

I stood in an octagonal room not more than twenty feet across. Its eight sides were covered with silken hangings of exquisite texture. They were sea-green and woven in each was an undersea picture—fishes strangely shaped and coloured swimming through a forest of feathery kelp . . . anemones waving tentacles over mouths that were like fantastic flowers . . . a gold and silver school of winged snakes guarding their castles of royal coral. In the centre of the room a table was set with antique crystal, translucent porcelain and archaic silver gleaming under the light of tall candles.

I thrust my hand into the hanging by which I had entered, drew it aside. There was no sign of a door. . . . I heard laughter, like the laughter of little ruthless waves, the laughter of Dahut. . . .

She was at the far side of the octagonal chamber, holding one of the hangings half aside. There was another room there, for light streamed through and formed a faint rosy aureole around her head. And the beauty of her made me for a dozen heart-beats forget everything else in the world—even forget that there was a world. From white shoulders to white feet she was draped in a web-like gown of filmy green in flowing folds like the *stola* of the women of ancient Rome. Her feet were sandalled. Two thick braids of her pale gold hair dropped between her breasts, and through her drapings every lovely line and contour were plain. She wore no jewels—nor needed any. Her eyes both caressed and menaced me—and there was both tenderness and menace in her laughter.

She came towards me and put her hands on my shoulders. Her fragrance was like that of some strange flower of the sea, and touch and fragrance rocked me.

She said, and in the Breton tongue: 'So, Alain—you still are cautious. But to-night you go only when it is

my will that you go. You taught me my lesson well,
Alain de Carnac.'

I asked, stupidly, still under that numbing spell of her
beauty: ' When did I teach you anything, Demoiselle? '

She answered: 'Long . . . and long . . . and long
ago.'

And now I thought that the menace nigh banished
the tenderness in her eyes. The straight brows drew
together in unbroken line. She said, absently:

' I had thought that it would be easy to say that which
I have to say when I met you to-night, Alain. I thought
the words would pour from me . . . as the waters
poured over Ys. But I am confused . . . I find it difficult . . . the memories struggle against each other . . .
hate and love battle . . .'

By now I had got myself a little in hand. I said: 'I,
too, am confused, Demoiselle. I do not speak the Breton
tongue as you, and that, perhaps, is why I am dull to your
meaning. Could we not speak French or English? '

The truth was that the Breton language was a little
too—intimate; brought me too close to her mind. The
other languages would be a barrier. And then I
thought: a barrier against what?

She said, fiercely: 'No. And no longer call me
Demoiselle, nor de Keradel. You know me! '

I laughed and answered: 'If you are not the
Demoiselle de Keradel, then you are the sea-fay Melusine
. . . or Gulnar the Sea-born . . . and I am safe in your '
—I looked at the hangings—'aquarium.'

She said, sombrely: 'I am Dahut . . . Dahut the
White, Dahut of the Shadows . . . Dahut of ancient
Ys. Reborn. Reborn here '—she tapped her forehead.

And you are Alain de Carnac, my ancient love . . . my great love . . . my treacherous love. So—beware.'

Suddenly she leaned towards me; she pressed her lips to mine, savagely; so savagely that her small teeth bruised them. It was not a kiss one could be indifferent to. My arms held her, and it was as though I held flame sheathed in fair flesh. She thrust me from her with what was almost a blow, and so strongly that I stumbled back a step.

She walked to the table and filled from a ewer two slender glasses with pale yellow wine. She said, with mockery:

'To our last parting, Alain. And to our reunion.' And as I hesitated at the toast: 'Don't be afraid—it is no witch's potion.'

I touched her glass and drank. We sat, and at some signal I neither saw nor heard, two other of the oddly dressed servants came in and served. They did it in the olden way, kneeling. The wines were excellent, the dinner was superb. The Demoiselle ate and drank daintily. She spoke little, at times deep in thought, at times regarding me with that blend of tenderness and malice. I have never dined tête-à-tête with a pretty girl and had so little to say—nor with one who was so silent. We were, in fact, like two opponents in some game upon which vital issues hung, studying our moves, studying each other, before beginning it. Whatever the game, I had the uncomfortable feeling that the Demoiselle knew much more about it than I—had in all probability made the rules.

From the great room beyond the hidden door came muted music and singing. They were queer melodies, vaguely familiar. It was as though the singers were in that room, and yet far, far away. They were shadows of song and music. Shadows of song? Suddenly I thought of Dick's description of the singing of the shadow. A shiver went down my spine. I looked up from my plate to find Dahut's gaze upon me, amused, mockery in it. I felt wholesome anger begin to stir in me. The lurking fear of her vanished. She was a beautiful woman, and dangerous. That was all. But how dangerous rested with me. I had no doubt she knew what I was thinking. She summoned the servants and they cleared the table, leaving the wine. She said, matter-of-factly:

'We'll go out on the terrace. Bring the wine with you, Alain. You may need it.'

I laughed at that, but picked up a bottle and glasses and followed her through the hangings into the room of rosy light.

It was her bedroom.

Like the other it was octagonal, but, unlike it, the top was that of a true turret—that is, the ceiling did not run straight across. It lifted in a graceful cone. In fact, the two rooms made a double tower, and I surmised that the walls were false, having been built into what had been one large chamber. In this, they were hung with the same sea-green tapestries but with no figures upon them. As I walked slowly in, their hues seemed to change and shift, darkening here into ocean depths, lightening there into the pale emerald of shallows, while constantly within them moved shadows; shadowy shapes that floated up from the depths, then loitered, then languidly sank beneath the range of sight.

93

There was a low, wide bed, an ancient *armoire*, a table, two or three low stools, a curiously carven and painted chest, a couch. The rosy light streamed down from some cunningly hidden fixture in the turret's roof. I felt again the uncomfortable sense of familiarity that had come to me when I had looked upon the black pebble of the bracelet.

A casement opened upon the terrace. I set the wine upon the table and walked out upon the terrace, Dahut beside me. The tower was at the top of the building as I had thought, and at its south-east corner. At my right was the magical night panorama of New York. Far below, the East River was a belt of tarnished silver studded with the diamonded bands of bridges. About twenty feet beneath was another terrace, plain to the view since the building was of the step-back kind.

I said to the Demoiselle, jestingly: 'Is this like your tower in ancient Ys, Dahut? And was it from a balcony such as this that your servants hurled the lovers of whom you had tired?'

This was in questionable taste, but she had invited it; and, besides, the inexplicable anger was growing within me. She answered:

'It was not so high. Nor were the nights in Ys like these. You looked up into the skies to see the stars, instead of down upon the city. And my tower looked down upon the sea. Nor did I cast my lovers from it, since in—death—they served me better than in life. And not by casting them from any tower could I have brought that to be.'

She had spoken tranquilly; with evident sincerity. Whether she had spoken the truth or not, I had then no slightest doubt that what she had spoken she believed to *be* truth. I caught her by the wrists. I said:

'Did you kill Ralston?'

She answered with that same tranquillity: 'Why, yes.'

She pressed a sandalled foot on mine and leaned close to me, looking up into my eyes. Hot jealousy mingled with my wrath. I asked:

'Had he—been your lover?'

She said: 'He would not have been had I met you before I met him.'

'And those—others? You killed them?'

'Why, yes.'

'And were they too——'

'Not if I had met you——'

My hands ached to go round her throat. I tried to drop her wrists, and could not. It was as though she held them, clamped. I could not move a finger. I said:

'You are a flower of evil, Dahut, and your roots feed on hell——' I said: 'It was his money then that bought you, like any harlot?'

She leaned back and laughed; and her eyes laughed, and in the laughter of eyes and mouth was triumph. She said:

'In the old days you cared nothing about lovers who had gone before. Why do you care now, Alain? But no—it was not his money. Nor did he die because he had given it to me. I was tired of him, Alain . . . yet I liked him . . . and Brittis had had no amusement for a long, long time, poor child . . . if I had not liked him I would not have given him to Brittis. . . .'

I came back to sanity. Undoubtedly the Demoiselle was scoring off me for those suggestions of mine about her the night before. Her method might be a bit elaborate, but certainly it had been effective. I was more than a little ashamed of myself. I dropped her hands and laughed with her . . . but why and whence that anger and the devastating jealousy?

I thrust that doubt aside. I said, ruefully: 'Dahut, that wine of yours must have been more potent than I knew. I've been acting like a damned fool, and I ask forgiveness.'

She looked at me, enigmatically: 'Forgiveness? Now —I wonder—I am cold. Let us go in.'

I followed her into the turreted room. Suddenly I, too, felt cold, and a strange weakness. I poured some wine and drank it down. I sat upon the couch. There was a haziness about my thoughts, as though a cold fog had gathered round my brain. I poured another glass of the wine. I saw that Dahut had brought one of the stools and was sitting at my feet. In her hands was an old and many-stringed lute. She laughed again, and whispered:

'You ask forgiveness—and you do not know what it is that you ask.'

She touched the strings and began to sing. There was something archaic about that song—all weird, sighing minors. I thought that I ought to know that song; that I did know it; had heard it often and often—in just such a turret as this. I looked at the walls. The hues in the hangings were shifting more rapidly . . . changing from malachite depths to pallid shoals. And the shadows were rising more and more rapidly; were coming closer and closer to the surface before they sank again. . . .

96

Dahut said: ' You brought the bracelet I gave you? '

Passively, I thrust my hand into my pocket, drew out the bracelet and gave it to her. She fastened it round her wrist. The red symbol on the pebble gleamed as though traced in lines of fire. She said:

' You have forgotten I gave you that ... long and long and long ago ... lover I loved above all men ... lover I have hated above all men. And you have forgotten the name it bears. Well, hear that name once more, Alain de Carnac ... and remember what you ask me to forgive.'

She spoke a name. Hearing it, a million sparks seemed to burst in my brain—fireflies dissipating the cold fog that gripped it.

She spoke it again, and the shadows within the green tapestries rushed to the surface of the waves, twined arms, locked hands.

Round and round and round the walls they danced ... faster and ever faster ... shadows of women and of men. Hazily, I thought of the dancing girls in the ' House of the Heart's Desire', dancing in a circle to the drums of the Senussi sorcerers ... as these shadows were dancing to the luting of Dahut.

Faster and faster the shadows spun, and then they, too, began to sing; in faint whispering voices, shadows of voices ... and in the green tapestries the shifting colours became the surge and withdrawal of great waves, and the shadow-singing became the murmuring of waves, and then their song, and then a clamorous shouting.

Again Dahut spoke the name. The shadows sprang out of the tapestries and ringed me ... closer and closer. The shouting of the waves became the roaring of a tempest, beating me down and down—out and out.

CHAPTER IX

IN DAHUT'S TOWER—YS

HURRICANE roaring and clamour of the sea dwindled into the ordered beat of great waves breaking against some barrier. I was standing at a window in some high place looking out over a white-capped, stormy sea. The sunset was red and sullen. It made a wide path of blood across the waters. I leaned out of the window, eyes straining to the right to find something that ought still to be visible in the gathering dusk. I found it. A vast plain covered with immense upright stones; hundreds of them, marching from every side to a squat, rock-built temple like the hub of a gigantic wheel of which the monoliths were the spokes. They were so far away that they looked like boulders, then suddenly by some trick of mirage they quivered and swam close. The rays of the dying sun painted them so that they seemed splashed with blood and the squat temple to drip blood.

I knew that this was Carnac, of which I was the Lord. And that the squat temple was the Alkar-Az where the Gatherer in the Cairn came at the evocation of Dahut the White and the evil priests.

And that I was in ancient Ys.

Then the mirage quivered again and was gone. The dusk blotted out Carnac. I looked down upon Cyclopean walls against which long combers broke, shouting. They were enormously thick and high here, these walls; jutting out into the ocean like the prow of some ship of stone; they lessened as they fell back towards the mainland through shallows which were bare sands when the tides ebbed.

I knew the city well. A fair city. Temples and palaces of sculptured stone with tiled and painted roofs red and orange and blue and green adorned it, and dwellings of lacquered wood utterly unlike the rude homes of my clan. It was filled with hidden gardens where fountains whispered and strange flowers bloomed. It was clustered, this city, between the wave-beaten walls as though the land upon which it stood was a deck of a ship and the walls the bulwarks. They had built it on a peninsula that stretched far out into the sea. The sea menaced it always, and always was held at bay by the walls, and by sorceries of Ys. Out of the city ran a wide road, straight over the sands to the mainland, and straight to the evil heart of the circling monoliths—where my people were sacrificed.

They who had built Ys were not my people. It was not they who had raised the stones of Carnac. Our grandmothers had said their grandmothers had told how long and long ago the people who built Ys had come sailing in strangely shaped ships, had fortified the neck of the peninsula and had settled there; and now we were in thrall to them; and they had taken Carnac and on the trunk of its dark ritual had grafted branches that bore fruit of unnamable evil. I had come to Ys to lop those branches. And, if I lived thereafter, to put axe to trunk.

Bitterly did I hate these people of Ys, sorcerers and sorceresses all, and I had a plan to destroy them, one and all; to end the dreadful rites of the Alkar-Az and rid

99

the temple for ever of That which came in the wake of torment and death to my own people at the summoning of White Dahut and the priests of Ys. I thought all that while knowing at the same time that I was the Lord of Carnac and also Alan Caranac who had allowed himself to be caught in the wiles of the Demoiselle de Keradel, and was seeing only what she was willing him to see. At least, Alan Caranac knew that, but the Lord of Carnac did not.

I heard the sweetness of a lute touched lightly; heard laughter like little heartless waves, and a voice—the voice of Dahut!

'Lord of Carnac, the dusk hides your lands. And have you not looked long enough on the sea, beloved? *Her* arms are cold—*mine* are warm.'

I turned from the window, and for a moment ancient Carnac and ancient Ys seemed fantastic dreams. For I was still in that tower from which I had thought the dancing shadows had thrust me. It was the same room; rose-lighted, octagonal, hung with the same tapestries in which green shadows waxed and waned; and upon a low stool sat Dahut, lute in hand, draped in the same sea-green web, her braids falling between her breasts.

I said: 'You are a true witch, Dahut—to trap me like that again,' and turned to the window to look upon the familiar lights of New York.

But that was not what I said, nor did I turn. I found myself walking straight towards her, and instead of the words I had thought to speak, I heard myself saying:

'You are of the sea, Dahut . . . and if your arms are warmer, your heart is as merciless.'

And suddenly I knew that, whether dream or illusion,

100

this *was* Ys, and whilst the I that was Alan **Caranac** could see through the eyes, hear with the ears, and read the thought of this other part of me which was Lord of Carnac, I was powerless to control him and he was unaware of me. Yet I must abide by what he did. Something like an actor watching himself go through a play—but with the quite important difference that I knew neither the lines nor the situations. A most disturbing condition. I had a swift thought that Dahut ought either to have placed me under better hypnotic control or not to have tried hypnosis at all. I felt a faint disappointment in her. That idea shot up and out of my mind like a rocket.

She looked up at me, and her eyes were wet. She loosed her braids and covered her face with her hair and wept behind its curtain.

I said, coldly: 'Many women have wept as you do . . . for men you have slain, Dahut.'

She said: 'Since you rode into Ys from Carnac a month ago, I have had no peace. There is a flame in my heart that eats it. What to me or to you are the lovers who have gone before, since until you came never did I know love? I kill no more—I have banished my shadows——'

I asked, grimly: 'What if they do not accept their banishment?'

She threw back her hair; looked at me, sharply.

'What do you mean by that?'

I answered: 'I make serfs. I train them to serve me well and to acknowledge no other master. I feed and house them. Suppose, then, I feed them no longer, deny them shelter. Banish them. What will my hungry, homeless serfs do, Dahut?'

She said, incredulously: 'You mean my shadows may rebel against me?' She laughed, then her eyes narrowed, calculatingly. 'Still—there is something in what you say. And what I have made, I can—unmake.'

I thought that a sighing went round the room, and that for an instant the hues in the tapestries shifted more rapidly. If so, Dahut paid no heed, sat pensive. She said, musingly:

'After all, they do not love me—my shadows. They do my bidding—but they do not love me, who made them. No.'

I who was Alan Caranac smiled at this, but then I reflected that the I who was Lord of Carnac quite evidently took these shadows seriously, disconcertingly as matters of fact. . . .

She stood up, threw white arms around my neck, and the fragrance of her that was like some secret flower of the sea rocked me, and at her touch desire flamed through me. She said languorously:

'Beloved . . . who have swept my heart clean of all other loves . . . who have awakened me to love . . . why will you not love me?'

I said, thickly: 'I do love you, Dahut—but I do not trust you. How can I know your love will last . . . or that the time may not come when I, too, become a shadow . . . as did those others who loved you?'

She answered, lips close to mine: 'I have told you. I loved none of them.'

I said: 'There was one you loved.'

She swayed back, looked deep into my eyes, her own sparkling.

'You mean the child! You are jealous, Alain—and

therefore I know you love me. I will send away the child. Nay—if you desire, she shall be slain.'

And now I felt cold fury stifle all desire for this woman who held life so lightly against passion that she would turn her hand even against the daughter she had borne. Ah, but that was no secret even in Carnac. I had seen the small Dahut, violet-eyed, milk-white with the moon-fire in her veins—no mistaking who had given *her* birth, even had her mother denied her. But I mastered the fury—after all, it was but what I had expected, and it steeled me in my determination.

'No.' I shook my head. 'What would that mean except that you had tired of her—as you tired of her father—as you tired of all your lovers?'

She whispered, desperately, and if I ever saw true madness of love in a woman's face it was there in hers:

'What can I do? Alain—what can I do to gain your trust? . . . What can I do to make you believe? . . .'

I said: 'When the moon wanes, then is the feast of Alkar-Az. Then you will summon the Gatherer in the Cairn—and then will many of my people die under the mauls of the priests and many more be swallowed by the Blackness. Promise me you will not summon—It. Then I will trust you.'

She shrank away, lips white; she whispered: 'I cannot do that. It would mean the end of Ys. It would mean the end of—me. The Gatherer would summon—me . . . ask anything else, beloved . . . but that I *cannot* do.'

Well, I had expected her refusal; had hoped for it. I said: 'Then give me the keys to the sea-gates.'

She stiffened; I read doubt, suspicion, in her eyes; and

when she spoke, softness had gone from her voice. She said, slowly:

'Now why do you ask for them, Lord of Carnac? They are the very sign and symbol of Ys. They *are*—Ys. They were forged by the sea-god who led my forefathers here long and long and long ago. Never have they been in any hands except those of the Kings of Ys. Never may they be in any hands except those of a King of Ys. Why do you ask for—them?'

Ah—but this was the crisis. This was the moment towards which for long I had been working. I caught her up in my arms, tall woman that she was, and held her cupped in them. I pressed my lips to hers, and I felt her quiver and her arms lock round my neck and her teeth bruise my mouth. I threw back my head and roared laughter. I said:

'You yourself have said it, Dahut. I ask because they are the symbol of Ys. Because they are—you. Perhaps because I would hold them against any change of heart of yours, White Witch. Perhaps as a shield against your shadows. Double your guards at the sea-gates, if you will, Dahut. But'—again I held her close and set my mouth against hers—'I kiss you never again until those keys are in my hands.'

She said, falteringly: 'Hold me so another moment, Alain . . . and you shall have the keys . . . hold me . . . it is as though my soul were loosed from bondage . . . you shall have the keys. . . .'

She bent her head and I felt her lips upon my breast, over my heart. And black hate of her and red lust for her fought within me.

She said: 'Put me down.'

And when I had done this she looked at me long with soft and misty eyes; and she said again:

'You shall have the keys, beloved. But I must wait until my father is asleep. I shall see to it that he goes early to sleep. And the keys of Ys shall be in the hands of a King of Ys—for King of Ys you shall be, my own dear Lord. Now wait here for me——'

She was gone.

I walked to the window and looked out upon the sea. The storm had broken, was rising to tempest strength, and the long combers were battering, battering at the stone prow of Ys, and I could feel the tower tremble in the blast. Blast and sea matched the exultation in my heart.

I knew that hours had passed, and that I had eaten and had drunk. There was confused memory of a great hall where I had sat among gay people close to a dais where was the old King of Ys; and at his right Dahut; and at his left a white-robed, yellow-eyed priest, around whose forehead was a narrow band of gold and at whose girdle the sacred maul with which the breasts of my own people were beaten in before the Alkar-Az. He had watched me, malevolently. And the King had grown sleepy, nodding . . . nodding. . . .

But now I was in Dahut's tower. The storm was stronger and so were the surge and beat of waves on the stone prow of Ys. The rosy light was dim, and the shadows in the green hangings were motionless. Yet I thought that they were closer to the surface; were watching me.

In my hands were three slender bars of sea-green

metal, strangely notched and serrated; upon each the symbol of the trident. The longest was three times the space between my index finger and wrist, the shortest the length of my hand.

They hung from a bracelet, a thin band of silver in which was set a black stone bearing in crimson the trident symbol that was the summoning name of the sea-god. They were the keys of Ys, given by the sea-god to those who had built Ys.

The keys to the sea-gates!

And Dahut stood before me. She as like a girl in her robe of white, her slender feet bare, hair of silvery gold flowing over exquisite shoulders, and the rosy light weaving a little aureole around her head. I who was Alan Caranac thought: *She looks like a saint.* But I who was Lord of Carnac knew nothing of saints, and only thought: *How can I kill this woman, evil as I know her to be!*

She said, simply: 'Now can you trust, Lord of me?'

I dropped the keys and set my hands on her shoulders. 'Yes.'

She raised her lips to me, like a child. I felt pity— against all my knowledge of what she truly was and against my will I felt pity for her. So I lied. I said:

'Let the keys stay where they are, white flower. In the morning, before your father awakens, you shall take them back to him. It was but a test, sweet white flame.'

She looked at me gravely.

'If you wish it, so shall it be done. But there is no need. To-morrow you shall be King of Ys.'

I felt a little shock go through me, and pity fled. If that promise meant anything it meant that she was going to kill her father as remorselessly as she had offered to kill her child. She said dreamily:

'He grows old. And he is weary. He will be glad to go. And with these keys—I give you all of myself. With them—I lock behind me all life that I have lived. I come to you—virgin. Those I have slain I forget, as you will forget. And their shadows shall—cease to be.'

Again I heard that sighing whisper go round the room, but she did not—or if she did, she gave it no heed.

And suddenly she clasped me in her arms, and her lips clung to mine . . . nor were they virginal . . . and the desire of her swept like wild-fire through me. . . .

I had not been asleep. Knowing what I must do, I had not dared to sleep though sleep pressed heavy on my eyes. I had lain, listening to the breathing of Dahut, waiting for her to sink into deepest slumber. Yet I must have dozed, for suddenly I became conscious of a whispering close to my ear, and I knew that the whisper had not just begun.

I lifted my head. The rosy light was dim. Beside me was Dahut, one white arm and breast uncovered, hair a silken net upon her pillow.

The whispering continued; grew more urgent. I looked about the room. It was thronged with shadowy shapes that swayed and shifted like shadows in the waves. Upon the floor where I had thrown them lay the keys of Ys, the black pebble glimmering.

I looked again at Dahut—and looked and looked again. For over her eyes was a shadow as though of a hand, and over her lips another such shadow, and upon her breast was a shadow like a hand upon her heart, and around' knees and ankles were other shadowy hands, clasping them like fetters.

I slipped from the bed; dressed swiftly and threw my cloak over my shoulders. I picked up the keys.

One last look I took at Dahut—and almost my resolution broke. Witch or not—she was too fair to kill. . . .

The whispering grew fiercer; it threatened; it urged me on, implacably. I looked at Dahut no more—I could not. I passed out of her chamber—and I felt the shadows go with me, wavering before and around and after me.

I knew the way to the sea-gates. It led through the palace, thence underground to the vault at the end of the prow of stone against which the waves were thundering.

I could not think clearly—my thoughts were shadows —I was a shadow walking with shadows. . . .

The shadows were hurrying me, whispering . . . what were they whispering? That nothing could harm me . . . nothing stop me . . . but I must hurry . . . hurry.

The shadows were like a cloak, covering me.

I came upon a guard. He stood beside the passage I must take from the palace into the underground way. He stood there, as in a dream, staring vacantly, staring through me, as though I, too, were but a shadow. The shadows whispered—' Kill.' I thrust my dagger through him, and went on.

I came out of that passage into the ante-room of the vault of the gates. There was a man there, coming out of the vault. It was the white-robed priest with the yellow eyes. To him, at least, I was no shadow.

He stared at me and at the keys I held as though I were a demon. Then he rushed towards me, maul upraised, lifting a golden whistle to his lips to summon aid. The shadows swept me forward, and before it could touch his lips I had thrust my dagger through his heart.

And now the gate of the vault was before me. I took the smallest key, and at its touch in the slot that gate drew open. And again the shadows crowded before and around, and pushed me on.

There were two guards there. One I killed before he could draw weapon. I threw myself on the other, throttling him before he could cry alarm.

I thought that as we writhed the shadows wound themselves round him, smotheringly. At any rate, he soon lay dead.

I went on to the sea-gates. They were of the same metal as the keys; immense; ten times my height at the least, twice that as wide; so massive that it did not seem that they could have been forged by the hands of men —that they were indeed the gift of the sea-god as the people of Ys had told us.

I found the slits.

The shadows were whispering . . . first I must thrust in the larger key and turn . . . now the smaller and turn . . . and now I must cry out the name upon the pebble . . . once and twice and thrice . . . I cried that name. . . .

The massive valves shuddered. They began to open— inward. A thin sheet of water hissed through the opening, striking the opposite side of the vault like a sword.

And now the shadows were whispering to me to flee
. . . quickly . . . quickly. . . .

Before I could reach the doorway of the vault the split
between the opening valves was a roaring cataract.
Before I could reach the passage a wave struck me. On
its crest was the body of the priest, arms stretched out
to me as though in death he were trying to drag me
down . . . down under the smother. . . .

And now I was on a horse, racing over the wide road
to Carnac through howling tempest. In my arms was
a child, a girl whose violet eyes were open wide, and
blank with terror. And on and on I raced, with the
waves reaching out for me, clamouring behind me.

Above the tumult of wind and waves, another tumult
from Ys—the crashing of its temples and palaces, the
rape of its sea-walls and the death-cry of its people
blended into one sustained note of despair. . . .

CHAPTER X

AND OUT OF DAHUT'S TOWER

I LAY, eyes shut, but wide awake. I had battled back into this awakening, wrestling for mastery over another self that had stubbornly asserted its right to be. I had won, and the other self had retreated into my memories of Ys. But the memories were vivid and he was as strong as they; he was entrenched among them and he would live as long as they lived; waiting his chance. I was as spent as though that fight had been physical; and in my mind the Lord of Carnac and Alan Caranac and Dahut of ancient Ys and the Demoiselle de Keradel danced a witches' dance, passing in and out of each other, shifting from one to another—like the girls in the ' House of Heart's Desire '.

Time had passed between the moment of awakening and the moment when the death cry of Ys had smitten me in my flight over the sands. I knew that. But whether it had been minutes or millenniums I did not know. And other things had happened which I did not like remembering.

I opened my eyes. I had thought that I had been lying on a soft bed. I was not. I was standing fully dressed beside a window in a room of dim rosy light; a room like a turret . . . with octagonal walls covered by sea-green tapestries in which furtive shadows moved. And suddenly that other self became alert, and I heard a far-off clamour of waves racing towards me. . . .

I turned my head quickly and looked out of the

window. There was no stormy sea, no spuming combers beating upon great walls. I looked down upon bridge-bound East River and the lights of New York; looked and fed upon them, drawing strength and sanity from them.

Slowly I turned from the window. Upon the bed was Dahut. She was asleep, one white arm and breast uncovered and her hair a silken net upon her pillow. She lay there, straight as a sword, and in her sleep she smiled.

No shadowy hands held her. Around her wrist was the bracelet, and the black stone was like an unwinking eye, watching me. I wondered whether her eyes under the long curling lashes were also watching me. Her breasts rose and fell, like the slow lift and fall of waves in a slumbering sea. Her mouth, with the kiss of the archaic upon her lips, was peaceful. She was like a soul of the sea over which tempest had passed, leaving it sleeping. She was very lovely . . . and there was desire for her in my heart, and there was fear of her. I took a step towards her . . . to kill her now while she lay asleep and helpless . . . to set my hands round her throat and choke the black life out of the white witch . . . to kill her, ruthlessly, as she had killed. . . .

I could not do that. Nor could I awaken her. The fear of her stood like a barrier against awakening. The desire for her stood like another barrier against the urge to slay her. I drew back through the window and out upon the terrace.

I waited there for a moment, considering, watching Dahut's chamber for any movement. Witchcraft might be superstition—but what Dahut had twice done to me measured up fully to any definition of it. And I thought of what had happened to Dick—and of her calm confession about that. She had told the truth there, whether she had brought his death about by suggestion or by actual shadow. My own experiences had been too similar to doubt that. She had killed Ralston, and those other three. And how many more only she knew.

I gave up any idea of slinking through her turret and trying to find the hidden door to the great room from whence had come the shadowy singing. Maybe the shadows wouldn't be as helpful as they had been back in ancient Ys. Also, there was the ante-chamber of the elevators.

The truth was that the cold fear I felt of the Demoiselle seemed to paralyse all trust in myself. I was too vulnerable to her on her own picked field. And if I killed her, what possible reason could I offer? Ralston's death, shadows, witchcraft? The best I could expect was the mad-house. How could I prove such absurdities? And if I awakened her and demanded release—well, I couldn't see that working either. New York and ancient Ys were still too close together in my mind—and something whispered that the way I had taken in Ys was still the best way. And that was to go while she slept.

I walked to the edge of the terrace and looked over its coping. The next terrace was twenty feet below. I didn't dare risk the drop. I examined the wall. It had bricks jutting out here and there that I thought I could manage. I took off my shoes and hung them around my neck by the laces. I slid over the coping and with an occasional slip or two I landed on the lower terrace. Its windows were open and there was the sound of heavy sleeping from within. A clock struck two and the breathing stopped. A singularly formidable woman came to the casements, looked out, and slammed them shut. It occurred to me that this was no place for a hatless, coatless, shoeless fugitive to ask sanctuary. So I did the same crawl down to the next terrace, and that was all boarded up.

I climbed to the next, and that too was boarded. By this time my shirt was a wreck, my trousers ripped here and there, and my feet bare. I realized that I was rapidly getting in such shape that it would take all my eloquence to get away no matter what lucky break might come. I looked up at Dahut's terrace, and I thought the light was streaming more brightly from her windows. I hastily slipped over the coping and half-slid, half-fell upon the next terrace.

There was a brilliantly lighted room. Four men were playing poker at a table liberally loaded with bottles. I had overturned a big potted bush. I saw the men stare at the window. There was nothing to do but walk in and take a chance. I did so.

The man at the head of the table was fat, with twinkling little blue eyes and a cigar sticking up out of the corner of his mouth. Next him was one who might have been an old-time banker; then a lank and sprawling chap with a humorous mouth and a melancholy little fellow with an aspect of indestructible indigestion.

The fat man said: 'Do you all see what I do? All voting yes will take a drink.'

They all took a drink.

The fat man said: 'The ayes have it.'

The banker said: 'If he didn't drop out of an aeroplane, then he's a human fly.'

The fat man asked: 'Which was it, stranger?'

I said: 'I climbed.'

The melancholy man said: 'I knew it. I always said this house had no morals.'

The lanky man stood up and pointed a warning finger at me: 'Which way did you climb? Up or down?'

'Down,' I said.

'Well,' he said, 'if you came down, it's all right so far with us.'

I asked, puzzled: 'What difference does it make?'

He said: 'A hell of a lot of difference. We all live underneath here except the fat man, and we're all married.'

The melancholy man said: 'Let this be a lesson to you, stranger. Put not your trust in the presence of woman nor in the absence of man.'

The lanky man said: 'A sentiment, James, that deserves another round. Pass the rye, Bill.'

The fat man passed it.

I suddenly realized what a ridiculous figure I must make. I said: 'Gentlemen, I can give you my name and credentials, which you can verify by 'phone if necessary. I admit, I prefer not to. But if you will let me get out of this place you will be compounding neither misdemeanour nor felony nor any other crime. And it would be useless to tell you the truth, for you wouldn't believe me.'

The lank man mused: 'How often have I heard that plea of not guilty before, and in precisely those phrases.

Stand right where you are, stranger, till the jury decides.
Let us view the scene of the crime, gentlemen.'

They walked out to the terrace, poked at the overturned plant, scanned the front of the building, and
returned. They looked at me curiously.

The lanky man said: 'Either he has a hell of a nerve
to take a climb like that to save the lady's reputation—
or Daddy just naturally scared him worse than death.'

The melancholy man, James, said, bitterly: 'There's
a way to tell if it's nerve. Let him stack a couple of
hands against that God-damned fat pirate.'

The fat man, Bill, said, indignantly: 'I'll play with
no man who wears his shoes around his neck.'

The lanky man said: 'A worthy sentiment, Bill.
Another round on it.'

They drank.

I slipped on my shoes. This was doing me good. It
was about as far as possible from ancient Ys and the
Demoiselle. I said:

'Even under a torn shirt, ripped pants and footless
socks a fearless heart may beat. Count me in.'

The lanky man said: 'A peerless sentiment. Gentlemen, a round in which the stranger joins.'

We drank, and I needed it.

I said: 'What I'm playing for is a pair of socks, a
shirt, a pair of pants, an overcoat, a hat and a free and
unquestioned exit.'

The melancholy man said: 'What we're playing for
is your money. And if you lose you get out of here
how you can in the clothes you've got on.'

I said: 'Fair enough.'

I opened, and the lanky man wrote something on a

blue chip and showed it to me before he tossed it into the pot. I read: 'Half a sock.' The others solemnly marked their chips and the game was on. I won and lost. There were many worthy sentiments and many rounds. At four o'clock I had won my outfit and release. Bill's clothes were too big for me, but the others went out and came back with what was needful.

They took me downstairs. They put me in a taxi and held their hands over their ears as I told the taxi man where to go. That was a quartet of good scouts if ever there was one. When I was unsteadily undressing at the Club a lot of chips fell out of my pockets. They were marked 'Half a shirt': 'One seat of pants': 'A pant leg': 'One hat brim': and so on and so on.

I steered a wavering nor'-nor'-east course to the bed. I'd forgotten all about Ys and Dahut. Nor did I dream of them.

CHAPTER XI

DAHUT SENDS A SOUVENIR

IT was different when I woke up about noon. I was stiff and sore and it took about three pick-me-ups to steady the floor. The memories of the Demoiselle Dahut and of Ys were all too acute, and they had a nightmarish edge to them. That flight from her tower for example. Why hadn't I stayed and fought it out? I hadn't even the excuse of Joseph fleeing from Potiphar's wife. I had been no Joseph. Not that this troubled my conscience particularly, but the fact remained that I had made a most undignified exit and that each time I had met Dahut—with the problematical exception of Ys—she had worsted me. That outraged my pride.

Hell, the plain truth was that I had run away in terror and had let down Bill and let down—Helen. At that moment I hated Dahut as much as ever had the Lord of Carnac.

I managed a breakfast, and called up Bill.

Helen answered. She said with poisonous solicitude: 'Why, darling, you must have travelled all night to get back so early. Where did you go?'

I was still pretty edgy and I answered, curtly: 'Three thousand miles and five thousand years away.'

She said: 'How interesting! Not all by yourself, surely.'

I thought: *Damn all women!* and asked: 'Where's Bill?'

Helen said: 'Darling, you sound guilty. You weren't alone.'

I said: 'No. And I didn't like the trip. And if you're thinking what I'm thinking—yes, I'm guilty. And I don't like that either.'

Her voice changed; was filled with real concern; a little frightened: 'You mean that?—about three thousand miles and centuries away?'

I said: 'Yes.'

Again she was silent; then: 'With the—Demoiselle?'
'Yes.'

She said, furiously: 'The damned witch! Oh, if you'd only been with me . . . I could have saved you that.'

I said: 'Maybe. But not on some other night. Sooner or later it had to come, Helen. Why that is true I don't know—yet. But it is true.' For suddenly I had remembered that strange thought which had come to me—that I had drunk of the Demoiselle's evil long and long ago—and must drink again; and I knew that it had been a true thought.

I repeated: 'It had to be. And it is done.'

That I knew was a lie, and so did Helen. She said, a bit piteously: 'It's just begun, Alan.'

I had no answer to that.

She said: 'I'd give my life to help you, Alan——' Her voice broke; then, hurriedly: 'Bill said you were to wait at the Club for him. He'll be there about four.' She rang off.

Hardly had she done so than a boy brought me a letter. On the envelope was a tiny imprint of the trident. I opened it. It was in the Breton language.

'My elusive—friend! Whatever I may be—I am still a woman and therefore curious. Are you as insubstantial as—shadows, that doors and walls are nothing to you? You did not seem so—last night. I await you with all eagerness to-night—to learn.

'DAHUT.'

There was subtle threat in every line of that. Especially the part about the shadows. My anger rose. I wrote:

'Ask your shadows. Perhaps they are no more faithful to you now than they were in Ys. As for to-night— I am otherwise engaged.'

I signed it Alan Caranac and sent it off by messenger. Then I waited for Bill. I drew some comfort from the thought that the Demoiselle evidently knew nothing of how I had escaped from her turret. That, at least, meant her powers, whatever they might be, were limited. Also, if those damned shadows had any reality except in the minds of those who strayed into her web of suggestion, the idea I had planted might bring about some helpful confusion in her *ménage*.

Promptly at four, Bill came in. He looked worried. I laid the whole thing before him from start to finish, not even omitting the poker party. He read the Demoiselle's letter and my reply. He looked up.

'I don't blame you for last night, Alan. But I rather wish you had answered this—differently.'

'You mean accepted it?'

He nodded.

'Yes, you're pretty well forewarned now. You might

temporize. Play her along a bit . . . make her believe you love her . . . pretend you would like to join her and de Keradel. . . .'

'Sit in on their game?'

He hesitated, then said: 'For a little while.'

I laughed.

'Bill, as for being forewarned, if that dream of Ys she conjured up means anything, it means Dahut is a damned sight better forewarned than I am. Also, much better forearmed. As for temporizing with or playing her—she'd see through me in no time, or her father would. There's nothing to do but fight.'

He asked: 'How can you fight—shadows?'

I said: 'It would take me days to tell you all the charms, counter-charms, exorcisms and what not that man has devised for that sole purpose—Cro-Magnons and without doubt the men before them and perhaps even the half-men before *them*. Sumerians, Egyptians, Phœnicians, the Greeks and the Romans, the Celts, the Gauls and every race under the sun, known and forgotten, put their minds to it. But there is only one way to defeat the shadow sorcery—and that is not to believe in it.'

He said: 'Once I would have agreed with you—and not so long ago. Now the idea seems to me to resemble that of getting rid of a cancer by denying you have it.'

I said impatiently: 'If you had tried a good dose of hypnotism on Dick, counter-suggestion, he'd probably be alive to-day.'

He replied, quietly: 'I did. There were reasons I didn't want de Keradel to know it. Nor you. I tried it to the limit, and it did no good.'

And as I digested this, he asked: 'You don't believe in them, do you, Alan—in the shadows? I mean in their reality?'

'No,' I answered—and wished it were the truth.

'Well,' he said, 'your incredulity doesn't seem to have helped you much last night!'

I went to the window and looked out. I wanted to tell him that there was another way to stop the shadow sorcery. The *only* sure way. Kill the witch who did it. But what was the use? I'd had my chance to do that and lost it. And I knew that if I could relive the night—I would not kill her. I said:

'That's true, Bill. But it was because my disbelief was not strong enough. Dahut weakens it. That's why I want to keep away from her.'

He laughed.

'I'm still reminded of the cancer patient—if he could only have believed strongly enough that he had not got it, it couldn't have killed him. Well, if you won't go you won't. Now I've some news for you. De Keradel has a big place on Rhode Island. I found out about it yesterday. It's an isolated spot, miles from nowhere and right on the ocean. He keeps a yacht—sea-going. He must be almighty rich. De Keradel is up there now, which is why you had it all to yourself with the Demoiselle. Lowell sent yesterday for McCann and McCann is coming in to-night to talk things over. It's Lowell's idea, and mine, too, to have him go up and scout around de Keradel's place. Find out what he can from the people about. Lowell, by the way, has got over his panic. He's—rather deadly in his hatred for de Keradel, and that includes the Demoiselle. I told you he is all wrapped up in Helen. Thinks of her as a daughter. Well, he seems to think that she's in danger.'

I said: 'But that's a damned good idea, Bill. De Keradel spoke of some experiment he is carrying out. That's undoubtedly where he's working. His laboratory. McCann might find out a lot.'

Bill nodded.

' Why not come along and see him? '

I was about to accept when suddenly I had the strongest feeling that I must not. A tingling warning of danger, like some deep, hidden alarm going off. I shook my head.

'Can't do it, Bill. I've got work to do. You can tell me about it to-morrow.'

He got up.

'Thinking you might change your mind about that rendezvous with the Demoiselle? '

'No chance,' I answered. 'Give my love to Helen. And tell her I don't mean maybe. Tell her I'm taking no more journeys. She'll understand.'

I did spend that afternoon working; and that night. Now and then I had an uncomfortable feeling that some one was watching me. Bill called up next day to say that McCann had gone to Rhode Island. Helen got on the 'phone and said she had received my message and would I come up that night. Her voice was warm and sweet and somehow—cleansing. I wanted to go, but that deep hidden alarm was shrilling, peremptorily. I apologized—rather awkwardly. She asked:

' You haven't it in your stubborn head that you'd carry some witch taint with you, have you? '

I said: 'No. But I might carry danger to you.'

123

She said: 'I'm not afraid of the Demoiselle. I know how to fight her, Alan.'

I asked: 'What do you mean by that?'

She said, furiously: 'Damn your stupidity!' and hung up before I could speak.

I was puzzled, and I was troubled. The inexplicable warning to keep away from Dr. Lowell's and from Helen was insistent, not to be disregarded. At last I threw my notes into a bag with some clothes and sought shelter in a little hide-away hotel I knew, after having sent Bill a note telling him where he could find me but warning him not to tell Helen. I said I had the strongest reasons for this temporary disappearance. So I had, even though I didn't know what they were. That was Tuesday. On Friday I went back to the Club.

I found two notes from the Demoiselle. One must have come just after I had left for the hide-out. It read:

'There was a debt from you to me. In part you have paid it. There is not nor ever was a debt from me to you. Beloved—come to me to-night.'

The other had been delivered the day after. It read:

'I go to join my father in his work. When next I call you, see to it that you come. I have sent a souvenir that you may not forget this.'

I read and re-read those notes, wondering. In the first there was appeal, longing; the kind of letter any woman might write to some reluctant lover. In the other was menace. Uneasily, I paced the floor; then called up Bill.

He said: 'So you're back. I'll be right down.'

He was there in half an hour. He seemed a little on edge.

I aked: 'Anything new?'

He sat down and said casually, a bit too casually: 'Well, yes. She's pinned one on me.'

I said, stupidly: 'Who's done what?'

He answered: 'Dahut. She's pinned one of her shadows on me.'

My feet and hands were suddenly cold and I felt a thin cord draw tight round my throat. The letter in which Dahut had spoken of the souvenir she was sending lay open before me, and I folded it. I said:

'Tell me about it, Bill.'

He said: 'Don't look so panicky, Alan. I'm not like Dick and the others. It won't handle me so easily. But I'm not saying it's exactly—companionable. By the way, do you see something at my right? Something like a bit of dark curtain—fluttering?'

He was keeping his eyes upon mine, but the effort of will he was making to do it was plain. They were a bit bloodshot. I looked, intently, and said:

'No, Bill. I don't see a thing.'

He said: 'I'll just shut my eyes, if you don't mind. Last night I came out of the hospital about eleven. There was a taxi at the kerb. The driver was half asleep, hunched over the wheel. I opened the door and was about to get in when I saw some one—something— move in the far corner of the seat. The cab was fairly dark, and I could not determine whether it was a man or a woman. I said: "Oh, I beg your pardon. I thought the taxi empty." And I stepped back.

'The taxi man had awakened. He touched my

125

shoulder. He said: " O.K., boss, get in. I ain't got anybody." I said: "Sure you have." He flashed on the inside light. The cab was empty. He said: " I been waitin' here an hour, boss, on a chance. Just dozin'. Nobody got in. You seen a shadow."

'I stepped into the cab and told him where to take me. We had gone a couple of blocks when I thought some one was sitting beside me. Close to me. I had been looking straight ahead and turned quickly. I caught a glimpse of something dark between me and the window. Then—there was nothing, but I distinctly heard a faint rustling. Like a dry leaf being blown along a window in the night. Deliberately, I moved over to that side. We had gone another few blocks when I once more saw the movement at my left, and again there was a thin veil of deeper darkness between me and that window——

'The outline was that of a human body. And again as it flicked out I heard the rustling. And in that instant, Alan, I knew.

'I confess that I had a moment of pure panic. I called to the driver, about to tell him to take me back to the hospital. Then my nerve came back, and I told him to go ahead. I went into the house. I felt the shadow flitting with me as I entered. There was no one up. It accompanied me, impalpable, incorporeal, glimpsed only by its movement, until I went to bed. It was with me through the night. I didn't sleep much——'

He opened his eyes, and quickly shut them again.

'I thought that like Dick's shadow it would go with the dawn. This one didn't. It was still there when I woke up. I waited until they'd all had breakfast—after all, Alan, a little playmate like that was nothing to introduce to the family, you know.' He squinted at me sardonically. 'Also—it has other points of difference from Dick's. I gather that Dahut rather favoured him in that matter. I wouldn't call my pal—cosy.'

I asked: 'It's pretty bad then, Bill?'

He said: 'I can get along with it—unless it gets worse.'

I looked at my watch. It was five o'clock. I said: 'Bill, have you got de Keradel's address?'

Bill said: 'Yes,' and gave it to me.

I said: 'Bill, don't worry any more. I have an idea. Forget about the shadow as much as you can. If you haven't anything important, go home and go to sleep. Or would you rather sleep here a bit?'

He said: 'I'd rather lie down here for a bit. The damned thing doesn't seem to bother me so much here.'

Bill lay down on the bed. I unfolded the Demoiselle's last letter and read it again. I called up the telegraph company and found the nearest village to the de Keradel place. I got the telegraph office there on the 'phone and asked them if there was telephone communication with Dr. de Keradel. They said there was, but that it was a private wire. I said that was all right, I only wanted to dictate a telegram to the Demoiselle de Keradel. They asked—'the what?' I answered: 'Miss de Keradel.' I felt ironic amusement at that innocent 'Miss'. They said they could take it.

I dictated:

'Your souvenir most convincing, but embarrassing.

Take it back and I surrender unconditionally. Am at your command at any moment when assured this is done.'

I sat down and looked at Bill. He was asleep, but not very happily. I was wide awake but not very happy either. I loved Helen, and I wanted Helen. And I felt that what I had just done had lost Helen to me for ever.

The clock struck six. There was a ring on the telephone. It was long distance. The man to whom I had dictated the telegram spoke:

' Miss de Keradel got the message O.K. Here's one from her. It reads: " Souvenir withdrawn but returnable." You know what it means? '

I answered: ' Sure.' If he had expected me to go into details, he was disappointed. I hung up the 'phone.

I went over to Bill. He was sleeping more quietly. I sat watching him. In half an hour he was breathing peacefully, his face untroubled. I gave him another hour and then awakened him.

' Time to get up, Bill.'

He sat up and looked at me blankly. He looked around the room, and went over to the window. He stood there a minute or two, then turned to me.

' God, Alan! The shadow's gone! '

He said it like a man reprieved from death by torment.

CHAPTER XII

THE VANISHING PAUPERS

WELL, I'd expected results, but not quite so soon nor so complete. It gave me a fresh and disconcerting realization of Dahut's powers—whether of remote control by suggestion, as the Christian Scientists term it, or witchcraft. Such control would in itself savour of witchcraft. But certainly something had happened as the result of my message; and by the relief Bill was showing I knew how much he had understated the burden of the shadow upon him.

He looked at me, suspiciously. He asked: 'What did you do to me while I was asleep?'

'Not a thing,' I said.

'What did you want with de Keradel's address?'

'Oh, just curiosity.'

He said: 'You're a liar, Alan. If I'd been myself, I'd have asked that before I gave it to you. You've been up to something. Now what was it?'

'Bill,' I said, 'you're goofy. We've both been goofy over this shadow stuff. You don't even know you—had one.'

He said, grimly: 'Oh, I don't?' And I saw his hands clench.

I said, glibly: 'No, you don't. You've been thinking too much about Dick and de Keradel's ravings, and of what I told you of the Demoiselle's pretty little hypnotic experiment on me. Your imagination has got infected. Me—I've gone back to hard-headed, safe-

and-sane, scientific incredulity. There ain't no shadow. The Demoiselle is one top-notch expert hypnotist, and we've been letting her play us—that's all.'

He studied me for a moment.

'You never were good at lying, Alan.'

I laughed. I said: 'Bill, I'll tell you the truth. While you were asleep I tried counter-suggestion. Sent you deeper and deeper down until I got to the shadow —and wiped it out. Convinced your subconsciousness you'd never see it again. And you won't.'

He said slowly: 'You forget I tried that on Dick, and it didn't work.'

'I don't give a damn about that,' I said. 'It worked on you.'

I hoped he'd believe me. It would help build up his resistance if the Demoiselle tried any more of her tricks on him. Not that I was any too sanguine. Bill was a psychiatrist of sorts, knew far more about the quirks and aberrations of the human mind than I did, and if he hadn't been able to convince himself of the hallucinatory aspect of the shadows, how could I expect to?

Bill sat quietly for a minute or two, then sighed and shook his head.

'That's all you're going to tell me, Alan?'

'That's all I *can* tell you, Bill. It's all there is to tell.'

He sighed again, then looked at his watch.

'Good God, it's seven o'clock!'

I said: 'How about staying here for dinner? Or are you busy to-night?'

Bill brightened.

'I'm not. But I'll have to call up Lowell.' He took up the telephone.

I said: 'Wait a minute. Did you tell Lowell about my little party with the Demoiselle?'

He said: 'Yes. You don't mind, do you? I thought it might help.'

I said: 'I'm glad you did. But did you tell Helen?'

He hesitated. 'Well—not everything.'

I said, cheerfully: 'Fine. She knows what you left out. And it saves me the time. Go ahead and 'phone.'

I went downstairs to order dinner. I thought both of us were entitled to something extra. When I came back to the room Bill was quite excited. He said:

'McCann is coming to-night to report. He's found out something. He'll be at Lowell's about nine o'clock.'

I said: 'We'll get dinner and go up. I want to meet McCann.'

We had dinner. At nine o'clock we were at Lowell's. Helen wasn't there. She hadn't known I was coming, nor had Lowell told her about McCann. She had gone to the theatre. I was glad of that, and sorry. A little after nine McCann came in.

I liked McCann from the start. He was a lanky, drawling Texan. He had been the underworld leader Ricori's trusted bodyguard and handy man; a former cowpuncher; loyal, resourceful and utterly without fear. I had heard much of him when Bill had recounted the story of that incredible adventure of Lowell and Ricori with Madame Mandilip, the doll-maker, whose lover this de Keradel had been. I had the feeling that McCann took the same instant liking to me. Briggs brought in decanters and glasses. Lowell went over and locked the door. We sat at the table, the four of us. McCann said to Lowell:

'Well, Doc—I reckon we're headed for about the same kind of round-up we was last time. Only mebbe a mite worse. I wish the boss was around. . . .'

Lowell explained to me: 'McCann means Ricori—he's in Italy. I think I told you.'

I asked McCann: 'How much do you know?'

Lowell answered: 'Everything that I know. I have the utmost faith in him, Dr. Caranac.'

I said: 'Fine.'

McCann grinned at me. He said: 'But the boss ain't around, so I guess you'd better cable him you need some help, Doc. Ask him to cable these fellers'—he thrust a list of half a dozen names to Lowell—'an' tell 'em he wants 'em to report to me an' do what I say. An' ask him to take the next ship over.'

Lowell asked, uncertainly: 'You think that is justified, McCann?'

McCann said: 'Yeah. I'd even go as far as to put in that cable that it's a matter of life an' death, an' that the hag who made dolls was just a nursery figure compared to the people we're up against. I'd send that cable right off, Doc. I'll put my name to it, too.'

Lowell asked again: 'You're sure, McCann?'

McCann said: 'We're going to need the boss. That's certain, Doc.'

Bill had been writing. He said: 'How's this?' He passed the paper to McCann. 'You can put in the names of the people you want Ricori to cable.'

McCann read:

'Ricori. Doll-maker menace renewed worse than

before. Have urgent immediate need of you. Ask you return at once. In meantime cable (so-and-so) to report to McCann and follow implicitly his orders. Cable when can expect you.'

'That's O.K.,' McCann said. 'I guess the boss'll read between the lines without the life and death part.'

He filled in the missing names and handed it to Dr. Lowell.

'I'd get it right off, Doc.'

Lowell nodded and wrote an address on it. Bill ran the message off on the typewriter. Lowell unlocked the door and rang for Briggs; he came, and the message to Ricori was on its way.

'I hope to God he gets it quick an' comes,' said McCann, and poured himself a drink. 'An' now,' he said, 'I'll begin at the beginning. Let me tell the whole thing my own way, an' if you got questions, ask them when I'm through.'

He said to Bill: 'After you give me the layout, I head for Rhode Island. I got a sort of hunch, so I take along a big roll of bills. Most of 'em are fakes but imposing in the herd. An' I don't aim to dispose of the mavericks—just display 'em. I see by the road map there's a place called Beverly down that locality. It's the nearest place on the map to this de Keradel ranch. On beyond, it's empty country or big estates. So I head the car that way an' give her the spur. I get there about dark. It's a nice little village, old-fashioned, one street running down to the water, some stores, a movie. I see a shack with a sign Beverly House, an' figure to bed down there for the night. Far as I can see de Keradel an' his gal have got to ride through here to get to the ranch, an' mebbe they do some buying of their truck here. Anyway, I'm betting that there's talk going 'round, an' if so then the gent that runs this Beverly House knows all of it.

' So I go in an' there's an old fellow who looks like a cross between a goat an' a human question mark at the desk, an' I tell him I'm looking for shelter for the night an' maybe a day or so longer. He asks if I'm a tourist, an' I say no, an' hesitate, an' then say I got a piece of business on my mind. He pricks up his ears at that, an' I say where I come from we put our stake on the table before we play, an' pull out the roll. He waggles his ears at that, an' after I've talked him down about two bits on the tariff he's not only plumb curious but got quite a respect for me. Which is the impression I want.

' I go in an' have a darn good meal, and when I'm near through the old goat comes an' asks me how things is an' so on, an' I tell him fine an' to sit down. He does. We talk of this an' that, an' after a while he gets probing what my business is, an' we have some darn good applejack. I get confidential an' tell him I been nursing cows for years down Texas way, an' they've left me sitting mighty pretty. Tell him my grandpap came from round these parts an' I've got a yearning to get back.

' He asks me grandpap's name an' I tell him Partington, an' what I'd hoped to do was buy back the old house, but I was too late learning it was on the market, an' I'd found some Frenchman called de Keradel had bought it from the estate, an' so I supposed that was no good. But mebbe, I say, I could pick

134

up a place near, or mebbe the Frenchman would sell me some of the land. Then I'd wait till mebbe this Frenchman got tired of it an' I could pick the old house up cheap.'

Bill explained to me: ' This place de Keradel bought had belonged to the Partington family for generations. The last one died about four years ago. I told McCann all that. Go on, McCann.'

' He listened to this with a queer look on his face, half-scared,' said McCann. ' Then he opined my grandpap must have been Eben Partington who went West after the Civil War, an' I said I guessed so because pap's name was Eben, an' he seemed to hold quite a grudge against the family an' never talked much about 'em, which was mainly what made me want to get hold of the old place. I said I thought buying it back an' living in it might rile the ghosts of them who kicked grandpap out.

' Well, that was a shot in the dark, but it hit the mark. The old goat gets more talkative. He said I was a grandson of Eben all right, for the Partingtons never forgot a grudge. Then he said he didn't think there was a chance of me getting the old place back because the Frenchman had spent a lot of money on it, but there was a place right close he knew of that I could get an' if I'd put it in his hands he'd get me the lowest price for it. Also, he was sure I couldn't buy in on the Partington ranch, an' with that same queer look said he didn't think I'd like it there if I could. An' he kept staring at me as though he was trying to make up his mind about something.

' I said I'd set my mind on the old homestead, which

I always understood was a pretty fairish size for the East though mebbe not so sizable out West. An' I asked what was the improvements the Frenchman had put in, anyway. Well, the old goat got a map an' showed me the layout. It's a big chunk of land sticking out into the sea. There's a narrow neck about a thousand feet across before the land spreads out. Outside that it spreads a fantail which I figure's got two or three thousand acres in it.

'He tells me the Frenchman's built a twenty foot high wall across that thousand foot neck. There's a gate in the middle. But nobody gets through it. Anything that goes from the village, including the mail, is took in by the guards. Foreigners, he says; funny little dark men who always have the money ready an' say nothing no way. He says they take in a lot of supplies in their boat. Also, they got a farm an' livestock —cattle an' sheep an' such, an' hosses an' a pack of big dogs. He says: "Nobody ain't seen the dogs, except one man, an' he——"

'Then he shuts up all of a sudden as though he's saying too much, an' that funny scared look comes on his face. So I file that for reference but don't press him none.

'I ask him if nobody ain't been inside an' knows what it looks like, an' he says: "Nobody round here has been except the man who——" Then he shuts up again, so I figure he's referring to the man who seen the dogs, an' I get more curious about him.

'I say that with all that coast-line I don't see why people can't slip in an' look around a bit without anybody knowing. But he tells me it's all rock, an' only three places where you can land a boat, an' that these three

136

places are guarded like the gate. He looks at me suspicious an' I say: "Oh, yes, now I remember pap told me about that." An' I'm afraid to ask much more on that line.

'I ask casual what other improvements there are, and he says they made a big rockery. I ask what anybody wants making a rockery in a place where nature has been so prodigal with rocks. He takes another drink an' says, this is a different kind of rockery, an', he says, mebbe it ain't a rockery but a cemetery, an' that funny scared look comes on his face plainer than ever.

'We have some more applejack an' he tells me that his name is Ephraim Hopkins, an' he goes on to say about a month after the Frenchman moves in there's a couple of fishermen coming home when their engine goes wrong right off the point where the house stands. The Frenchman's yacht has just dropped her anchor an' she's lightering a lot of men to the house landing. The fishermen drift a while an' while they're doing it, they figure more'n a hundred men must have been landed.

'Well, he says, about a month after that a Beverly man named Jim Taylor is driving along at night when his headlights pick up a feller staggering along the road. This man gives a yelp when he sees the lights, an' tries to run but he falls down. Taylor gets out an' sees he ain't got nothing on but his underclothes an' a pouch tied round his neck. He's fainted. Taylor picks him up an' carts him to this Beverly House. They pour liquor in him an' he comes to, but he's an Eyetalian who don't speak much English, an' he acts like he's scared half to death. All he wants is to get some clothes an' get away. An' he opens the pouch an' shows money.

137

They get out of him that he's run off from this de Keradel place. Got to the water and swum till he figured he was past the wall, then come to land. He says he's a stone-cutter an' one of a big gang brought in on the boat. He says they're putting up a big rockery there, cutting out stones an' standing 'em up like giant's tombstones all in circles around a house they're building in the middle. Says these stones are twenty, thirty feet high——'

I felt something like a cold hand pass through my hair. I said: ' Say that again, McCann! '

He said, patiently: ' Better let me go on an' tell this in my own way, Doc.'

Bill said: ' I know what you're thinking, Alan. But let McCann go on.'

McCann said: ' The Eyetalian won't tell what scared him. Just jabbers, and shivers, an' keeps crossing himself. They get he's telling 'em the house in the middle of the stones is cursed. Tells 'em it's the Devil's house. They pour more liquor in him an' he says the Devil is taking his toll. Says out of more'n a hundred men that come with him, half have died by stones falling on 'em. Says nobody knows where their bodies went afterwards. Says the gang was recruited from distant cities an' nobody knew each other. Says about fifty more have since been brought in. Says only men without any families were hired.

' Then all of a sudden he gives a screech an' ducks an' covers his head with his hands an' runs out the door an' disappears before anybody can foller. And two days after, says the old goat, they find him washed up on the shore about a mile away.

'He tells me they all figure the Eyetalian's drunk or crazy. But I don't believe him. He looks too agitated. It don't take any eagle eye to see there's something queer here. He says, though, that some of the lads cruise around in boats trying to get a look at this rockery. But they can't see nothing. That don't mean it ain't there, because the rocks are steep around the point an' where they ain't there's big trees growing.

'Anyway, they bury the Eyetalian an' pay their taxes to the poor-farm with his money. I'm telling you about that poor-farm later,' said McCann.

'Well, it seems to me that by then the old goat gets the sudden idea what he's been telling me ain't selling talk for that place he's picked out for me. Anyway, he shuts up and waggles his beard and considers me. So I say that every word he's said only makes me more interested. Tell him there's nothing I like better than a good mystery, an' the more I hear him the more I yearn to settle right down close to a real live one. We take another drink, an' I say if he can only dig up some more stuff like he's been telling me, I'm as good as sold. Also, I'm paying cash. Also, that to-morrow we'll go an' take a look at this ranch he's got in mind. I feel it's better to let all this sink in, so we have another drink an' I go to bed. I notice he's looking at me darned peculiar as I go.

'The next day—that's Wednesday—he's up bright an' early, pert an' panting. We pile into his bus an' start out. After a bit he starts telling me about this feller that seen the dogs. 'Lias Barton, he calls him. He says 'Lias is more curious than ten old maids peeking out behind the curtains at a house with a bride just

moved in. Says curiosity is like a disease with 'Lias.
Says he'd pull out a plug in Hell for a look in, even if
he knew it'd squirt in his face. Well, 'Lias gets brooding and brooding over this wall an' what's behind it.
He's been all over the old Partington place dozens of
times an' he knows darned well what it's like, but this
wall's like his wife putting a veil over her face sudden.
He'd know he'd see the same old face but he'd have to
lift it just the same. An' for the same reason 'Lias just
has to look over that wall.

'He knows there ain't a chance by day, but he recon-
noitres an' crawls around, an' at last he picks a place
down near the water. Eph says there's breasts of rock
each end of the wall into which the wall is built, an' you
can't get over 'em from the water. 'Lias figures he can
row down, slip to land and climb the wall. So he
picks a night when it's full moon but clouds obscuring
the moon frequent. He packs a light ladder an' sculls
down cautious. He lands an' puts up his ladder an'
when the moon's under a cloud he swarms up. An'
there he is on top the wall. He draws up the ladder an'
flattens out an' peers round. It's 'Lias's idea to drop the
ladder on the other side an' prospect. He waits till the
moon comes out again an' he sees it's an open meadow
below him dotted with big bushes. He waits till
another cloud comes an' he unslings the ladder an'
starts down——

'An' when he gets to this point in his story, Eph shuts
up an' heads the bus to the side of the road where we
halt. I say: "Yeah, an' what then?" Eph says:
"Then we pick him up next morning rowing 'round and
'round the harbour an' crying: 'Keep 'em off me—keep

'em off me! ' We take him in," he says, " an' get him
calmed down some an' he tells us what I've told you."

' An' then,' said McCann, ' an' then '—he poured
himself a drink and gulped it—' an' then the old goat
shows he's the best liar or the best actor I ever rode
range with. For he says after that 'Lias goes like this
—an' Eph's eyes roll an' his face twitches an' he sort of
whimpers—" Hear the piping! Oh, hear the piping like
birds! Oh, God—look at 'em running and hiding in the
bushes! Hiding and piping! God—they look like men
—but they ain't men. Look at 'em run an' hide! . . .

' " What's that? It sounds like a hoss . . . a big hoss
. . . galloping . . . galloping! Christ! Look at her
. . . with her hair streaming . . . look at the blue eyes
an' white face of her . . . on the hoss . . . the big black
hoss!

' " Look at 'em run . . . an' hear 'em pipe! Hear
'em pipe like birds! In the bushes . . . running from
bush to bush. . . .

' " Look at the dogs . . . they ain't dogs. . . . Christ!
keep 'em off me! Christ! keep 'em off me! The
hounds of Hell . . . dear Jesus . . . keep 'em off me! " '

McCann said: ' He made me crawl. I'm telling you
I'm crawling now.

' Then he started the bus an' went on. I managed to
ask: " Then what? " He says: " That's all. That's all
we can get out of him. Ain't never been the same since.
Mebbe he just fell off the wall an' hit his head. Mebbe
so—mebbe not. Anyway 'Lias ain't curious no more.
Goes round the village sort of wide-eyed an' lonesome.
Get him started an' he'll do for you what I just did."
He cackled—" But better."

'I said, still crawling: "If what looked like men wasn't, an' the dogs that looked like dogs wasn't, then what the hell were they?"

'He says: "You know as much as I do."

'I say: "Oh, yeah. Anyway, ain't you got any idea of who was the gal on the big black hoss?"

'He says: "Oh, her—sure. That was the Frenchman's gal."'

Again the icy hand ruffled my hair, and my thoughts ran swiftly. . . . Dahut on the black stallion . . . and hunting—what . . . and with—what? And the upright stones and the men who had died raising them . . . as they did of old . . . as of old in Carnac. . . .

McCann's narrative was going smoothly on. He said: 'We ride along quiet after that. I see the old goat is pretty agitated, an' chewing his whiskers. We come to the place he's been telling about. We look around. It's a nice place all right. If I was what I say I was, I'd buy it. Old stone house, lots of room—for the East. Furniture in it. We amble around an' after a while we come in sight of this wall. It's all the old goat said it was. It'd take artillery or TNT to knock it down. Eph mutters not to pay attention to it, except casual. There's big gates across the road that look like steel to me. An' while I don't see nobody I get the idea we're being watched all the time. We stroll here an' stroll there, an' then back to the other place. An' then the old goat asks me anxious what I think of it, an' I say it's all right if the price is, an' what is the price. An' he gives me one that makes me blink. Not because it's high but because it's so low. It gives me the glimmer of another idea. Nursing that idea, I say I'd like to look at some other places. He shows me some, but half-hearted like, an' the idea grows.

'It's late when we get back to the village. On the way we run across a man who draws up to talk. He says to the old goat: "Eph, there's four more gone from the poor-farm."

'The old goat sort of jitters an' asks when. The other man says last night. He says the superintendent's about ready to call in the police. Eph sort of calculates an' says that makes about fifty gone. The other man says, yeah, all of that. They shake their heads an' we go on. I ask what's this about the poor-farm, an' Eph tells me that it's about ten miles off an' that in the last three months the paupers have been vanishing an' vanishing. He's got that same scared look back, an' starts talking about something else.

'Well, we get back to the Beverly House. Thar's quite a bunch of villagers in the front room, an' they treat me mighty respectful. I gather that Eph has told 'em who I'm supposed to be, an' that this is a sort of committee of welcome. One man comes up an' says he's glad to see me but I've been too slow coming home. Also, they've all got the news about these vanishing paupers, an' it's plain they don't like it.

'I get my supper, an' come out, an' there's more people there. They've got a sort of look of herding for comfort. An' that idea of mine gets stronger. It's that I've been wronging Eph in thinking all he wants is a profit from me. I get the flattering idea that they're all pretty plumb scared, an' what they think is that mebbe I'm the man who can help 'em out in whatever's scaring them. After all, I suppose the Partingtons in their time was big guns 'round here, an' here I am, one of 'em, an' coming back providentially, as you might say, just at the right time. I sit an' listen, an' all the talk goes 'round the poor-farm an' the Frenchman.

'It gets around nine o'clock an' a feller comes in. He says: "They picked up two of them missing paupers." Everybody sort of comes close, an' Eph says: " Where? " An' this feller says: " Bill Johnson's late getting in, an' he sees these two floating off his bow. He hooks an' tows 'em. Old Li Jameson's at the wharf an' he takes a look. He says he knows 'em. They're Sam an' Mattie Whelan who've been at the poor-farm for three years. They lay 'em out on the wharf. They must have drowned themselves an' been hitting up against a rock for God knows when," says this feller.

' " What d'you mean, hitting up against a rock? " asks Eph. An' the feller says they must have been because there ain't a whole bone in their chests. Says the ribs are all smashed, an' the way it looks to him they must have been pounding on a rock steady for days. Like as if they'd been tied to it. Even their hearts are all mashed up——'

I felt sick, and abreast of sickness a bitter rage; and within me I heard a voice crying: 'So it was done in the old days . . . so they slew your people . . . long ago——' Then I realized I was on my feet, and that Bill was holding my arms. McCann was on his feet, too, but there was little surprise on his face, and even then I wondered how much more he knew than he was telling us.

I said: 'All right, Bill. Sorry, McCann,' and poured myself a drink.

McCann said, mildly: 'Okay, Doc, you've got your reasons. Well, just then into the room comes a gang-ling sort of feller with empty eyes an' a loose mouth. Nobody says a word, just watches him. He comes over to me an' stares at me. He starts to shake, an' he whispers to me: "She's riding again. She's riding on the black horse. She rode last night with her hair streaming behind her an' her dogs around her——"

'Then he lets out the most God-awful screech an' starts bowing up an' down like a jumping-jack, an' he yells—"But they ain't dogs! They ain't dogs! Keep 'em off me! Dear Jesus . . . keep 'em off me!"

'At that there's a bunch around him saying "Come along, 'Lias, now come along," an' they take him out, still screeching. Them that's left don't say much. They look at me solemn, an' pour down a drink or two an' go. Me'—McCann hesitated—'me, I'm feeling a mite shaky. If I was the old goat I could give you an idea how 'Lias yelped. It was like a couple of devils had pincers on his soul an' was yanking it loose like a tooth. I drank a big one an' started for bed. Old Eph stops me. He's putty-white an' his beard is quivering. He trots out another jug an' says: "Stay up awhile, Mr. Partington. We've an idea we'd like you to settle here with us. If that price don't suit you, name your own. We'll meet it."

'By that time it don't take a master-mind to tell this is a pretty well-scared village. An' from what I know before an' what I've heard since I don't blame 'em. I say to Eph: "Them paupers? You got an idea where they're going to? Who's taking them?"

' He looks around before he answers, then he whispers: " De Keradel."

' I says: " What for? " An' he whispers: " For his rockery."

' Earlier I might have laughed at that. But somehow now I don't feel like it. So I tell him I'm interested, but I got to go back to New York to-morrow an' I'll think it over, an' why don't they get the police to look into things. He says the village constable's as scared as any, an' there ain't no evidence to get out a search warrant, an' he's talked to a couple of country officers but they think he's crazy. So the next morning I check out saying I'll be back in a day or two. There's quite a little delegation sees me off an' urges me to come back.

' I'm mighty curious to see that place behind the wall, an' especially what Eph calls the rockery. So I run down to Providence where I've got a friend with a hydroplane, an' we fix it to ride over the de Keradel place that night. We go along the coast. It's a moonlight night, an' we sight it about ten o'clock. I get out the glasses as we come close. We're flying about five hundred feet up. It's clear, but there's a fog rising about this point as we get closer. A quick fog, too, that looks as if it's trying to beat us to it.

' There's a big boat lying off the point, too, in a sort of deep cove. They flash searchlights up at us, whether trying to blind us or to find out who we are I don't know. I give my friend the word and we duck the lights. I've got my glasses up an' I see a long rambling stone house half hid by a hill. Then I see something that sort of makes me feel creepy—like old 'Lias's wailing. I don't just know why. But it's a lot of big stones

146

all doing ring-a-roses around a bigger grey heap of stones in the middle. The fog's swirling all around like snakes, an' there's lights flickering here an' there . . . grey sort of lights . . . rotten . . .'

McCann stopped and lifted a drink with a none too steady hand. 'Rotten sort of lights is right. Like they're . . . decaying. An' there appears to be something big an' black squatting on the big grey heap . . . without no shape to it . . . shadowy. An' it quivers an' wavers . . . an' the standing stones are like they're reaching up to pull us down to this squatting thing. . . .'

He set the glass down with a hand even less steady. 'Then we're over an' zooming away. I look back an' the fog's covered everything——'

He said to Lowell: 'I'm telling you, Doc, that never at no time with the Mandilip hag did I feel as slimy as when we flew over that place. The Mandilip hag had a line into Hell all right. But this is Hell itself—I'm telling you!'

CHAPTER XIII

SUMMONS FROM DAHUT

'WELL, that's all.' McCann lighted a cigarette and looked at me. 'But I got the idea what I've been telling makes a lot more sense to Dr. Caranac than it does to me. Me—I know it's black poison. Mebbe he knows just how black. For instance, Doc, why did you shy so when I made mention of them two paupers?'

I said: 'Dr. Lowell, you won't mind if I have a little talk with Bill. McCann, I apologize to you in advance. Bill, come over here in the corner. I want to whisper to you.'

I took Bill out of earshot, and asked: 'Just how much does McCann know?'

Bill answered: 'All that we know about Dick. He knows de Keradel's connexion with the doll-maker. And that would be enough for him, if he knew nothing else.'

'Anything about my experiences with the Demoiselle?'

'Certainly not,' said Bill, stiffly. 'Both Lowell and myself thought too much of the confidential element entered into them.'

'That,' I said, keeping solemn with an effort, 'was true delicacy. But have you spoken to any one except me about the shadowy visitation your imagination drew upon you?'

Bill exclaimed: 'Imagination hell! But no—I haven't.'

'Not even to Helen?'

'No.'

'Fine,' I said. 'Now I know where I stand.'

I went back to the table and apologized again to McCann. I said to Lowell:

'You remember de Keradel spoke to us of a certain experiment he contemplated? Its purpose the evocation of some god or demon worshipped long ago? Well, from McCann's story I would say that his experiment must be rather far advanced. He has set up the standing stones in the order prescribed by the ancient ritual, and he has built in their centre the Great Cairn. The House of the Blackness, The Shrine of the Gatherer, The Alkar-Az——'

Lowell interrupted, eagerly: 'You have identified that name? I recall that when first you spoke it de Keradel showed consternation. You evaded his questions. Did you do that to mystify him?'

I said: 'I did not. I still do not know how that name came into my mind. Perhaps from that of the Demoiselle—as other things may have come later—or perhaps not. The Demoiselle, you will also recall, suggested to him that I had—remembered. Nevertheless, I know that what he has built in the heart of the monoliths is the Alkar-Az. And that, as McCann truly says, it is black poison.'

McCann asked: 'But the two paupers, Doc?'

I said: 'It may be that they were beaten by the waves against the rocks. But it is also true that at Carnac and at Stonehenge the Druid priests beat the breasts of the sacrifices with their mauls of oak and stone and bronze until their ribs were crushed and their hearts were pulp.'

McCann said, softly: ' Jesus! '

I said: ' The stone-cutter who tried to escape told of men being crushed under the great stones, and of their bodies vanishing. Recently, when they were restoring Stonehenge, they found fragments of human skeletons buried at the base of many of the monoliths. They had been living men when the monoliths were raised. Under the standing stones of Carnac are similar fragments. In ancient times men and women and children were buried under and within the walls of the cities as those walls were built—sometimes slain before they were encased in the mortar and stone, and sometimes encased while alive. The foundations of the temples rested upon such sacrifices. Men and women and children . . . their souls were fettered there for ever . . . to guard. Such was the ancient belief. Even to-day there is the superstition that no bridge can stand unless at least one life is lost in its building. Dig around the monoliths of de Keradel's—rockery. I'll stake all I have that you'll discover where those vanished workmen went.'

McCann said: ' That poor-farm's on the water. It wouldn't be hard to take them away by boat.'

Lowell objected sharply: ' Nonsense, McCann. How could they be taken secretly? You're surely not suggesting that de Keradel could steam in, gather the paupers on his boat and sail away without any one being aware of it? '

McCann said, placatingly: ' Well now, Doc, there wouldn't be much of a trick in that. I've seen 'em snaked out of penitentiaries. Guards can always be fixed, you know.'

I said: ' There are other ways. They might slip away

of their own volition. Who knows what de Keradel might promise them—if they slipped away to him?'

Lowell said: 'But how could he get to them? How establish contact?'

Bill answered, quietly: 'By the shadows of Dahut!'

Lowell thrust his chair back violently. He said: 'Preposterous! I acknowledge that such an abnormal suggestion as we have been considering might have been effective in Ralston's case. But to assert that a collective hallucination could be induced which would draw away half a hundred inmates of it is—preposterous!'

'Well, anyway,' drawled McCann, 'they went.'

I said: 'De Keradel is an enthusiast, and thorough. Like Napoleon, he knows that you cannot make an omelet without breaking eggs; nor can you have meat without cattle; nor human sacrifices without humans. How did he get his workmen? He engaged an agent who collected men without family—and therefore with nobody to care whether they turned up again or did not. Also, they came from widely separated parts and they did not know each other. Why? Because that reduced to a minimum any chance of inquiry concerning them. What became of those who were left after they had finished his—rockery? Who knows—and who cares? Were any of them allowed to go after they had finished their work? I doubt it. Otherwise, why all these peculiar precautions? Again—who knows and who cares?'

Bill said: 'You mean he used them for——'

I interjected: 'For his experiment, of course. Or as McCann's old goat put it—for his rockery. They were laboratory subjects. Well, the supply runs short. He

F   151

hasn't enough. For one reason or another he doesn't want to bring in any more that way. Still, he must have more subjects. For a show such as he proposes putting on, he may need quite a crowd. Where could he get them with the least risk? Not by stealing them from around the countryside. That would raise hell. Not from a prison—because even ten men vanishing from a prison would raise even more hell. Also, he needs women as well as men. Who is the least missed person in the world? A pauper. And here close at hand is a reservoir of them. And so—the paupers vanish.'

McCann said: 'It sounds right. But what about them dogs that ain't dogs that sent 'Lias mad?'

I thought: *Riding on her stallion black, at her feet her shadow pack*——

I answered: 'Your guess about that is as good as mine, McCann. What are you going to do with these men, if Ricori puts them under your command? What plan have you in mind?'

He settled himself in his chair.

'Well, it's this way. If the boss turns 'em over to me, it means he's going to come back. An' when the boss makes up his mind, he moves quick. Now these lads I named are handpicked an' none afraid of Hell or its angels. Handy with the Tommy-guns an' what not, but they ain't a bad-looking or a bad-behaved lot—ordinarily. Now what I'm figuring is that if this de Keradel's up to the tricks we've been talking of, something's likely to happen that'll give us a hold on him. I got a hunch the floating off of them two paupers was a mistake. He don't want nothing that'll point a finger at him. All right, maybe he'll make another mistake. An' we'll be there.

'The Beverly people'll be damned glad to see me. I been a mite modest about how much they took to me. I go back with a couple of the lads an' tell Eph I'll try out for a bit that house he offered me. Then in a day or two the rest filter in. Just coming up to stay with McCann for the fishing an' the rest. We'll fish around all right, an' sort of ride an' tramp an' scout. By the time the boss gets here we'll have the lay of the land. Then, after you've shown him, he'll tell us what to do further.'

Dr. Lowell said: 'McCann, all of this will cost money. I cannot consent to it unless you permit me to defray the expenses.'

McCann grinned.

'Don't worry about that, Doc. The house won't cost us nothing. Eph an' his friends'll see to that. As for the lads—well, I look after some things for the boss an' he's left me plenty of funds. The boss'll pay for the party. An' should the party get rough, well '—there was a lawless glint in McCann's eyes—' from what you and Doc Bennett tell me there ought to be good pickings at the de Keradel joint.'

Lowell exclaimed, shocked: 'McCann! '

I laughed; nevertheless I studied McCann. Suddenly I had an uneasy feeling that he might not be so disinterested after all. Straightforward enough he seemed, and his story supported our every suspicion—but wasn't it just a little too pat. He and Ricori had been gangsters and racketeers, operating ruthlessly outside the law. I had no doubt that in the main his story was true; that

153

he had found a village filled with fear and rumour. But this might be nothing more than the gossip of a small community whose curiosity and resentment had been aroused by being barred from a place to which they had enjoyed free ingress for generations. In many parts of rural New England it is a neighbourhood affront to pull down the window shades at night. Families have been ostracized and preached against in the churches for doing it. Unless you are doing something wrong, why cover the windows so the neighbours can't look in? The same argument might be at the bottom of the Beverly unrest. Their imaginations painted what might be going on behind the de Keradel wall. And tale after tale would grow stronger in the telling.

How easy for a quick-witted crook to take advantage of such a situation; bring in a gang and set up head-quarters in this house between the village and the isolated de Keradel place. Then, on some manufactured evidence or without it, under pretence of ridding the villagers of their terror, with their rear protected by these superstitious allies, to storm the wall, raid the house and loot it. Its guards once overcome, there would be none to interfere. Perhaps McCann had in-formation as to the extent of the 'pickings' beyond Bill's surmises as to what had been secured from Ralston and the others. Perhaps he had already apprised Ricori of the opportunity, and the cable he had induced Lowell to send was only a blind.

These thoughts ran through my mind in a fraction of the time it has taken to tell them. I said:

'It sounds first-rate. But what you need is somebody inside the place who will keep in touch with you.'

McCann said, emphatically: 'That's one thing can't be done.'

I said: 'Wrong. I know somebody who will do it.'

He grinned.

'Yeah? Who?'

I said: 'Me.'

Lowell leaned forward, staring at me incredulously. Bill whitened, and little beads of sweat came out on his forehead.

McCann's grin faded. He asked: 'How you going to get in?'

I said: 'By the front door, McCann. I have, in fact, an invitation from Mademoiselle de Keradel. I've accepted it. I'm afraid I forgot to tell you that, Bill.'

Bill said, grimly: 'I'm afraid you did. So . . . *that* . . . was why you wanted de Keradel's address? And *that* was what you did while I was asleep . . . and *that* was why . . .'

I said, airily: 'I haven't the slightest idea what you're talking about, Bill. The Demoiselle, no matter what else she may be, is a damned interesting lady. I'd been thinking over what you suggested a few days ago—about sitting in and so on. It just happened that the invitation came while you were asleep, and I immediately accepted. And that's all.'

He said, slowly: 'And immediately the——'

I said, hastily: 'Nothing to that, Bill. Forget it. Now as I see the situation——'

McCann interrupted, his eyes narrowed and face hardened: 'Seems to me you know this de Keradel gal better'n anybody told me, Dr. Caranac. Seems to me you know a hell of a lot you've not come clean with.'

I said, cheerfully: 'A hell of a lot is right, McCann. And that's the way it stays. Take me or leave me. You'll have your gang outside the wall. I'll be inside. If you want me to co-operate, fine. If you don't, I'd just as soon play a lone hand. What are you afraid of?'

He flushed, and his hands went down to his hips in a swift, stiff motion. He drawled:

'I ain't afraid—but I like to know the brand of man I work for.'

I laughed.

'Take it from me, McCann, whatever it is, it's not the Double-Cross. But you'll have to leave it at that.'

Bill said, still sweating: 'I can't let you do that, Alan.'

I said: 'Listen. Either de Keradel and the Demoiselle brought about the suicide of Dick and the others—or they did not. If they did—they accomplished it by some dark knowledge they possess, or by hypnotic suggestion. In either case, no evidence could be brought against them that any court would consider. So that's out. But if de Keradel is actually carrying on that devilish experiment he hinted, and if he is luring, stealing or otherwise securing human sacrifices to complete that experiment, then he's leaving himself open to perfectly tangible evidence and a charge of murder. Therefore a drop with a noose around his neck. And so'—I winced at the thought—'is the Demoiselle. The only place to get that evidence is up there in Rhode Island. McCann's plan is good, but he's outside the wall, and he could not have the advantages that some one inside would have for observation. It happens that I am not only invited to go inside, but uniquely fitted for doing so.' I couldn't help giving Bill a sardonic grin at that. 'Also, Bill, if there is danger, I have a real conviction that I run less risk by accepting the Demoiselle's invitation than I do by refusing it.'

And that was true enough, I thought. If I obeyed Dahut's summons, I'd probably lose Helen for ever. But if I didn't—well, I would just as probably lose her anyway. And I didn't like to think of what might happen to her and to Bill in the process. At that time incredulity and absolute conviction of the Demoiselle's unholy powers revolved in my mind like a two-sailed windmill. And sometimes so fast that I found myself both believing and disbelieving at the same time.

Bill said: 'You were always a rotten bad liar, Alan.'

McCann stuck out his hand.

'Okay, Doc. I'm sorry I said it. You don't need tell me nothing more. What d'you want me to do?'

I was really moved by that. I took his hand and said: 'I'm sorry, too, McCann.'

McCann asked: 'What for?'

I said: 'For something I'd been thinking. Come down to the Club with me and we'll map out some line. We won't talk here because from now on I want Dr. Bennett to keep out of this.'

Bill said, hotly: 'The hell I will. When McCann goes up there I go with him.'

I said: 'I know what I'm talking about. I'll play this game with McCann. And with Ricori—if he comes over. But you're out of it, Bill. I don't want you even to talk to Ricori. Let Dr. Lowell do all the explaining.'

Bill said stubbornly: 'I go with McCann.'

I said: 'You poor boob, do you think it's you I'm considering? It's—Helen.'

He dropped at that, and again I saw his face whiten and the little beads of sweat come out on his forehead. He said, slowly:

'So—*that's* it.'

I said: 'That's *exactly* it. Think it over and see how right I am. Nothing doing, Bill. You're out.' I turned to Dr. Lowell. 'I have the best of reasons for what I am saying. I am hoping you will support me. I don't think there's much danger for you. But for Helen and Bill—a lot.'

I got up; I looked at Bill and laughed. I said: 'You've the look of somebody who sees his best friend pacing from the condemned cell towards that Little Green Door from which none returneth. It's nothing of the sort, Bill. I'm going to visit a charming lady and her perhaps insane but nevertheless brilliant father. I expect to have a most interesting time. And if papa gets too crazy I have McCann to fall back on. If I want you, I'll call on you. There are mails and telephone. Come on, McCann.'

We went down, the four of us, to the hall. I said: 'Also, Bill, don't tell Helen anything about this until I give you the word.'

And just then the door opened and Helen came in.

Her eyes widened, and she looked distressed. She said: 'Hello, darling. Why didn't somebody tell me you were coming to-night? I'd not have gone out.'

She put her arms round my neck and kissed me. Her lips were soft and warm, and there was a fragrance about her—not like some unknown sea-bloom but flowers blossoming on a breast of earth.

I said: 'I didn't know it myself until after you'd gone, angel.'

She said: 'Well, you're coming right back. I've a lot to talk to you about.'

I wanted to be with Helen, right enough—but someway, to-night, I didn't want to talk to her. I cast an involuntary glance of appeal at McCann.

McCann caught it. He said: 'Sorry, Miss Helen, but we got to get right out.'

Helen looked at him.

'Hello, McCann. I didn't notice you. What are you going to do with this man of mine?'

'Anything you say, Miss Helen.' McCann was grinning, but I had the idea he was speaking absolute truth, and that whatever Helen ordered he would certainly do his best to accomplish.

Bill said: 'Alan has to go, Helen.'

She took off her hat and smoothed the copper helmet of her hair. She asked, quietly:

'The de Keradel affair, Alan?'

I nodded and she went a little white. I said: 'It's nothing very important, but, honestly, I can't stay. Let's make a day of it to-morrow, Helen. Meet me at Marguens and take lunch. Then we'll ride around a bit and get supper and go to some show or other. I haven't been to a theatre for three years.'

She looked at me for a long minute or two, then rested her hands on my shoulders.

'All right, Alan. I'll meet you there—at two. But —be there.'

As I went out I swore to myself that come hell or high water, I'd be there. Summons from Dahut notwithstanding. If Bill had to entertain one of her shadows for a few hours—well, he'd have to stand it.

Down at the Club, McCann and I had a few drinks and I told him a few more things. I said I thought both de Keradel and his daughter were a bit crazy, and the reason I'd been invited down was because she had a wild idea we'd been in love with each other a few thousand years ago. He listened, silently. When I was done, he said:

'Them shadders, Doc. You think they're real?'

I said: 'I don't see how they can be. But certainly the people who see them think they are.'

He nodded, absently.

'Well, they got to be treated as if they're real. But how can you put the heat on a shadder? The people responsible for 'em are real, though. An' you can always put the heat on them.'

He said, shrewdly: 'This de Keradel gal, now—how do you feel about her? I hear she's mighty ornamental. Feel safe—going down there?'

I flushed at that. I said, coldly: 'When I need a guardian, McCann, I'll let you know.'

He answered as coldly: 'I didn't mean it that way. Only—I ain't aiming to see Miss Helen get any crooked deal.'

That stung me. I began, unthinkingly: 'If it wasn't for Miss Helen——' then shut up.

He leaned over towards me, his eyes less hard.

'I thought so. You're scared for Miss Helen. That's why you're going. But mebbe that ain't just the way to protect her.'

I said: 'All right, McCann, tell me a better.'

He said: ' Why not leave it to me an' the hands? '

' I know what I'm about, McCann,' I told him.

He sighed and got up.

' Well, soon's we hear from the boss you an' me's got to get together on signals an' how to meet down there. There'll be boats fishing at the end of the walls, for one thing. When do you figure on visiting? '

' When I'm sent for.'

He sighed again, shook my hand solemnly, and left. I went to bed, and slept soundly. The next morning at nine Bill called me up to say that Ricori had cabled the necessary instructions, and that he was flying from Genoa to Paris that day to catch the *Mauretania*, and would be in New York in a week. McCann 'phoned the same news, and we made an engagement for that midnight to go over details of our team work.

I spent a gorgeous day with Helen. I met her at Marguens and said:

' This day is yours and mine, darling. We're not going to think about anything else. To hell with the de Keradels. This is the last mention of them.'

She said, sweetly: ' To hell with them suits me perfectly, darling.'

It was, as I have said, a gorgeous day, and long before it was over I knew just how much I was in love with her; how utterly lovely and desirable she was. Every time the thought of the Demoiselle crept out of the far corner of my mind into which I had thrust her, I pushed her back with a pang of hatred. At half-past eleven I bade good-bye to Helen at Lowell's door. I asked:

' How about to-morrow? '

She said: ' All right—if you can.'

I asked: ' Why the devil couldn't I? '

She said: ' This day's over, Alan. You'll not be rid of Dahut so easily.' I started to answer; she stopped me. ' You don't know how much I love you. Promise me—if you need me . . . come to me . . . at any time . . . in any—shape! '

I caught her in my arms.

' In any shape—what the devil do you mean by that? '

She drew my head down, pressed her lips to mine— savagely, tenderly, passionately, all in one—for long. She thrust me from her, and I saw that she was crying. She threw open the door, then turned for a moment.

' You *don't* know how much I love you! '

She closed the door. I went down to the waiting cab and rode to the Club, cursing the Demoiselle more comprehensively than I had since ancient Ys—if and when that had been. McCann hadn't arrived, but a telegram had. It was from Dahut, and read:

' The yacht will be waiting for you at the Larchmont Club at noon to-morrow. Her name is *Brittis*. I will meet you. Sincerely hope you will come prepared for indefinite stay.'

Well—that was that. I did not miss the nuance of the name, nor the mockery in that ' indefinite stay '. Helen was reality, and Dahut was shadow. But I knew that now shadow had become the true reality. With a sinking of the heart; with forebodings against which I raged, impotently; with sorrow for Helen as though I were bidding her farewell for ever; with bitter hatred against this woman who was half-contemptuously sum- moning me—I knew I could do nothing but obey her.

CHAPTER XIV

BEHIND DE KERADEL'S WALL

I HAD one of my valises packed when McCann was
announced. He squinted at it with surprise.

'You ain't going away to-night, Doc?'

With a sudden impulse towards frankness, I pushed
over to him the Demoiselle's telegram. He read it
stolidly; looked up.

'This just come? Thought you told Doc Bennett
you'd already had an invitation?'

'This,' I explained patiently, 'is merely a confirma-
tion of an engagement previously made, setting a
definite time for one left indefinite before—as you will
see if you read it over again carefully.' I began to pack
the other valise.

McCann re-read the telegram, watched me silently
for a while, then said mildly:

'Doc Bennett had one of them shadders trailing him,
didn't he?'

I turned to him sharply: 'What makes you think that?'

He went on, as though he had not heard me: 'An'
he lost it down here with you, didn't he?'

'McCann,' I said, 'you're crazy. What gave you
that idea?'

He sighed, and said: 'When you an' him was
arguing last night about you going down an' staying
with this de Keradel, I got a mite puzzled. But when
I see this telegram, I ain't puzzled no more. I get the
answer.'

'Fine,' I said, and resumed packing. 'What is it?'

He said: 'You traded something for Doc Bennett's shadder.'

I looked at him and laughed.

'You've grand ideas, McCann. What have I to trade, and with whom and for what?'

McCann sighed again, and put a finger on the Demoiselle's name. 'With her.' He pointed to the 'indefinite stay' and said: 'An' you traded this for his shadder.'

'McCann '—I went over to him—'he did think a shadow was following him. But that may have been only because he has been thinking too much about this whole queer matter. And he has much the same idea as you about how he was relieved of the—obsession. I want you to promise me that you will say nothing of your own suspicions to him—and especially nothing to Miss Helen. If one or the other should speak to you about it, do your best to discourage the notion. I have good reasons for asking this—believe me I have. Will you promise?'

He asked: 'Miss Helen don't know nothing about it yet?'

'Not unless Dr. Bennett has told her since we left,' I answered. Uneasily I wondered whether he had, and cursed my stupidity for not getting his promise that he wouldn't.

He considered me for a time, then said: 'Okay, Doc. But I've got to tell the boss when he comes.'

I laughed, and said: 'Okay, McCann. By that time the game may be all over—except for the post-mortems.'

He asked, sharply: 'What do you mean by that?'

164

I answered: 'Nothing', and went on with my packing. The truth was I didn't know myself what I had meant.

He said: 'You figure on getting there some time tomorrow evening. I'll be up at the old goat's with some of the lads long before dusk. Probably won't get to this house I been telling you of until next day. But nothing's likely to happen right off. You got any plans how we're going to get together?'

'I've been thinking about that.' I stopped the packing, and sat on the bed. 'I'm not so sure how much I'm going to be under surveillance, or what liberty I'll have. The situation is—well, unusual and complicated. Obviously, I can't trust to letters or telegrams. Telegrams have to be telephoned and telephones can be tapped. Also, letters can be opened. I might ride to the village, but that doesn't mean I could get in touch with you when I got there, because I don't think I'd be riding alone. Even if you happened to be there, it would be highly impolitic to recognize and talk to you. The de Keradels are no fools, McCann, and they would realize the situation perfectly. Until I've been on the other side of de Keradel's wall and studied the ground, I can suggest only one thing.'

'You talk like you been sentenced an' bound for the Big House,' he grinned.

'I believe in looking for the worst,' I said. 'Then you're never disappointed. That being so—put this down, McCann—a telegram to Dr. Bennett which reads "Feeling fine. Don't forget to forward all mail," means that you're to get over that wall despite hell or high water as quick as you can and up to the house as

165

quick as you can, and damn the torpedoes. Get that, McCann?'

'Okay,' he said. 'But I got an idea or two likewise. First—nobody's going to keep you from writing after you get there. Okay again. You write an' you find some excuse to get to the village. You get out to this Beverly House I been telling you about an' go in. Don't matter who's with you, you'll find some way to drop that letter on the floor or somewhere. You don't have to give it to nobody. After you go they'll comb the place through to find it. An' I'll get it. That's one line. Next—there'll be a couple of lads fishing around the north side of that wall all the time—that's the left end of it coming from the house. There's a breast of rock there, an' I don't see why you can't climb up that to look at the surroundings, all by yourself. Hell, you're *inside* the wall an' why should they stop you? Then if you've written another note an' put it in a little bottle an' casually throw some stones an' among 'em the bottle, the lads being on the look-out for just such stuff will just as casually rope it in.'

'Fine,' I said, and poured him a drink. 'Now all you have to do is to tell Dr. Bennett to look out for that message and bring up your myrmidons.'

'My what?' asked McCann.

'Your gifted lads with their Tommies and pine-apples.'

'That's a grand name,' said McCann. 'The boys'll like it. Say it again.'

I said it again, and added: 'And for God's sake, don't forget to give that message straight to Dr. Bennett.'

He said: 'Then you ain't going to talk to him before you go?'

I said: 'No. Nor to Miss Helen either.'

He thought over that for a bit, then asked: 'How well you armed, Doc?'

I showed him my 32-automatic.

He shook his head. 'This is better, Doc.' He reached under his left arm-pit and unstrapped a holster. In it was an extraordinarily compact little gun, short-barrelled, squat.

'It shoots a 38,' he said. 'Ain't nothing under armour plate stands up against that, Doc. Carry your other but stick this under your arm. Keep it there, asleep or awake. Keep it hid. There's a few extra clips in that pocket of the holster.'

I said: 'Thanks, Mac.' And threw it on the bed.

He said: 'No. Put it on an' get used to the feel of it.'

'All right,' I said. And did so.

He took another drink, leisurely; he said, gently: 'Of course there's one straight easy way out of all this, Doc. All you need do when you sit at the table with de Keradel an' his gal is to slip that little cannon loose an' let 'em have it. Me an' the lads'd cover you.'

I said: 'I'm not sure enough for that, Mac. Honestly—I'm not.'

He sighed again, and rose.

'You got too much curiosity, Doc. Well, play your hand your own way.' At the door he turned. 'Anyway, the boss'll like you. You got guts.'

He went out. I felt as though I'd been given the accolade.

I dropped a brief note to Bill, simply saying that

when one had made up one's mind to do something, there was no time like the present to do it, and that therefore I was making myself one of the de Keradel *ménage* on the morrow. I didn't say anything about the Demoiselle's telegram, leaving him to think I was on my way solely of my own volition. I told him McCann had a message that was damned important, and that if and when he received it from me to forward it quick, according to directions.

I wrote a little letter to Helen. . . .

The next morning I left the Club early—before the letters could be delivered. I taxied leisurely to Larchmont; arrived at the Club shortly before noon, and was told that a boat from the *Brittis* was awaiting me at the landing-stage. I went down to the boat. There were three men on it—Bretons or Basques, I couldn't tell which, oddly enough. Rather queer-looking—stolid faces, the pupils of their eyes unusually dilated, skins sallow. One turned his eyes up to me and asked, tonelessly, in French:

'The Sieur de Carnac?'

I answered, impatiently: 'Dr. Caranac.' And took my place in the stern.

He turned to the two: 'The Sieur de Carnac. Go.'

We shot through a school of small fry and headed for a slim, grey yacht. I asked: 'The *Brittis*?' The helmsman nodded. She was a sweet craft, about a hundred and fifty feet over all, schooner rigged and built for speed. I doubted McCann's estimate of her ocean-going capabilities.

The Demoiselle was standing at the head of the

ladder. Considering the manner of my last parting
with her, there were obvious elements of embarrass-
ment in this meeting. I had given them considerable
thought, and had decided to ignore them, or pass them
over lightly—if she would let me. It was no picture
of a romantic hero I had made sliding down from her
tower, and I was still somewhat sensitive as to its
undignified aspects. I hoped her arts, infernal or otherwise, hadn't enabled her to reconstruct that spectacle.
So when I had climbed the ladder, I simply said with
cheerful idiocy:

'Hello, Dahut. You're looking—beautiful.'

And so she was. Nothing at all like the Dahut of
ancient Ys; nothing at all like a shadow queen; nothing
at all like a witch. She had on a snappy white sport
suit, and there was no aureole, evil or otherwise, about
her pale gold hair. Instead there was a tricky little
green knit hat. Her great violet eyes were clear and
ingenuous with not a trace of the orchid hell sparks.
In fact, to outward appearance only an extraordinarily
beautiful woman with no more high explosive about
her than any beautiful woman would naturally carry.
But I knew different.

She laughed, and held out her hand.

'Welcome, Alain.'

She glanced at my two bags with a small enigmatic
smile, and led me down to a luxurious little cabin.
She said, matter-of-factly:

'I'll wait for you on deck. Don't be long. Lunch
is ready.' And she was gone.

The yacht was already under way. I looked out of the
port-hole and was surprised to see how far we were from

the Club. The *Brittis* was speedier than I had surmised. In a few minutes I went up on deck and joined
the Demoiselle. She was talking to the captain, whom
she introduced to me by the good old Breton name of
Braz; and me to him as the 'Sieur de Carnac'. The
captain was of stockier build than the others I had
seen, but with the same stolid expression and the same
abnormally dilated eyes. I saw the pupils of his eyes
suddenly contract, like a cat's, and a curiously
speculative gleam come into them . . . almost as
though it were recognition.

I knew then that what I had taken for stolidity was
not that at all. It was—withdrawal. This man's consciousness lived in a world of its own, his actions and
responses to the outer world instinctive only. For some
reason that consciousness had looked out from its inner
world into this under the spur of the ancient name.
From its own world . . . or from another's into which
it had been sent?

And were the other men upon this boat under that
same strange duress?

I said: 'But, Captain Braz, I prefer to be called
Dr. Caranac—not the Sieur de Carnac.'

I watched him closely. He did not respond, his face
impassive, his eyes wide and blank. It was as though
he had not heard me.

The Demoiselle said: 'The Sieur de Carnac will make
many voyages with us.'

He bent and kissed my hand. He answered, tonelessly, as had the boatman: 'The Sieur de Carnac does
me great honour.'

He bowed to the Demoiselle and walked away. I

watched him, and felt a shiver along my spine. It was exactly as though an automaton had spoken; an automaton of flesh and blood who had seen me not as I was but as some one else had bidden him.

The Demoiselle was regarding me with frank amusement.

I said, indifferently: 'You have perfect discipline, Dahut.'

Again she laughed.

'Perfect, Alain. Let us go to lunch.'

We went to lunch. That, too, was perfect. Somewhat too perfect. The two stewards who served us were like the others I had seen; and they served us on bent knees. The Demoiselle was a perfect hostess. We talked of this and that . . . and steadily I forgot what she probably was, and thought of her as what she seemed to be. Only towards the last did that which was buried deep in both our minds crop up. The blank-eyed stewards had knelt, and gone. I said, half to myself:

'Here feudal and the modern meet.'

She answered, quietly: 'As they do in me. But you are too conservative in naming feudal times, Alain. My servants go further back than that. As do I.'

I said nothing. She held her wineglass against the light, turned it to catch the colours, and added, casually:

'As do you!'

I lifted my own glass, and touched hers with its rim: 'To ancient Ys? If so, I drink to it.'

She answered gravely: 'To ancient Ys . . . and we drink to it.'

We touched glasses again, and drank. She set down

her glass and looked at me, faint mockery in her eyes and, when she spoke, within her voice:

'Is it not like a honeymoon, Alain?'

I said, coldly: 'If so—it would be somewhat lacking in novelty, would it not?'

She flushed a little at that. She said: 'You are rather —brutal, Alain.'

I said: 'I might feel more like a bridegroom if I felt less like a prisoner.'

Her straight brows drew together, and for a moment the hell sparks danced in her eyes. She dropped her eyes and said, demurely, although the angry flush still stained her cheeks:

'But you are so—elusive, my beloved. You have such a gift for disappearance. There was nothing for you to fear—that night. You had seen what I had willed you to see, done as I had willed . . . why did you run away?'

That stung; the sleeping wrath and hate against her that I had known since I met her flared up; I caught her wrists.

'Not because I *feared* you, white witch. I could have strangled you while you slept.'

She asked, tranquilly, and tiny dimples showed beside her lips: 'Why didn't you?'

I dropped her hands.

'I may still. That was a wonderful picture you painted in my sleeping mind.'

She stared at me, incredulously.

'You mean . . . you do not think it was real? That Ys was not—real?'

'No more real, Dahut, than the world in which the

minds of the men on this boat live. At your command
—or your father's.'

She said, sombrely: 'Then I must convince you of its
reality.'

I said, rage still hot within me: 'Nor more real than
your shadows, Dahut.'

She said, yet more sombrely: 'Then of those, too, you
must be convinced.'

The moment I had said that about the shadows I was
sorry for it. Her reply did nothing to reassure me. I
cursed myself. This was no way to play the game.
There was no advantage to be gained by quarrelling
with the Demoiselle. It might, indeed, bring down
upon those I was trying to protect precisely what I was
trying to save them from. Was that the meaning
behind her promise to convince me? She was pledged
so far as Bill was concerned and here I was in payment
—but she had made no pledges as to Helen.

If I was to play my game, it must be to the limit; con-
vincingly; with no reservations. I looked at Dahut and
thought, with a sharp pang of compunction for Helen,
that if the Demoiselle were a willing partner it would have
its peculiar compensations. And then I thrust Helen out
of my mind, as though she might read that thought. . . .

And there was only one way to convince a woman. . . .

I stood up. I took the glass from which I had drunk
and I took Dahut's glass and threw them to the cabin
floor, splintering. I walked to the door and turned the
key. I went to Dahut and lifted her from the chair
and carried her to the divan beneath the port-hole. Her
arms clung round my neck, and she raised her lips to
mine . . . her eyes closed. . . .

I said: 'To hell with Ys and to hell with its mysteries. I live to-day. . . .'

She whispered: 'You love me?'

I answered: 'I do love you.'

'No!' She pushed me away. 'In the long ago you loved me. Loved me even though you killed me. And in this life it was not you but the Lord of Carnac who for a night was my lover. Yet this I know—again in this life you must love me. But must you again kill me? I wonder, Alain . . . I wonder . . .'

I took her hands, and they were cold; in her eyes there was neither mockery nor amusement; there was vague puzzlement and vague dread. Nor was there anything of the witch about her. I felt a stirring of pity—what if she, like the others upon this boat, were victim of another's will? De Keradel's, who called himself her father. . . . Dahut who lay there looking at me with the eyes of a frightened maiden . . . and she was very beautiful. . . .

She whispered: 'Alain, beloved—better for you and better for me if you had not obeyed my summons. Was it because of that shadow I sent your friend . . . or had you other reasons?'

That steadied me. I thought: *Witch, you are not so clever.*

I said, as though reluctantly: 'There was another reason, Dahut.'

She asked: 'And that?'

'You,' I said.

She bent towards me, took my chin in one soft hand and held my face close to hers.

'You mean that?'

174

I said: 'I may not love you as the—Lord of Carnac did. But I am tempted to try.'

She leaned back at that, laughing—little rippling waves of laughter, careless and cruel.

'You woo me strangely, Alain. Yet I like it. What do you truly think of me, Alain?'

I said: 'I think of you as a garden that was planned under the red Heart of the Dragon ten thousand years before the Great Pyramid was built and its rays fell upon the altar of its most secret shrine . . . a strange garden, Dahut, half of the sea . . . with trees whose leaves chant instead of whisper . . . with flowers that may be evil and may not be, but certainly are not wholly of the earth . . . whose birds sing strange songs . . . whose breath is more of ocean than of land . . . difficult garden to enter . . . more difficult to find its heart . . . most difficult, once entered, to find escape.'

She bent to me, eyes wide and glowing; kissed me.

'You think that of me! And it is true . . . and the Lord of Carnac never saw me so truly . . . you know more than he . . .'

She fastened my wrists, her breast against mine.

'The red-haired girl—I forget her name—is she not a garden, too?'

Helen!

I said, indifferently: 'A garden of earth. Fragrant and sweet. But no difficulty there about finding your way out.'

She dropped my wrists, and sat for a time silent; then said, abruptly: 'Let us go up on deck.'

I followed her, uneasily. Something had gone amiss, something I had said or had not said about Helen. But

175

what the devil it could have been, I did not know. I looked at my watch. It was after four. There was a fog, but the yacht seemed not to mind it; instead of diminishing, it seemed to me that the speed had increased. As we sat on the deck-chairs, I mentioned this to the Demoiselle. She said, absently:

'It is nothing. There can be no danger.'

I said: 'The speed seems rather dangerous.'

She answered: 'We must be at Ys by seven.'

I echoed, stupidly: 'Ys?'

She said: 'Ys. It is so we have named our home.'

She sank back into silence. I watched the fog. It was an odd fog. It did not swirl past us as fog normally does. It seemed to go with us, to accommodate its pace to ours. . . .

To move with us.

The wide-eyed, vacant-faced sailors padded past. I began to have a nightmarish sort of feeling that I was on a ship of ghosts, a modern Flying Dutchman, cut off from the rest of the world and sped on by unseen, unheard, unfelt winds. Or being pushed along by some gigantic swimmer whose hand was clasped about the stern of this boat . . . and whose breath was the fog that shrouded us. I glanced at the Demoiselle. Her eyes were shut, and she seemed to be fast asleep. I closed my own eyes. . . .

When I opened them, the yacht had stopped. There was no sign of fog. We lay in a little harbour between two rocky headlands. Dahut was shaking me by the shoulders. I was outlandishly sleepy. The sea air, I drowsily thought. We dropped into a tender, and landed at a dock. We climbed up steps, interminably,

176

it seemed to me. A few yards from the top of the steps was a long rambling old stone house. It was dark, and I could see nothing beyond it but the banks of trees, half-stripped of their leaves by the autumn.

We went into the house, met by servants, wide-pupilled, impassive, as those who manned the *Brittis*. I was taken to my room, and a valet began to unpack my bags. In the same torpor, I dressed for dinner. The only moment of real consciousness I had was when I put my hand up and felt McCann's holster under my arm-pit.

I have the vaguest recollection of the dinner. I know that de Keradel greeted me with the utmost politeness and hospitality. During the dinner, he talked on and on, but what he was talking about I'm damned if I knew. Now and then I was acutely aware of the Demoiselle, her face and big eyes swimming out of the haze that gripped me. And now and then I thought that I must have been drugged—but whether I had or hadn't been didn't seem to matter. There was one thing that I was acutely conscious did matter, however —and that was how I answered de Keradel's questions. But another sense, or another self, unaffected by what had so paralysed my normal ones, seemed to have taken charge of that, and I had the comfortable feeling that it was doing it most satisfactorily.

And after a while I heard Dahut say: 'But, Alain, you are so sleepy. Why, you can hardly keep your eyes open. It must be the sea air.'

I replied, solemnly, that it must indeed be the sea air and apologized for my dullness. I had a dim perception of the solicitous readiness with which de Keradel

177

accepted the feeble excuses. He, himself, took me to my room. At least, I was hazily aware that he accompanied me to some place where there was a bed. I rid myself of my clothes by sheer habit, dropped into the bed and in an instant was sound asleep.

I sat up in my bed, wide awake. The strange drowsiness was gone; the irresistible torpor lifted. What had awakened me? I looked at my watch, and it was a few minutes after one. The sound that had awakened me came again—a distant muffled chanting, as though from far under earth. As though from far beneath the old house.

It passed slowly from beneath the house, rising, approaching; becoming ever plainer. A weird chanting, archaic, vaguely familiar. I got up from the bed, and went to the windows. They looked out upon the ocean. There was no moon, but I could see the grey surges breaking sullenly against the rocky shore. The chanting grew louder. I did not know where was the switch to turn on the electric light. There had been a flashlight in one of my bags, but these had been unpacked; their contents distributed.

I felt around in my coat and found a box of matches. The chanting was dying away, as though those singing were passing far beyond the house. I lighted a match, and saw a switch beside the wall. I pressed it, and without result. I saw my flashlight on a table beside the bed. I clicked the catch, but no ray streamed forth. Suspicion began to take hold of me that these three things were linked—the strange sleepiness, the useless flash, the unresponsive switch. . . .

McCann's gun! I felt for it. There it was, nestling under my left arm-pit. I looked at it. The magazine was full and the extra clips safe. I went to the door and cautiously turned the key. It opened into a wide, old-fashioned hall at the end of which dimly glimmered a great window. The hall was curiously—uneasy. That is the only word for it. It was filled with whisperings and rustlings—and shadows.

I hesitated; then stole to the window and looked out. There was a bank of trees through whose half-bare branches I could see across a level field. Beyond that level field was another bank of trees. From beyond them came the chanting.

There was a glow through and over these trees—a grey glow. I stared at it . . . thinking of what McCann had said . . . like light decaying . . . rotten. . . .

It was exactly that. I stood there, gripping the window, watching the putrescent glow wax and wane . . . wax and wane. And now the chanting was like that dead luminescence transformed to sound. . . .

And then a sharp scream of human agony shot through it. . . .

The whisperings in the hall were peremptory. The rustlings were close. The shadows were pressing around me. They pressed me from the window, back to my room. I thrust the door shut against them, and leaned against it, wet with sweat.

Leaning against it, I heard again that scream of anguish, sharper, more agonized. And suddenly muffled.

Again the torpor swept over me. I crumpled down at the edge of the door, and slept.

CHAPTER XV

BEHIND DE KERADEL'S WALL—*continued*

SOMETHING was dancing, flittering, before me. It had no shape, but it had a voice. The voice was saying, over and over again: ' Dahut . . . beware of Dahut . . . Alan, beware of Dahut . . . give me release, Alan . . . but beware of Dahut . . . Alan, give me release . . . from the Gatherer . . . from the Blackness. . . .'

I tried to focus upon this flittering thing, but there was a brilliance about it into which it melted and was lost; a broad aureole of brilliance, and only when I turned my eyes from it could I see the thing dancing and flittering like a fly caught in a globule of light.

But the voice—I knew the voice.

The thing danced and flittered; grew larger but never assumed definite shape; became small, and still was shapeless . . . a flittering shadow caught in a brilliance. . . .

A shadow!

The thing whispered: ' The Gatherer, Alan . . . the Gatherer in the Cairn . . . do not let It eat me . . . but beware, beware of Dahut . . . free me, Alan . . . free . . . free . . .'

Ralston's voice!

I lifted myself to my knees, crouching, hands on the floor; my eyes fixed upon the brilliance—straining to focus this whispering, flittering thing that spoke with the voice of Ralston.

The brilliance contracted—like the eyes of the captain

of the *Brittis*. It became the knob of a door. A knob of brass glimmering in the light of dawn.

There was a fly upon the knob. A bluebottle; a carrion-fly. It was crawling over the knob, buzzing. The voice I had thought that of Dick was drained down into the buzzing; became one with it. There was only a bluebottle flittering and buzzing upon a shining brass door-knob. The fly left the knob, circled me and was gone.

I staggered to my feet. I thought: *Whatever you did to me there on the boat, Dahut, it was a first-class job.* I looked at my wrist-watch. It was a few minutes after six. I opened the door, cautiously. The hall was shadowless; tranquil. There was not a sound in the house. It seemed to sleep, but I didn't trust it. I closed the door quietly. There were great bolts at top and bottom which I dropped into place.

There was a queer emptiness in my head, and I could not see clearly. I made my way to the window and drew deep breaths of the sharp morning air, the tang of the sea strong within it. It made me feel better. I turned and looked at the room. It was immense and was panelled in old wood; tapestries, colours softened by centuries, fell here and there. The bed was ancient, carved and postered and canopied. It was the chamber of some castle in Brittany, rather than that of a New England manse. At my left was an *armoire*, ancient as the bed. Idly, I opened a drawer. There upon my handkerchiefs lay my pistol. I pulled it open. Not a cartridge was in the chamber.

I looked at it, unbelievingly. I knew that I had loaded it when I had placed it in one of my bags. Abruptly, its emptiness linked itself with the useless flash, the unresponsive switch, the strange sleepiness. It jarred me wide awake. I put the gun back in the drawer and went and lay down on the bed. I hadn't the slightest doubt that something other than natural cause had induced the stupor. Whether it had been suggestion by Dahut while I lay asleep on the deck, or whether she had given me some soporific drug with my lunch, made no difference. It had not been natural. A drug? I remembered the subtle drug the Tibetan lamas administer—the drug they name 'Master of the Will' which weakens all resistance to hypnotic control and renders the minds of those to whom it is given impotent against command, wide-open to hallucination. All at once the behaviour, the appearance, of the men on the boat, the servants in this house, fell into an understandable pattern. Suppose that all were being fed with such a drug, and moved and thought only as the Demoiselle and her father willed them to move and think? That I was surrounded by human robots, creatures who were reflections, multiplications, of the de Keradels?

And that I, myself, was in imminent peril of the same slavery?

Belief that something like this was the truth became stronger the more I thought over it. I strove to recall the conversation with de Keradel the night before. I could not—but I still retained the conviction I had passed the ordeal successfully; that the other sense or self which had taken charge had not allowed me to be betrayed. Deep within, I felt that assurance.

Suddenly, as I lay there, I felt other eyes upon me, knew that I was being watched. I was facing the windows. I drew a deep breath, sighed as one does in deep sleep, and turned with arm over face. Under its cover, with scarcely opened lids, I watched. In a few moments a white hand stole from behind a tapestry, drew it aside, and Dahut stepped into the room. Her braids fell below her waist, she wore the sheerest of silken negligees and she was incomparably lovely. She slipped to the bottom of the bed, soundlessly as one of her shadows, and stood studying me. I forced myself to breathe regularly, as though in soundest slumber. She was so lovely that I found it rather difficult. She came to the side of the bed and leaned over me. I felt her lips touch my cheek as lightly as the kiss of a moth.

Then, as suddenly, I knew she was gone.

I opened my eyes. There was another scent, unfamiliar, mingling with the breath of the sea. It was oddly stimulating. Breathing it, I felt the last traces of lethargy vanish. I sat up, wide awake and alert. There was a shallow metal dish on the table beside the bed. Piled on it was a little heap of fern-like leaves. They were smouldering, and from their smoke came the invigorating scent. I pressed out the sparks and instantly smoke and scent disappeared.

Evidently this was an antidote to whatever had induced the other condition; and quite as evidently there was no suspicion that I had not slept uninterruptedly throughout the night.

And possibly, it occurred to me, the shadow-crowded, rustling hall and the bluebottle that had buzzed with the voice of Ralston might have been by-products of this hypothetical drug; the subconsciousness fantastically picturing under its influence, as it does in dream, chance sounds in terms of what has been engrossing the consciousness.

Maybe I really had slept through the night. Maybe I had only dreamed I had gone out into the shadow-crowded hall . . . and had fled from it and dropped down beside the door . . . had only dreamed the chanting.

But if there had been nothing they had wanted me to be deaf and blind to—then why had they bundled me up in that blanket of sleep?

Well, there was one thing I knew I had not dreamed. That was Dahut slipping into the room with the leaves.

And that meant I had not acted precisely as they had expected, else I would not have been awake to see her. There was one lucky break, whatever the cause. I would be able to use those leaves later, if they repeated the bundling.

I went over to the tapestry and raised it. There was no sign of opening, the panelling seemingly solid. Some secret spring existed, of course, but I postponed hunting for it. I unbarred the door; the bars were about as much a guarantee of privacy as one wall in a room with the other three sides open. I took what was left of the leaves, put them in an envelope and tucked them in McCann's holster. Then I smoked half a dozen cigarettes and added their ashes to those on the dish. They appeared about the same, and they were about what would have remained if all the leaves had burned. Maybe nobody would bother to check—but maybe they would.

By then it was seven o'clock. I wondered whether

I ought to get up and dress. How long was it supposed
to be before the antidote took effect? I had no means
of knowing and no desire to make the least mistake.
To sleep too long would be far safer than to wake too
soon. I crawled back into bed. And I did go to sleep,
honestly and dreamlessly.

When I awakened there was a man laying out my
clothes; the valet. The dish that had held the smoking
leaves was gone. It was half-past eight. I sat up and
yawned, and the valet announced with antique humility
that the Lord of Carnac's bath was ready. Despite all
that the Lord of Carnac had on his mind, this combination of archaic servility and modern convenience made
me laugh. But no smile answered me. The man stood,
head bent, wound up to do and say certain things.
Smiling had not been in his instructions.

I looked at his impassive face, the blank eyes which
were not seeing me at all as I was, nor the world in
which I lived, but were seeing me as another man in
another world. What that world might be, I suspected.

I threw a robe over my pyjamas and locked the bath-
room door against him; unstrapped McCann's holster
and hid it before bathing. When I came out I dismissed
him. He told me that breakfast would be ready a little
after nine, and bowing low, departed.

I went to the *armoire*, took out my gun and snapped
it open. The cartridges were in place. Furthermore,
the extra clips lay neatly beside where it had been.
Had I also dreamed that it had been emptied? A
suspicion came to me. If I were wrong, I could explain
it as an accident. I carried the gun to the window,
aimed it at the sea and touched the trigger. There was

only a sharp crack as the cap exploded. In the night the cartridges had been made useless and, without doubt, had been restored to the pistol during my later sleep.

Well, here was warning enough, I thought grimly, without any buzzing bluebottle, and put the gun back. Then I went down to breakfast, cold with anger and disposed to be brutal if I had the chance. The Demoiselle was waiting for me, prosaically reading a newspaper. The table was laid for two, so I judged her father had business elsewhere. I looked at Dahut, and as always admiration and a certain tenderness reluctantly joined my wrath and my rooted hatred of her. I think I have mentioned her beauty before. She was never more beautiful than now—a dewy freshness about her, like the dawn; her skin a miracle, clear-eyed, just the right touch of demureness . . . not at all the murderess, harlot and witch I knew her in my heart to be. Clean.

She dropped the paper and held out her hand. I kissed it, ironically.

She said: 'I do hope you slept soundly, Alan.'

And that had just the right touch of domesticity. It irritated me still more. I dropped into my chair, spread my napkin over my knees.

'Soundly, Dahut. Except for a big bluebottle that came and whispered to me.'

Her eyes narrowed at that, and distinctly I saw her tremble. Then she dropped her eyes, and laughed.

'You're joking, Alan.'

I said: 'I am not. It was a big bluebottle that whispered and buzzed, and buzzed and whispered.'

186

She asked quietly: 'What did it whisper, Alan?'

'To beware of you, Dahut.'

She asked, again quietly: 'Were you awake?'

Now, regaining caution, I laughed: 'Do bluebottles whisper to people who are awake? I was sound asleep and dreaming—without doubt.'

'Did you know the voice?' Her eyes lifted suddenly and held mine.

I answered: 'When I heard it I seemed to know it. But now, awake, I have forgotten.'

She was silent while the blank-eyed servants placed this and that before us. Then she said, half wearily:

'Put away your sword, Alan. For to-day, at least, you do not need it. And to-day, at least, I carry no weapons. I pledge you this, and you can trust me— for to-day. Treat me to-day only as—one who loves you greatly. Will you do this, Alan?'

It was said so simply, so sincerely, that my anger fled and my distrust of her weakened. For the first time I felt a stirring of pity.

She said: 'I will not even ask you to pretend to love me.'

I said, slowly: 'It would not be hard to love you, Dahut.'

The violet of her eyes was misted with tears. She said: 'I—wonder——'

I said: 'A bargain. We meet for the first time this morning. I know nothing of you, Dahut, and to-day you will be to me only—what you seem to be. Perhaps by to-night I will be your—slave.'

She said, sharply: 'I asked you to put down your sword.'

I had meant nothing more than what I had said. No innuendo. . . . But now I heard again the voice that had changed to the buzzing of a fly—'*Beware* . . . *beware of Dahut* . . . *Alan, beware of Dahut.* . . .' And I thought of the blank-eyed, impassive men . . . slaves to her will or to her father's. . . .

I would not put away the sword—but I would hide it.

I said, earnestly: 'I haven't the slightest idea what you mean, Dahut. Really I haven't. I meant precisely what I said.'

She seemed to believe me. And on that basis, piquant enough considering what had gone before in New York and ancient Ys, our breakfast continued. It had its peculiar charm. Before it was done I found myself dangerously close several times to thinking of the Demoiselle exactly as she wanted me to think of her. We dawdled, and it was eleven when we ended. She suggested a ride around the place, and with relief I went up to change my clothes. I had to snap my gun a few times and look at the leaves in McCann's holster to clear my mind of disarming doubts. Dahut had a way with her.

When I came down she was in riding-breeches, her hair braided round her head like a helmet. We went to the stables. There were a dozen first-class horses. I looked around for the black stallion. I didn't see it, but there was a box stall where it might have been. I picked out a sweet roan and Dahut a leggy bay. What I wanted most to see was de Keradel's 'rockery'. I didn't see it. We trotted along a well-made bridle-path which gave occasional vistas of the water, but most of the time the rocks and trees shut off the ocean. It was

a peculiar lay-out and one better adapted for solitude
I have never seen. We came at last to the wall, turned
and rode along it. Wicked, inverted *chevaux de frise*
guarded the top, and there were a couple of wires that
I suspected of carrying heavy voltage. They could not
have been there when 'Lias had scaled the wall. I
thought that probably he had taught a lesson as well
as received one. And here and there stood one of the
swarthy little men. They had clubs, but how otherwise
armed they were I could not tell. They knelt as we
passed them.

We came to a massive gate, and there was a garrison
of half a dozen. We rode past the gate and came to
a wide, long meadow-land dotted with stunted bushes,
crouching like cowering men. It came to me that this
must be where the unfortunate 'Lias had encountered
the dogs that weren't dogs. Under the sun, the brisk
air and the exhilaration of riding, that story had lost
many of its elements of reality. Yet the place had a
frightened, forbidding aspect. I mentioned this casually
to Dahut. She looked at me with a secret amusement
and answered as casually:

' Yes—but there is good hunting here.'

She rode on without saying what kind of hunting.
Nor did I ask; for there had been that about her answer
which had abruptly restored my faith in 'Lias's veracity.

We came to the end of the wall, and it was built in
the rock as McCann had said. There was a big breast of
the rock which shut off a view of what lay beyond. I said:

' I'd like to take a look from here.'

And before she could answer I had dismounted and
climbed the rock. From the top, it was open ocean. A

couple of hundred yards from shore were two men in a small fishing-boat. They raised their heads as they saw me, and one drew out a hand-net and began dipping with it.

Well, McCann was on the job.

I scrambled down and joined Dahut. I asked: 'How about riding back and going out of the gate for a canter? I'd like to see more of the countryside.'

She hesitated, then nodded. We rode back and through the garrison and out upon a country road. In a little while we sighted a fine old house, set well back among big trees. A stone wall protected it from the road, and lounging beside one of its gates was McCann.

He watched us come, imperturbably. Dahut passed without a glance. I had hung back a few paces, and as I went by McCann I dropped a card. I had hoped for just this encounter, and I had managed to scribble on it:

'Something very wrong but no definite evidence yet. About thirty men. Think all well-armed. Barbed and charged wires behind wall.'

I drew up beside the Demoiselle and we rode on a mile or so. She halted, and asked:

'Have you seen enough?'

I said, yes, and we turned back. When we went by McCann he was still lounging beside the gate as though he had not moved. But there was no paper on the road. The garrison had seen us coming, and the postern was swinging open. We returned to the house the same way we had gone. I had got not a glimpse of the 'rockery'.

Dahut was flushed with the ride, full of gaiety. She

said: 'I'll bathe. Then we'll have lunch on the boat—go for a little cruise.'

'Fine,' I said. 'And I hope it doesn't make me as sleepy as it did yesterday.'

Her eyes narrowed, but my face was entirely innocent. She smiled: 'It won't, I'm sure. You're getting acclimatized.'

I said, morosely: 'I hope so. I must have been pretty dull company at dinner last night.'

She smiled again: 'But you weren't. You pleased my father immensely.'

She went into the house laughing.

I was very glad I had pleased her father.

It had been a thoroughly delightful sail with a thoroughly charming girl. Only when one of the tranced crew knelt as he passed did I feel the sinister hidden undertow. And now I sat at dinner with de Keradel and the Demoiselle. De Keradel's conversation was so fascinating that he had made me forget that I was a prisoner. I had discussed with him much that I had wished to on the night Bill had persuaded me to be so objectionable. If at times his manner was irritatingly too much like that of a hierophant instructing a neophyte in elementary mysteries, or if he calmly advanced as fact matters which modern science holds to be the darkest of superstitions, investing them with all the authenticity of proven experience—it made no difference to me. The man's learning was as extraordinary as his mind, and I wondered how in one short life he could have acquired it. He spoke of the rites of Osiris, the black worship of Typhon whom the Egyp-

tians also named Set of the Red Hair, the Eleusinian
and the Delphic mysteries as though he had witnessed
them.   Described them in minutest detail—and others
more ancient and darker, long buried in age-rotten
shrouds of Time.   The evil secrets of the Sabbat were
open to him, and once he spoke of the worship of Kore,
the Daughter, who was known also as Persephone, and
in another form as Hecate, and by other names back,
back through the endless vistas of the ages—the wife of
Hades, the Queen of the Shades whose daughters were
the Furies.

It was then I told him of what I had beheld in the
Delphian cave when the Greek priest with the pagan
soul had evoked Kore . . . and I had watched that
majestic—that dreadful—form taking shape in the swirls
of smoke from what was being consumed upon her
thrice ancient altar. . . .

He listened intently, without interrupting, as one to
whom the story held no surprise.   He asked:

' And had She come to him before? '

I answered: ' I do not know.'

He said, directly to the Demoiselle: ' But even if so,
the fact that She appeared to—to Dr. Caranac—is most
significant.   It is proof that he——'

Dahut interrupted him, and I thought there was some
warning in the glance she gave him:

' That he is—acceptable.   Yes, my father.'

De Keradel considered me.

' An illuminating experience, indeed.   I am wondering, in the light of it, and of other things you have told
me—I am wondering why you were so—so hostile—to
such ideas the night we met.'

I answered, bluntly: 'I was more than half drunk—
and ready to fight anybody.'

He bared his teeth at that, then laughed outright.

'You do not fear to speak the truth.'

'Neither when drunk nor sober,' I said.

He scrutinized me silently, for moments. He spoke,
more as though to himself than to me:

'I do not know . . . she may be right . . . if I could
wholly trust him it would mean much to us . . . he has
curiosity . . . he does not shrink from the dark wisdom
. . . but has he courage. . . ?'

I laughed at that, and said, baldly: 'If I did not have
—would I be here?'

'Quite true, my father.' Dahut was smiling mali-
ciously.

De Keradel struck down his hand like one who has
come at last to a decision.

'Carnac, I spoke to you of an experiment in which I
am deeply interested. Instead of being a spectator,
willing or unwilling . . . or no—spectator, whichever I
might decide'—he paused as though to let the covert
menace of this sink in—'I invite you to participate with
me in this experiment. I have good reason to believe
that its rewards, if successful, will be incalculably great.
My invitation is not disinterested. I will admit to you
that my experiment has not as yet met with full success.
I have had results—but they have not been what I
hoped. But what you have told me of Kore proves that
you are no barrier to the materialization of these Beings
—Powers or Presences, or if you prefer, discarnate,
unknown energies which can take shape, become substance, in accordance with laws discoverable to man—

and discovered.   Also, you have within you the ancient
blood of Carnac and the ancient memories of your race.
It may be that I have missed some slight detail that your
—stimulated—memory will recall.   It may be that with
you beside us this Being I desire to evoke will appear in
all its power—and with all that implies of power for us.'

I asked: 'What is that Being?'

He said: 'You, yourself, named it.   That which in
one of its manifold shapes came to the Alkar-Az of
ancient Carnac as it came to the temples of my own
people ages before Ys was built or the stones of Carnac
raised—the Gatherer in the Cairn—the Blackness——'

If I felt cold creep along my skin he did not know
it.   It was the answer I had been expecting and I was
prepared.

I looked long at Dahut, and he, at least, misinter-
preted that look, as I had hoped he would.   I struck my
own hand down upon the table.

'De Keradel, I am with you.'

After all, wasn't that why I had come there?

CHAPTER XVI

THE MAEL BENNIQUE

D E KERADEL said: 'We drink to that!'
He unlocked a cupboard and took from it decanter half-filled with a green liqueur. The stopper was clamped and difficult to withdraw. He poured three small glasses and quickly clamped the stopper down. I raised my glass.

He checked me: 'Wait!'

There were little bubbles rising through the green drink; like atoms of diamonds; like splintered sun-rays shot back by crystals lying in still shadows. They rose more and more quickly, and suddenly the green drink fumed; then became quiescent; pellucid.

De Keradel lifted his glass.

'Carnac, you join us of your own will?'

The Demoiselle said, her glass close to mine: 'It is of your own will you join us, Alain de Carnac?'

I answered: 'Of my own will.'

We touched glasses and drank.

That was a strange drink. It tingled through brain and nerve, and immediately there was born of it an extraordinary sense of freedom; swift sloughing of inhibitions; a blowing away of old ideas as though they had crumbled to dust and, like dust, had been puffed from the surface of consciousness. As though I were a serpent which had abruptly shed an outworn skin. Memories grew dim, faded away, readjusted themselves. I had an indescribable sense of liberation. . . . I could do anything, since, like God, there existed for me neither good nor evil. Whatever I willed to do that I could do, since there was neither evil nor good but only my will. . . .

De Keradel said: 'You are one with us.'

The Demoiselle whispered: 'You are one with us, Alain.'

Her eyes were closed, or seemed to be; the long lashes low upon her cheeks. Yet I thought that beneath them I saw a glint of purple flame. And de Keradel's hands covered his eyes, as though to shield them, but between his fingers I thought I saw them gleaming. He said:

'Carnac—you have not asked me what is this Gatherer—this Being I would evoke in Its completeness. Is it because you know?'

'No,' I answered; and would have followed by saying that I did not care—except that suddenly I knew I did care; that of all things it was what I thirsted to know.

He said: 'A brilliant Englishman once formulated perfectly the materialistic credo. He said that the existence of man is an accident; his story a brief and transitory episode in the life of the meanest of planets. He pointed out that of the combination of causes which first converted a dead organic compound into the living progenitors of humanity, science as yet knows nothing. Nor would it matter if science did know. The wetnurses of famine, disease and mutual slaughter had gradually evolved creatures with consciousness and intelligence enough to know that they were insignificant. The history of the past was that of blood and tears, stupid acquiescence, helpless blunderings, wild revolt

and empty aspirations. And at last, the energies of
our system will decay, the sun be dimmed, the inert and
tideless earth be barren. Man will go down into the
pit, and all his thoughts will perish. Matter will know
itself no longer. Everything will be as though it never
had been. And nothing will be either better or worse
for all the labour, devotion, pity, love and suffering of
man.'

I said, the God-like sense of power stronger within
me: 'It is not true.'

'It is partly true,' he answered. 'What is not true
is that life is an accident. What we call accident is
only a happening of whose causes we are ignorant.
Life must have come from life. Not necessarily such
life as we know, but from some Thing, acting
deliberately, whose essence was—and is—life. It is true
that pain, agony, sorrow, hate and discord are the
foundations of humanity. It is true that famine,
disease and slaughter have been our nurses. Yet it is
equally true that there are such things as peace,
happiness, pity, perception of beauty, wisdom . . .
although these may be only of the thickness of the
film on the surface of a woodland pool which mirrors
its flowered rim—yet, these things do exist . . . peace
and beauty, happiness and wisdom. They *are*.

'And therefore'—de Keradel's hands were still over
his eyes, but through the masking fingers I felt his
gaze sharpen upon me, penetrate me—'therefore I hold
that these desirable things must be inherent in That
which breathed life into the primeval slime. It must
be so, since that which is created cannot possess attributes other than those possessed by what creates it.'

Of course, I knew all that. Why should he waste effort to convince me of the obvious? I said, tolerantly:

' It is self-evident.'

He said: ' And therefore it must also be self-evident that since it was the dark, the malevolent, the cruel side of this—Being—which created us, our only approach to It, our only path to Its other self, must be through agony and suffering, cruelty and malevolence.'

He paused, then said violently: ' Is it not what every religion has taught? That man can approach his Creator only through suffering and sorrow? Sacrifice. . . . Crucifixion! '

I answered: ' It is true. The baptism of blood. The purification through tears. Rebirth through sorrow. Christ on the Cross! '

The Demoiselle murmured: ' Chords that must be struck before we may attain the supreme harmonies.'

There was a mocking note to that; I turned to her quickly. She had not opened her eyes, but I caught the derisive curving of her lips.

De Keradel said: ' The sacrifices are ready.'

I said: ' Then let us sacrifice! '

De Keradel dropped his hands. The pupils of his eyes were phosphorescent; his face seemed to retreat until nothing could be seen but those two orbs of pale blue fire. The Demoiselle raised her eyes, and they were two deep pools of violet flame; her face a blur beyond them. I did not think that strange—then.

There was a mirror at the back of the sideboard. I looked into it and my own eyes were shining with the same feral fires; golden; my face a blurred setting from which yellow, gleaming eyes stared back at me. . . .

Nor did that seem so strange, either—not then.

De Keradel repeated: ' The sacrifices are ready.'

I said, rising: ' Let us use them! '

We went out of the dining-room and up the stairs. The inhuman exaltation did not wane; it grew stronger; more ruthless. Life was to be taken, but what was the life of one or the lives of many if they were rungs of a ladder up which I could climb out of the pit into the sun? Force recognition from That which had lived before life . . . command It . . . the Creator?

With de Keradel's hand upon my arm I passed into my room. He bade me strip and bath, and left me. I stripped, and my hand touched something hanging to my left arm-pit. It was a holster in which was an automatic. I had forgotten who had given it to me, but whoever it was had told me it was important . . . most important; not to be lost nor given up . . . essential. I laughed. This toy essential to one about to summon the Creator of life? I tossed it into a corner of the room. . . .

De Keradel was beside me, and I wondered vaguely why I had not seen him come into the room. I had bathed, and· was stark naked. He was wrapping a breech-clout of white cotton around my loins. He laced sandals on my feet, and he drew my arms through the sleeves of a robe of thick fine cotton. He stood back, and I saw that he was clothed in the same white robes. There was a broad belt either of black metal or ancient wood around his middle. There was a similar cincture around his breast. They were inlaid with symbols in silver . . . but whoever saw silver shift and change outline . . . melt from this rune into another . . . as these did? Around his forehead was a black chaplet of oak leaves, and from his belt swung a long black knife, a black maul, a black and oval bowl and a black ewer. . . .

Dahut was watching me, and I wondered why I had not seen her enter. She wore the robe of thick white cotton, but the girdle around her waist was of gold, and on it the shifting symbols were red; and of red gold was the fillet that bound her hair and the bracelets upon her arms. In her hand was a golden sickle, razor-edged.

They fastened around my waist another black and silver symbolled belt, and set upon my head a chaplet of the black oak leaves. De Keradèl drew from his belt the maul and put it in my hand. I shrank from its touch and dropped it. He picked it up and closed my fingers round it. I tried to unclose them and could not, although the touch of the maul was loathsome. I raised the maul and looked at it. It was heavy and black with age . . . like the belt . . . like the chaplet. It was shaped all of one piece, as though carved from the heart of oak; shaft in centre, ends of its massive head blunt. . . .

The *mael bennique!* The beater in of breasts! Heart-crusher! And I knew that its blackness was less from age than from red baptisms.

My exaltation ebbed. Something deep within me was stirring, tearing at its fetters, whispering to me . . . whispering that it had been to stop the beating of this maul that I had gone from Carnac long and long ago to slay Dahut . . . that whatever else I did I must not use the maul . . . but also that I must go on, go on as I had in lost Ys . . . meet and even steep myself in this ancient evil, so that . . . so that . . .

De Keradel's face was thrust into mine, mouth snarling, hell-fire flaming in his eyes.

'You are one with us, Bearer of the Maul!'

Dahut's hand closed round mine; her cheek touched me. The exaltation swept back; the deep revolt forgotten. But some echo of it remained. I said:

'I am one with you—but I will not wield the maul.'

Dahut's hand pressed and my fingers were loosed and I threw the thing from me.

De Keradel said, deadly: 'You do as I command Pick up the maul.'

Dahut said, sweetly, but with voice as deadly as his own: 'Patience, my father. He shall bear the bowl and the ewer and do with them as is prescribed. He shall feed the fires. Unless he wields the *mael* of his own will, it is useless. Be patient.'

He answered her, furiously: 'Once before you betrayed a father for your lover.'

She said, steadily: 'And may again . . . and if so what can you do, my father?'

His face writhed; he half raised his arm as though to strike her. And then crept into his eyes that same fear as had shown there on the night we had met when he had spoken of Powers summoned to aid and obey, and she had added—'or to command us.'

His arm dropped. He picked up the maul, and gave to me the bowl and ewer. He said, sullenly:

'Let us go.'

We went out of that room, he on one side of me and Dahut on the other. Down the stairs we went. A score of the servants were in the great hall. All wore the white robes and they held unlighted flambeaux. They sank upon their knees as we approached them. De Keradel pressed upon the wall and a section slid open, revealing wide stone steps winding down and down. Arm in arm, Dahut and de Keradel and I trod them, the servants behind us, until we faced what seemed to be a wall of solid stone. Here again de Keradel pressed, and a part of the wall slid up slowly and silently like a curtain.

It had masked a portal to a vast chamber hewn out of the solid rock. Through the portal stole a penetrating pungent odour, and from beyond it came the murmur of many voices. The light that filled it was dim but crystal clear—like a forest twilight. There were a hundred or more men and women facing us, and their eyes wide-pupilled and blank—rapt—looking into another world. But they saw us. There were cubicles all around the cavern, and others came out of them; women who carried babies in their arms; women at whose skirts children clung. Babies and children were wide-eyed too, small faces rapt and impassive; dreaming. And men and women wore that ancient dress.

De Keradel raised the maul and shouted to them. They answered the shout and rushed towards us, throwing themselves upon their faces as we drew near; crawling to and kissing my feet, the feet of de Keradel, the slim and sandalled feet of Dahut.

De Keradel began a chant, low-voiced, vibrant—archaic. Dahut joined him, and my own throat answered . . . in that tongue I knew and did not know.

The men and women lifted themselves to their knees. They joined, full-throated, in the chant. They lifted themselves to their feet and stood swaying to its cadence. I studied them. They were gaunt-faced and old, most of them. Their garb was what I had known in ancient Carnac, but their faces were not those of Carnac's sacrifices.

There was a glow in their breasts, over their hearts. But in too many it was dim and yellowed; flickering towards extinction. Only in the babies and the children was it clear and steady.

I said to de Keradel: 'Too many are old. The fire of life is dim within them. The essence of life which feeds the wicks runs too low. We need younger sacrifices—those in whom the fire of life is strong.'

He answered: 'Does it matter—so long as there is life to be eaten?'

I said, angrily: 'It does matter. We must have youth. Nor are these of the old blood.'

He looked at me for the first time since I had refused to pick up the maul. There was calculation in the glowing eyes, and satisfaction and approval. He looked at Dahut, and I saw her nod to him, and she murmured:

'I am right, my father . . . he is one with us, but . . . patience.'

De Keradel said: 'We shall have youth—later. All we need of it. But now we must do with what we have.'

Dahut touched my hand, and pointed. At the far end of the cavern a ramp led up to another door. She said:

'Time goes—and we must do with what we have—now.'

De Keradel took up the chant. We walked, the three of us, between the ranks of swaying, chanting men and women. The servants with the flambeaux fell in behind us, and behind them trooped the singing sacrifices. We ascended the ramp. A door opened smoothly. We passed through it into the open air.

De Keradel stepped ahead, his chanting fuller voiced, challenging. The night was cloudy and thin wisps of fog eddied around us. We crossed a broad, open stretch and entered a grove of great oaks. The oaks sighed and whispered; then their branches began to toss and their leaves soughed the chant. De Keradel raised his maul and saluted them. We passed out of the oaks.

For an instant ancient time and this time and all times reeled around me. I stopped my chanting. I said, strangled:

'Carnac—but it cannot be! Carnac was—*then* . . . and this is *now*! '

Dahut's arm was round my shoulders; Dahut's lips were upon mine; she whispered:

'There is no *then* . . . there is no *now* . . . for us, beloved. And you are *one* with *us*.'

Yet still I stood and looked; while behind me the chanting became ever fainter, faltering and uncertain. For there was a level space before me over which great monoliths marched; not leaning nor fallen as at Carnac now; but lifting straight up, defiant, as in Carnac of old. Scores of them in avenues like the spokes of a tremendous wheel. They marched and circled to the gigantic dolmen, the Cairn, that was their heart. A crypt that was truly an Alkar-Az . . . greater than that which I had known in most ancient Carnac . . . and among and between the standing stones danced the wraiths of the fog . . . the fog was a huge inverted bowl covering the Cairn and the monoliths. And against the standing stones leaned shadows . . . the shadows of men. . . .

Dahut's hands touched my eyes, covered them. And abruptly all strangeness, all comparisons of memory, were gone. De Keradel had turned, facing the sacrifices, roaring out the chant, black maul raised high, the symbols on black belt and cincture dancing like quicksilver. I raised the bowl and ewer and roared the chant. The faltering voices gathered strength, roared out to meet us. Dahut's lips were again on mine. . . .

'Beloved, you are *one* with *us*.'

The oaks bent, and waved their boughs, and shouted the chant.

The servants had lighted their flambeaux and stood like watching dogs on the fringes of the sacrifices. We entered the field of the monoliths. In front of me strode de Keradel, maul held high, raised to the Cairn as the priest raises the Host to the Altar. Dahut was beside me, singing . . . singing . . . her golden sickle uplifted. Thicker grew the walls of the great inverted bowl of the fog above and around us; and thicker grew the fog-wraiths dancing among and circling the monoliths. Darker became the shadows guarding the standing stones.

And the sacrifices were circling the monoliths, dancing around them in the ancient measures as though hand in hand with the fog-wraiths. The servants had quenched their torches, for now the corposants had begun to glimmer over the standing stones. The witch lights. The lamps of the dead. Faintly at first, but growing ever stronger. Glimmering, shifting orbs of grey phosphorescence of the greyness of the dead. Decaying lights, and putrescent.

And now I stood before the great Cairn. I looked into its vault; empty; untenanted—as yet. Louder was the chanting as the sacrifices danced between and around the monoliths. Coming ever closer. And more lividly gleamed the corposants, lighting the path of the Gatherer.

The chanting muted; became a prayer; an invocation. The sacrifices pressed upon me; swaying; murmuring; rapt eyes intent upon the Cairn . . . and seeing—what?

There were three stones close to the entrance to the chamber of the Cairn. The middle one was a slab of granite, longer than a tall man, and at about where the shoulders of a man lying upon it would be, there was a rounded ridge of stone like a pillow. It was stained—like the maul; and the stains ran down its sides. At its left was another stone; lower; squat; hollowed shallowly and channelled at its lower end as though to let some liquid escape from it. And at the right of the long slab was a more deeply hollowed stone black with fire.

There was a curious numbness creeping through me; a queer sense of detachment as though a part of me, and the most vital part, were stepping aside to watch some play in which another and less important self was to be an actor. At the same time, that lesser part

knew perfectly well what it had to do. Two of the
white-robed servants handed me small bunches of twigs,
small bundles of leaves, and two black bowls in which
were yellow crystals and lumps of resinous gum. With
the twigs I built the fire on the blackened altar as the
ancient rites prescribed . . . well did I remember how
the priests of Ys had made that fire before the Alkar-
Az at Carnac. . . .

I struck the flint, and as the twigs blazed I cast on
them leaves and crystals and gums. The strangely
scented smoke rose and wound around us and then
went streaming into the Cairn as though sucked by a
strong draught.

Dahut glided past me. There was a woman close by
with a child in her arms. Dahut drew the child from
her, unresisting, and glided back to the squat altar.
Through the smoke I caught the flash of the golden
sickle, and then de Keradel took the black bowl and ewer
from me. He set them beneath the gutter of the squat
altar. He gave them to me, and they were filled. . . .

I dipped my fingers into the bowl and sprinkled what
filled it over the threshold of the Cairn. I took the
ewer and poured what it held from side to side of that
threshold. I went back to the altar of the fire and fed
it from red hands.

Now de Keradel was standing at the squat altar.
He raised a small body in his arms, and cast it into
the Cairn. Dahut was beside him, rigid, golden sickle
upraised—but the sickle was no longer golden. It was
red . . . like my hands. . . .

The smoke from the sacred fire swirled between and
around us.

De Keradel cried a word—and the chant of the prayer ended. A man shambled from the sacrifices, eyes wide and unwinking, face rapt. De Keradel caught him by the shoulders, and instantly two of the servants threw themselves upon this man, tore off his clothing and pressed him naked down upon the stone. His head fell behind the stone pillow—his chest strained over it. Swiftly de Keradel pressed upon a spot on the neck, and over the heart, and under the thighs. The sacrifice lay limp upon the slab . . . and de Keradel began to beat upon the naked lifted breast with the black maul. Slowly at first . . . then faster and faster . . . harder . . . to the ancient prescribed rhythm.

There was a shrilling of agony from the man on the stone. As though fed by it, the corposants flared wanly. They pulsed and waned. The sacrifice was silent, and I knew that de Keradel had pressed fingers against his throat . . . the agony of the sacrifice must not be articulate since agony that is voiceless is hardest to bear, and therefore most acceptable to the Gatherer. . . .

The maul crashed down in the last stroke, splintering ribs and crushing heart. The smoke from the fire was swirling into the Cairn. De Keradel had raised the body of the sacrifice from the slab . . . held it high over his head. . . .

He hurled it into the Cairn, while fast upon its fall came the thud of a smaller body, hurled after it. . . .

From the hands of Dahut! And they were stained red and dripping—like my own.

There was a buzzing within the Cairn, like hundreds of carrion-flies. Over the Cairn the fog blackened. A formless shadow dropped through the fog and gathered over the Cairn. It had no shape, and it had no place in space. It darkened the fog and it squatted upon the Cairn—yet I knew that it was but a part of something that extended to the rim of the galaxy of which our world is a mote, our sun a spark . . . and beyond the rim of the galaxy . . . beyond the universe . . . beyond, where there is no such thing as space.

It squatted upon the Cairn, but it did not enter.

Again the golden sickle flashed in the hand of Dahut; and again de Keradel filled the ewer and the bowl and gave them to me. And again, numbly, I walked through the smoke of the altar fire and sprinkled the red drops from the bowl into the Cairn, and poured the red contents of the ewer from side to side of its threshold.

De Keradel held up the black maul, and cried out once more. A woman came out of the sacrifices, an old woman, wrinkled and trembling. The acolytes of de Keradel stripped her, and he threw her upon the stone . . . and swung the black maul down upon her withered breasts . . . and again and again. . . .

And he swung her body up and out and through the portal of the Cairn . . . and others came running to him . . . and them he slew with the black maul . . . no longer black but dripping crimson . . . and hurled them into the Cairn. . . .

The squatting darkness on the Cairn was no longer there. It had seeped through the great stones that roofed it, but still its shadow stained the fog reaching up and up like a black pillar. The chamber of the Cairn was thick with the Blackness. And the smoke

from the altar fire no longer clothed Dahut and de
Keradel and I, but streamed straight through into the
Cairn.

The buzzing ceased; all sound died everywhere; a
silence that was like the silence of space before ever a
sun was born took its place. All movement ceased.
Even the drifting fog-wraiths were motionless.

But I knew that the formless darkness within the
Cairn was aware of me. Was aware of me and weigh-
ing me with a thousand eyes. I felt its awareness;
malignant—more cruel beyond measurement than even
human cruelty. Its awareness streamed out and flicked
over me like tiny tentacles . . . like black butterflies
testing me with their antennae.

I was not afraid.

Now the buzzing began again within the Cairn,
rising higher and higher until it became a faint,
sustained whispering.

De Keradel was kneeling at the threshold, listening.
Beside him stood Dahut, listening . . . sickle in hand
. . . sickle no longer golden but red. . . .

There was a child upon the squat altar, crying—not
yet dead. . . .

Abruptly the Cairn was empty . . . the fog above it
empty of the shadow . . . the Gatherer gone.

I was marching back between the standing stones,
Dahut and de Keradel beside me. There were no
corposants over the monoliths. The flambeaux flared
in the hands of the servants. Behind us, chanting and
swaying, danced those who were left of the sacrifices.
We passed through the oaks, and they were silent.

The curious numbness still held me, and I felt no horror of what I had seen—or of what I had done.

The house was before me. It was strange how its outlines wavered . . . how misty and unsubstantial they seemed. . . .

And now I was in my own room. The numbness that had deadened all emotional reactions during the evocation of the Gatherer was slowly giving way to something else—not yet defined, not yet strong enough to be known. The exaltation which had followed the green drink ebbed and flowed in steadily decreasing waves. I had an overpowering sense of unreality—I moved, unreal, among unreal things. What had become of my robe of white? I remembered that de Keradel had stripped it from me, but where and when I could not think. And my hands were clean—no longer red with blood ... the blood of . . .

Dahut was with me, feet bare, white skin gleaming through a silken shift that held no concealment. The violet fires still flickered faintly in her eyes. She put her arms round my neck, drew my face down to hers, set her mouth on mine. She whispered:

'Alan . . . I have forgotten Alain de Carnac . . . he has paid for what he did, and he is dying . . . it is you, Alan—you that I love. . . ."

I held her in my arms, and within them I felt the Lord of Carnac die. But I, Alan Caranac, was not yet awake.

My arms closed tighter round her . . . there was the fragrance of some secret flower of the sea about her . . . and there was the sweetness of new-learned or long-forgotten evil in her kisses. . . .

CHAPTER XVII

THE BOWL OF SACRIFICE

I AWAKENED as though escaping from some singularly unpleasant dream. I could not remember what the dream had been, but I knew it had been—rotten. It was a stormy day, the surges hammering against the rocky shores, the wind wailing, and the light that came through the windows was grey. I raised my left arm to look at my watch, but it was not there. Nor was it on the table beside the bed. My mouth was dry, and my skin was dry and hot. I felt as though I had been drunk for two days.

Worst of all was my fear that I would remember the dream.

I sat up in bed. Something was missing besides my watch—the gun under my arm-pit—McCann's gun. I tried to remember. There had been a green drink which had sparkled and effervesced—after that, nothing. There was a fog between the green drink and now. The fog hid what I feared to have uncovered.

Fog had been in the dream. The pistol had been in the dream, too. When I had taken the green drink I had still had the gun. There was a flash of memory—after the drink the gun had seemed absurd, inconsequential, and I had thrown it into a corner. I jumped out of the bed to look for it——

My foot struck against a black and oval bowl. Not all black—there were stains along its sides, and inside it was a viscous scum.

The bowl of sacrifice!

Abruptly the fog lifted . . . and there was the dream
. . . if dream it had been . . . stark and clear in each
dread detail. I recoiled from it, not only sick of soul
but nauseated of body. . . .

If it had been no dream, then was I damned and
trebly damned. If I had not killed, I had acquiesced
in killing. If I had not beaten in the breasts of the
sacrifices with my own hands, I had not lifted a hand
to save them—and I had fed the fires that were their
funeral torches.

Equally with Dahut and de Keradel, I had summoned
that black and evil Power . . . equally with them I was
murderer, torturer . . . thrall of Hell.

What was there to prove it a dream? Illusion suggested
by de Keradel and Dahut while my will lay quiescent
under the spell of the green drink? Desperately out of
the damning memories I tried to sift some evidence that
it had been only a dream. There had been the flaring of
the feral phosphorescence in their eyes—and in mine.
A physiological peculiarity which man does not com-
monly possess, nor could any drink create the layer of
cells which causes it. Nor does humanity bear within
its breasts, over its hearts, perceptible lumens bright in
youth and dimmed and yellow in age. Yet they had
glowed in the breasts of the sacrifices!

Nor where, except in dream, do oaks chant as though
their leafed boughs have voices?

But—there was the blood-stained bowl! Could that
materialize from a dream?

No . . . but de Keradel or Dahut might have placed
it there to make me, waking, believe the dream had been

real. And dream or no dream—I was tainted with their evil.

I got up and searched for the automatic. I found it in the corner of the room where I had tossed it. Well, that much had been true. I strapped the holster under my arm. My head felt like a hive, my brain a honeycomb in and out of which lame bees of thought went buzzing aimlessly. But a cold, implacable hatred, a loathing of de Keradel and his witch daughter held steady in the shaken fabric of my mind.

The rain lashed the windows, and the gale cried around the old house. Somewhere a clock struck a single clanging note. Whether it was the half-hour or the full I could not tell. A straight thought struck through the aimless ones. I took a pinch of the leaves out of the holster and chewed them. They were exceedingly bitter. I swallowed them—and almost instantly my head was clear.

There was no use in hunting out de Keradel and killing him. In the first place, I could give no real defence for doing so. Not unless there was a heap of bodies in the Cairn, and I could open the cavern of the paupers. I had not the slightest belief that I could find that cavern or that there would be any bodies. Killing de Keradel would seem the act of a madman, and for doing so a mad-house would be the best I could expect. Also, if I killed him, there would yet be the blank-eyed servants to reckon with.

And Dahut . . . I doubted whether I could shoot down Dahut in cold blood. If I did—there still would be the servants. They would kill me . . . and I had no especial desire to die.

The face of Helen came before me . . . and still less did I desire to die.

Also, there was the necessity of knowing whether what I had been visualizing had been dream or reality. It was most necessary that I know.

Some way, somehow, I must get in touch with McCann. Whether dream or reality, I must continue to play the game, not allow myself to be trapped again. At any rate, I must seem to believe in its reality; convince de Keradel that I did so believe. For no other reason could he or Dahut have left the bowl beside my bed.

I dressed, and picked up the bowl and went downstairs, holding it behind me. De Keradel was at the table, but the Demoiselle was not. I saw that it was a little after one. He looked up at me, sharply, and said :

' I trust you slept well. I gave orders that you should not be disturbed. It is a desolate day, and my daughter sleeps late.'

I laughed : ' She should—after last night.'

He asked : ' What do you mean ? '

' No need to fence longer with me, de Keradel,' I answered, ' after last night.'

He asked, slowly : ' What do you remember of last night ? '

' Everything, de Keradel. Everything—from your convincing disquisition upon the dark begetting of life, its darker delivery, its darkest evolution—and the proof of it in what we summoned to the Cairn.'

He said : ' You have dreamed.'

' Did I dream this ? '

I set the stained bowl upon the table. His eyes

widened; he looked from it to me and back again to the bowl. He asked:

'Where did you find that?'

I answered: 'Beside my bed. When I awoke not long ago.'

The veins upon his temples swelled and began to throb. He whispered: 'Now why did she do that. . . .'

I said: 'Because she is wiser than you. Because she knows I should be told the truth. Because she trusts me.'

He said: 'As once before she trusted you—and to her cost and to her father's.'

'When I was Lord of Carnac,' I laughed. 'The Lord of Carnac died last night. She told me so.'

He looked at me, long.

'How did the Lord of Carnac die?'

I answered, brutally: 'In your daughter's arms. And now she prefers—me.'

He pushed back his chair, walked to the window and stared out at the driving rain. He came back to the table and sat quietly down.

'Caranac, what did you dream?'

I said: 'A waste of time to answer that. If it was a dream, you dictated it, and therefore know. If it was no dream, you were there.'

He said: 'Nevertheless, I ask you to tell me.'

I studied him. There was something strange about this request, made apparently in all sincerity. It threw a totally unexpected monkey-wrench of doubt into the simple machinery of my deductions. I sparred for time.

'After I've eaten,' I answered.

Not once while I breakfasted did he speak to me; nor,

when I looked at him, were his eyes on me. He seemed deep in not particularly pleasant thoughts. I tried to fish the monkey-wrench out of my calculations. His surprise and anger when I produced the bowl had seemed genuine. If so, then obviously he had not put it beside me. Therefore it was not he who had wished to awaken my memory—either of dream or reality.

Then it must have been Dahut. But why should she want me to remember if her father did not? The only answer seemed to be that they were in conflict. Yet it might mean something else, far wider reaching. I had respect for de Keradel's mentality. I did not believe he would ask me to tell him something he already knew. At least not without a reason. Did his question mean that he had taken no part in the summoning of the Gatherer? That there had been no sacrifices . . . that all had been illusion . . . and that he had taken no part in the creation of the illusion?

That all had been the work of Dahut alone?

But wait! Might it not also mean that the green drink, after it changed me into what I had become, had also been supposed to make me forget? And that for some reason I had been partly immune to its effect? That now de Keradel wanted to know to what extent it had failed . . . to compare my memories with what he knew had occurred?

Yet there was the bowl . . . and twice I had seen fear in his eyes when Dahut had spoken to him. And what was the rift between the pair . . . and how could I take advantage of it?

Could any one except Dahut have left beside me the sacrificial bowl . . . could any—*thing*?

I heard the voice of Ralston changing to the buzzing of a fly . . . I heard Dick's voice crying out to me . . . *' Beware, beware of Dahut . . . give me release . . . from the Gatherer . . . Alan.'*

And the room darkened as though the dripping clouds had grown heavier . . . or had filled with shadows. . . .

I said: 'Dismiss the servants, de Keradel. I'll tell you.'

And when he had done so, I did tell him. He listened without interrupting, expression unchanged, pale eyes now glancing out of the windows, now fixed on mine. When I was through, he asked, smiling:

'Do you think it dream—or real?'

'There is this '—I threw the stained bowl on the table.

He took it, and examined it, thoughtfully. He said: 'Let us first assume your experiences were real. Under that assumption, I am sorcerer, warlock, priest of evil. And I do not like you. Not only do I not like you, but I do not trust you. I am not deceived by your apparent conversion to our aims and purposes. I know that you came here only because of your fear of what might befall your friends if you did not. In short, I am fully aware of my daughter's command to you, and what led up to it. I could—get rid of you. Very easily. And would, were it not for one obstacle. My daughter's love for you. In awakening those memories which were her most ancient mother's in Ys . . . in resolving her into that ancient Dahut . . . obviously I could not pick and choose among her memories. They must, for my purposes, be complete. I must revive them all. Unfortunately, the Lord of Carnac was in them. Most unfortunately she met you, whose ancient father was that same Lord of Carnac. To destroy you would mean a complete and most probably abortive rearrangement of all my plans. It would infuriate her. She would become my enemy. Therefore you—continue to be. Is this plain?'

'Admirably so,' I said.

'What then—still assuming I am what you think— am I to do? Obviously, make you *particeps criminis*. A partner in my crimes. You cannot denounce me without denouncing yourself. I give you a certain drink which deadens your inhibitions against this and that. You become *particeps criminis*. Helpless to denounce, unless you want the same halter around your neck as would encircle mine. Doubtless,' he said, courteously, ' all this has occurred to you.'

'It has,' I answered. 'But I would like to put a few questions to you—in your character of sorcerer, warlock, priest of evil—assumed or otherwise, of course.'

'In that character,' he said, gravely, ' ask.'

'Did you bring about the death of Ralston?'

'I did not,' he said. 'My daughter did. It is she who commands the shadows.'

'Was the shadow which whispered him to his death— real?'

'Real enough to cause his death,' he replied.

'You become ambiguous,' I said. 'I asked was it real?'

He smiled: 'There is evidence that he thought so.'

'And the other three?'

'Equally as real. It was the unexpected linking of those cases by Dr. Bennett that prompted our visit to

Lowell . . . an exceedingly unfortunate visit, I repeat, since it resulted in my daughter meeting you. The admission, Caranac, is in my character of warlock, only.'

'Why, in that character, did you kill them?'

'Because we were temporarily in need of funds. You will recall there was difficulty in getting gold out of Europe. We had killed many times before—in England, in France, and elsewhere. Dahut needs amusement—so do her shadows. And they must feed—now and then.'

Could he be speaking truth—or was he playing with me? I said, coldly, hoping to bomb him out of his calm:

'You profit well by your daughter's whoredom.'

He laughed outright at that.

'What is whoredom to one who is warlock, sorcerer and priest of evil?'

'Those who marched last night to the Cairn—still assuming the sacrifices reality—the paupers——'

He interrupted me: 'Paupers! Why do you call them that?'

Now I laughed: 'Aren't they?'

He recovered his poise.

'Always under the same conditions of response, the majority of them, yes. And now you would ask me how I—collected—them. That, my dear Caranac, was remarkably simple. It involved only the bribing of an orderly or two, the administering to the paupers of a certain drug, a little whispering to them by my daughter's shadows, their slipping away under the guidance of those shadows to where my boat lay waiting for them. And they were here—and very happy to be here, I assure you . . . between sacrifices.'

He asked, suavely: 'Have I given tangible form to the vaguest of your suspicions, hardened into certainty those not so vague? Is not all this credible conduct for a sorcerer and his witch daughter?'

I did not answer.

He said: 'Speaking still in this capacity, my dear Caranac, assuming that you leave here, tell this story to others, bring down upon me man's law—what would happen? They would find no sacrifices, either dead in the Cairn or alive in the Cavern. There would be no Cavern. I have provided for all that. They would find only a peaceful scientist, one of whose hobbies is to reproduce Carnac in miniature. He would show them the standing stones. His entirely charming daughter would accompany and entertain them. You—if you were here—would be merely a lunatic dissonance. Whether you were here or not— what would happen to you thereafter? You would not die . . . but very heartily would you wish to die . . . if mind enough remained to formulate a wish.'

His lips were smiling, but his eyes were pale blue ice.

'I am still speaking as sorcerer, of course.'

I asked: 'Why did you come here for your experiment, de Keradel? Could you not have carried it on better in Carnac, before the ancient Cairn—the path to which the Gatherer knew well?'

He answered: 'All paths are known to the Gatherer. And how could I have had freedom to open that ancient path in a land where memory still lingers? Where could I have got the sacrifices—or carried on the ritual without interruption? It was not possible. Therefore I came here. Where the Gatherer is unknown—as yet.'

I nodded; that was reasonable enough. I asked, bluntly: 'What do you expect to gain?'

He laughed: 'You are too naïve, Caranac. That I will not tell you.'

Anger and remorse swept away my caution. I said: 'You'll never have my aid again in that black work, de Keradel.'

'So!' he said, slowly. 'So! And so I thought. But I will not need you again, Caranac. The *rapprochement* last night was almost perfect. So perfect . . . that I may not even need . . . again . . . Dahut.'

He had said that last musingly, more as though sealing by words a secret thought than speaking to me. And once more I had the feeling of dissension between the two . . . and fear of Dahut driving him . . . driving him to what . . .

He leaned back and roared with laughter; his eyes and lips both laughing, without malice or evil.

'That is one side of the matter, Dr. Caranac. And now I give you the other side, the common-sense side. I am an able psychiatrist, and adventurous. I am an explorer, but not of the jungles nor the deserts of this world. I explore the brains of men which are thousands of worlds. Mostly, I admit, they are distressingly similar; yet now and then there is one sufficiently different to justify the labour of exploration. Let us suppose that I have heard of you—as a matter of fact, Caranac, I know the history of your family better than you do yourself. Still, I have no desire to meet you until I read your interview in the case of this Ralston, whom I know not at all. It arouses my curiosity, and I decide to explore—you. What is my best approach without

exciting your suspicions? The most favourable, un-
guarded, entrance into the particular territory of your
brain which I wish to survey? I read that you are a
friend of Dr. Bennett, who has interesting ideas upon
the death of this same Ralston and others. I read that
he is with Dr. Lowell, a brother psychiatrist upon
whom I have long been intending to call. So I do call
upon him, and what more natural that I should receive
a dinner invitation for myself and my daughter. And,
as I expect, there are you and Dr. Bennett.

'Very well, then. You are a connoisseur of warlocks,
a student of sorcery. I turn the conversation in that
direction. You have spoken to the pressmen of shadows,
and to my delight I find that Dr. Bennett is obsessed by
the same idea. Better still, he is half convinced of
sorcery's reality. You two are so thoroughly *en rapport*
that not only do I find entrance to your mind doubly
easy, but his also open to me.'

He paused as though inviting comment. I made
none. Something of the amiability faded from his face.
He said:

'I have called myself an explorer of minds, Caranac.
I can cut my trails through them even as other explorers
cut theirs through the jungles. Better. Because I can
control the—vegetation.'

Again he paused, and when again I made no comment, asked with edge of irritation:

'You understand me?'

I nodded. 'I follow you perfectly.' I did not add that
not only did I follow him but was a bit ahead of
him.

He said: 'I now suggest to you—in my character of

psychiatrist, Caranac, not of sorcerer—that my whole experiment has been centred upon awakening those memories which have come down to you from ancestors who did make sacrifices to a Demon-god. Ancestors who made those very sacrifices in which last night it seemed to you you participated. That which you thought you saw upon the Cairn and within the Cairn was the image of that Demon-god, the image the imaginations of your ancestors created long centuries ago . . . that, and nothing more. I suggest that from the moment we met, little which has seemed reality to you has been wholly so—a tapestry of dark ancestral memories and innocent realities of which I have been the weaver. There is no Gatherer . . . there are no creeping Shadows . . . no hidden lair beneath this house. My daughter, who shares in my experiments, is in truth what sometimes she has seemed to you to be . . . a woman of to-day's world, sophisticated, certainly . . . but no more witch nor harlot than the Helen you called your antique coin. And finally, that you are a guest here, only. No prisoner, and under no compulsion to remain other than your own imagination—stimulated, as I have admitted, by my own passion for research.'

He added with barely discernible irony: '*And* my daughter's.'

Now it was I who walked to the window, and stood with my back to him. Absently, I noted that the rain had stopped and the sun was breaking through the clouds. He was lying—but in which of his two interpretations were the lies the fewer? No sorcerer could have set the stage of Dahut's towers in New York and Ys, nor have directed my experiences there, real or

224

imagined; nor been fugleman to what had happened after the rites of last night. Only a sorceress could have managed those things.

Also there were other weak spots to that second explanation. But the one indissoluble rock on which it split was that McCann, flying over this place, had also seen the corposants, the rotting lights of the dead . . . had seen the black and formless shape squatting upon the Cairn . . . glimpsed figures weaving among the standing stones before the fog had covered all.

Which of the two stories did de Keradel want me to believe? Which was it better for me to pretend to believe? That he had never really trusted me, I knew. Was this a sort of Lady or the Tiger trap? Which door ought I to open?

I turned to him with what I hoped was the precise mixture of chagrin and admiration. I said:

'Frankly, de Keradel, I don't know whether to be disappointed or relieved. After all, you know, you did take me up on the mountain and show me the kingdoms of Earth, and a part of me rejoiced exceedingly at the prospect and was perfectly willing to sign over to you. If a tenderer part is set at ease because it was mirage, still—the sterner part wishes it had been true. And I am divided between resentment that you should make me the subject of such an experiment, and admiration for your perfect workmanship.'

I sat down and added, carelessly: 'I take it that now you have made everything plain, the experiment is ended.'

The pale blue eyes dwelt upon me; he answered, slowly: 'It is ended—so far as I am concerned.'

Well did I know it wasn't, and well did I know I was as much a prisoner as ever; but I lighted a cigarette, and asked:

'I suppose, then, I am free to go whenever I choose?'

'An unnecessary question'—the pale eyes narrowed—'if you have accepted my common-sense interpretation of your experiences.'

I laughed: 'It was an echo of my servitude to you. One does not so quickly feel himself free of such fetters of illusion as you forge, de Keradel. By the way, I'd like to send a telegram to Dr. Bennett.'

'I am sorry,' he said, 'but the storm has broken the wire between us and the village.'

I said: 'I am sure it has. But what I would like to wire Dr. Bennett is that I like it here, and intend to remain as long as I am welcome. That the matter in which we have been so interested has been explained to my complete satisfaction, and to drop it. That there is nothing for him to worry about, and that I will amplify all this later by letter.'

Pausing, I looked him straight in the eyes: 'We would collaborate in that letter—you and I.'

He leaned back, appraising me with expressionless face, but I had not missed the flicker of astonishment when I had made my proposal. He was nibbling at the bait, although he had not yet swallowed it. He asked:

'Why?'

'Because of—you,' I said, and walked over to him. 'De Keradel, I *want* to stay here. With you. But not as one held by—ancestral memories. Not by an imagination stimulated or guided by you or your daughter. Nor by suggestion nor—sorcery. I want to stay here wide-awake and all myself. Nor have the charms of your daughter anything to do with that desire. I care little for women, de Keradel, except for the naked lady they name Truth. It is because of you, solely because of you, that I want to stay.'

Again he asked: 'Why?'

But he had taken the bait. His guard had dropped. Every symphony has its chord, and every chord its dominant note. So has every man and every woman. Discover that note, and learn just how and when to sound it—and man or woman is yours. De Keradel's dominant was vanity—egotism. I struck it heavily.

'Never, I think, has a de Carnac named a de Keradel —Master. Never asked to sit at a de Keradel's feet and learn. I know enough of the histories of our clans to be sure of that. Well, it has come to pass. All my life I have sought to lift Truth's veil. I think you can do that, de Keradel. Therefore—I would stay.'

He asked, curiously: 'Which of my two stories do you believe?'

I laughed: 'Both and neither. Otherwise would I deserve to be your acolyte?'

He said, almost wistfully: 'I wish I could trust you . . . Alain de Carnac! There is much that we could do together.'

I answered: 'Whether you trust me or do not, I cannot see how I, being here, can harm you. If I should disappear . . . or, for example, appear to have killed myself . . . or seem to have gone insane . . . that, of course, might harm you.'

He shook his head, absently; with a chillingly convincing indifference.

'I could be rid of you very easily, de Carnac . . . and there would be no necessity for explanations . . . but I wish I could trust you.'

I said: ' If you have nothing to lose by it—why not? ' He said, slowly: ' I will.'

He picked up the bowl of sacrifice in his hands, and weighed it. He dropped it on the table. Stretching both hands out towards me but without touching me, he did with them that to which, knowing what was in my heart against him, I could not respond. It was an immemorially ancient gesture, a holy gesture that had been taught to me in Tibet by a lama whose life I had saved . . . and the way de Keradel made that gesture defiled it, although it still held within it the obligation . . . an obligation beyond life. . . .

Dahut saved me. A sudden flood of sunshine poured into the room. She came through it towards us. If anything could have made me believe without reservation de Keradel's second and common-sense version, it would have been Dahut walking through that sunshine. She had on her riding-breeches and boots, and a sea-green silk shirt that just matched the colour of her eyes, and a beret on her silver-gilt hair that was exactly the same green. Coming through the sunshine towards me like this, she knocked de Keradel and everything else out of my head.

She said: ' Hello, Alan. It's cleared. Let's take a canter.'

She saw the bowl of sacrifice. Her eyes dilated so that I could see the whites both above and below them . . . and how the orchid hell sparks danced. . . .

De Keradel's face whitened. Then comprehension

came into it . . . a warning, a message, darted from him to her. The Demoiselle's lids dropped, the long lashes swept her cheeks. All this in a split second. I said, carelessly, as though I had observed nothing:

' Fine. I'll change my clothes.'

I had known that de Keradel hadn't put that bowl of sacrifice beside me. Now I knew that Dahut hadn't, either.

Then who had?

I stepped into my room . . . again I seemed to hear the buzzing . . . *'Alan, beware of Dahut. . . .'*

Maybe the shadows were going to be kind to me again.

CHAPTER XVIII

THE HOUNDS OF DAHUT

WHATEVER the mystery of the bowl, Dahut's invitation was a break I hadn't hoped for. I got into my riding togs with haste. I had the idea that the conversation between her and her father would not be entirely amicable, and I didn't want her to have time to change her mind about that gallop. Probably I would not be able to get to the village, but I ought to be able to make the rock where the patient fishermen waited.

I wrote a note to McCann:

'Be at the rock to-night from eleven until four. If I don't show up, be there to-morrow night between the same hours. Same holds for night after to-morrow. If you haven't heard from me then, tell Ricori from me to use his own judgment.'

Ricori should have landed by then. And if by then I had not been able to get a message to McCann, it would mean I was in a tight corner—if, indeed, I was in any shape to be in any corner whatsoever. I banked upon Ricori's resourcefulness and ruthlessness as adequate to meet de Keradel's own. Also, he would act swiftly. I wrote the note in duplicate, since after all I might be able to get to the village. I put one in a two-ounce bottle, stoppering it tightly. The other I put in my pocket.

230

I went downstairs whistling, thus giving warning of my approach. I went into the room as though I had not a care nor a suspicion in the world. Nor was I entirely acting. I did have a heady sense of elation; somewhat like that of a fighter who has lost round after round with an opponent whose style has been devastatingly unfamiliar, but who suddenly gets the key to it and feels he can meet it.

The Demoiselle was standing beside the fire-place, switching at her boots with her quirt. De Keradel was still at the head of the table, scrunched down a bit, more stolid than I had seen him. The bowl of sacrifice was nowhere in sight. The Demoiselle was rather like a beautiful wasp; de Keradel a quite small Gibraltar repelling stings. I laughed as that comparison came into my head.

Dahut said: 'You are gay.'

I said: 'Indeed I am. Gayer'—I looked at de Keradel—'than I have been for years.'

She did not miss that look, nor his faint answering smile.

She said: 'Let us go. You are sure you will not join us, my father.'

De Keradel shook his head: 'I have much to do.'

We went out to the stables. She took the same leggy bay, and I the roan. For a time she rode a little ahead of me, silent; then dropped back. She said:

'You are as gay as though you rode to meet a loved woman.'

I said: 'I hope to meet her. But not on this ride, Dahut.'

She whispered: ' Is it—Helen? '

' No, Dahut—although Helen has many of her attributes.'

' Who is she? '

' You don't know her very well, Dahut. She wears no clothes, except a veil over her face. Her name is Truth. Your father has promised me to lift her veil.'

She reined closer; grasped my wrist.

' He promised that—to you? '

I said, casually: ' Yes. And he rather more than intimated that he need not call you in to assist.'

' Why do you tell me this? ' Her fingers tightened on my wrist.

' Because, Dahut, I am exceedingly anxious to meet this naked lady Truth with no veil over her face. And I have a feeling that unless from now on I answer all questions with perfect candour, our meeting will be delayed.'

She said, dangerously: ' Do not play with me. Why did you tell me that? '

' I am not playing with you at all, Dahut. I am only being bluntly honest. So much so that I will give you my secondary reason.'

' And that? '

' Divide—and rule,' I answered.

She stared at me, uncomprehendingly.

' They tell a story in India,' I said. ' It is one of their *jatakas*—animal fables. Tiger Queen and Lion King could not agree. Their enmity upset the jungle. At last they made a bargain. They were to sit on the pans of a balance suspended just over a pool filled with crocodiles. The heavier one, obviously, would drop into the water, to the delight of the crocodiles. Tiger Queen and Lion King sat on the scales. Each weighed exactly the same. But an ant had hidden himself mid-beam with a grain of sand in his mandibles. "Ho," he cried. "Who bids? And what is bid?" This he cried, this humble ant, to Tiger Queen and Lion King. And a grain of sand in his mandibles was life or death to one of them.'

Dahut asked, breathlessly: 'Which lived?'

I laughed: 'The story does not say.'

She knew what I meant, and I watched the colour creep into her cheeks and the sparks dance in her eyes. She dropped my wrist. She said:

'My father is truly pleased with you, Alan.'

'I think you told me that once before, Dahut—but no gaiety followed.'

She whispered: 'And I seem to have heard you speaking like this before . . . and there was no gaiety thereafter for me. . . .' Again she grasped my wrist. 'But I am not pleased, Alan.'

'I am sorry, Dahut.'

She said: 'Despite his wisdom, my father is rather—ingenuous. I am not.'

'Fine,' I said, heartily. 'Nor am I. I loathe ingenuousness. But I have not as yet observed any *naïveté* about your father.'

Her grip upon my wrist tightened.

'This Helen . . . how much does she resemble the naked but veiled lady of your quest?'

My pulse leaped. I could not help it; she felt it. She said, sweetly:

233

'You do not know? You have had no opportunity, I take it, for . . . comparison.'

There was mercilessness in the rippling of the little waves of her laughter.

'Continue to be gay, my Alan. Perhaps, some day, I may give you that opportunity.'

She tapped her horse with her quirt, and cantered off. I ceased feeling gay. Why the devil had I allowed Helen to be brought into the talk? Not choked off mention of her at the beginning? I followed Dahut close, but she did not look at me, nor speak. We went along for a mile or two, and came out on that haunted meadow of the crouching bushes. Here she seemed to regain her good-humour, dropped back beside me. She said:

'Divide—and rule. It is a wise saying, that. Whose is it, Alan?'

I said: 'So far as I know, some old Roman's. Napoleon quoted it.'

'The Romans were wise, very wise. Suppose I told my father that you had put this thought into my head?'

I said, indifferently: 'Why not? Yet if it has not already occurred to him, why forearm him against yourself?'

She said, thoughtfully: 'You are strangely sure of *yourself* to-day.'

'If I am,' I answered, 'it is because there is nothing but the truth in me. So if there are any questions upon the tip of your lovely tongue whose truthful answers might offend your beautiful ears—do not ask them of me.'

She bent her head, and went scudding over the
meadow. We came to the breast of rock which I had
scaled on our first ride. I dropped from my horse and
began to climb. I reached the top, and turning, saw
that she, too, had dismounted and was looking up at
me, irresolutely. I waved to her, and sat down upon
the rock. The fishing-boat was a few hundred yards
away. I threw a stone or two idly into the water, then
flipped out the small bottle in which was the note to
McCann. One of the men stood up, stretched, and
began to pull up the anchors. I called out to him:

'Any luck?'...

Dahut was standing beside me. A ray of the setting
sun struck the neck of the small bottle, and it glinted.
She watched it for a moment, looked at the fishermen,
then at me.

I said to her: 'What is that? A fish?' And threw
a stone at the glint.

She did not answer; stood studying the men in the
boat. They rowed between us and the bottle, turned
the breast of rock and passed out of sight. The bottle
still glinted, rising and falling in the swell.

She half lifted her hand, and I could have sworn that
a ripple shot across the water straight to the bottle, and
that an eddy caught it, sending it swirling towards us.

I rose, and took her by the shoulders, raised her face
to mine and kissed her. She clung to me, quivering.
I took her hands, and they were cold, and helped her
down the breast of rock. Towards the bottom, I lifted
her in my arms and carried her. I set her on her feet
beside her horse. Her long fingers slipped round my
throat, half strangling me; she pressed her lips to mine

in a kiss that left me breathless. She leaped on the bay, and gave it the quirt, mercilessly. She was off over the meadow, swift as a racing shadow.

I hesitated, wondering whether to ascend the breast again to see if McCann's men had come back and retrieved the bottle. I decided I'd better not risk it, and rode after Dahut.

She kept far ahead of me, never looking back. At the door of the old house she flung herself from the back of the bay, gave it a little slap, and went quickly in. The bay trotted over to the stables. I turned across the field and rode towards the grove of oaks. I remembered it so well that I knew precisely when I would reach its edge and face the monoliths.

I reached the edge, and there were the standing stones, a good two hundred of them lifting up from a twenty-acre plain and hidden from the sea by an irregular and pine-thatched granite ridge. They were not grey as they had been under fog. They were stained red by the setting sun. In their centre squatted the Cairn, sullen, enigmatic and evil.

The roan would not pass the threshold of the grove. He raised his head and sniffed at the wind and whinnied; he began to shiver and to sweat, and his whinny grew shrill with fear.

He swerved and swung back into the oaks. I gave him his head.

Dahut sat at the head of the table. Her father had gone somewhere on the yacht and might not return that night, she had said. I wondered, but not aloud, if he were collecting more paupers for the sacrifices.

He had not been there when I had come in from the ride. Nor, until I had sat down at the table, had I seen Dahut. I had gone up to my room and bathed and dressed leisurely. I had set my ear to the tapestry and had searched again for the hidden spring; and had heard and found nothing. A kneeling servant had announced that dinner was ready. It interested me that he did not address me as his Lord of Carnac.

Dahut wore a black dress, for the first time since I had met her. There wasn't much of it, but what there was showed her off beautifully. She looked tired; not wilty or droopy, but in some odd fashion like a sea flower that was at its best at high tide and was now marking time through the low. I felt a certain pity for her. She raised her eyes to mine, and they were weary. She said:

'Alan, do you mind—I'd rather talk commonplace to-night.'

Inwardly, I smiled at that. The situation was somewhat more than piquant. There was so little we could talk about other than commonplace that wasn't loaded with high explosive. I approved of the suggestion, feeling in no mood for explosions. Nevertheless, there was something wrong with the Demoiselle or she would never have made it. Was she afraid I might bring up that matter of the sacrificial bowl, perhaps—or was it that my talk with de Keradel had upset her? Certainly she had not liked it.

'Commonplace it is,' I said. 'If brains were sparks, mine to-night wouldn't even light a match. Discussion of the weather is about the limit of my intelligence.'

She laughed: 'Well, what do you think of the weather, Alan?'

I said: 'It ought to be abolished by Constitutional amendment.'

'And what makes the weather?'

'Just now,' I answered, 'you do—for me.'

She looked at me, sombrely.

'I wish that were true—but take care, Alan.'

'My mistake, Dahut,' I said. 'Back to the commonplace.'

She sighed, then smiled—and it was hard to think of her as the Dahut I had known, or thought I had known, in her towers of Ys and New York . . . or with the golden sickle red in her hand. . . .

We stuck to commonplaces, although now and then perilous pits gaped. The perfect servants served us with a perfect dinner. De Keradel, whether scientist or sorcerer, did himself well with his wines. The Demoiselle ate little and drank hardly at all, and steadily her languor grew. I pushed aside the coffee, and said:

'The tide must be on the ebb, Dahut.'

She straightened, and asked sharply: 'Why do you say that?'

'I do not know. But always you have seemed to me of the sea, Dahut. I told you so that night I met you. So why should your spirit not rise and fall with the rise and fall of the tides?'

She got up abruptly, and her face was colourless.

'Good night, Alan. I am very tired. Sleep—without dreams.'

She was out of the room before I could answer her.

Why had that mention of the tides brought about

such a change in her, forced her to flight—for flight that swift departure had been? I could find no answer. A clock struck nine. I sat at the table for a quarter-hour more, the blank-eyed servants watching me. I stood up, yawning. I smiled drowsily at the butler and said to him in the Breton tongue:

'To-night I—sleep.'

He had been among the van of those who with their flambeaux had herded the sacrifices. He bowed low, no slightest change of expression to betray that he sensed the significance of what I had said. He held the curtains open for me. I felt his gaze upon me as I slowly went up the stairs to my room.

I paused for a moment in the hall and looked out of the window. There was a rack of thin clouds over the sky, half-veiling the moon, now a few nights past its full. It was a dimly luminous night, and a very silent one. There were no shadows in the wide, old-fashioned hall— whispering and rustling. I entered my room, undressed and went to bed. It was close to ten.

An hour went by while I lay there feigning sleep. Then that for which I had been waiting happened. Some one was in the room, and by the faint strange fragrance I knew it was Dahut, and that she stood close beside my bed. I felt her bend over me and listen to my breathing; her fingers, light as the touch of a moth, upon the pulse in my neck and upon the pulse in my wrist. I sighed, and turned, and seemed to sink again in deeper slumber. And I heard her sigh, and felt a touch upon my cheek that was not of fingers. The fragrance stole away, soundlessly. Yet I knew Dahut had paused before the tapestry, listening. For long

239

minutes she stood there, and then there was the faintest of clicks, and I knew that she had gone.

Nevertheless, I waited until the hands upon my watch-face pointed to eleven before I slipped out of bed, and drew on breeches, shirt, dark sweater and rubber shoes.

The driveway to the house ran straight to the guarded gates, a mile and a half away. I did not believe this was patrolled, and I purposed to follow it within half a mile of the gates, to strike off to the left, reach the wall and skirt it to the rock where McCann would be awaiting me. True, the keeper of the inn had said the breast could not be scaled from the water, but I had no doubt McCann would find a way. I should make it in half an hour, easily.

I stepped out into the hall, crept to the head of the stairs and looked down. A faint light was burning, but there was no sign of servants. I stole down the stairs and reached the front door. It was unlocked and un-bolted. I closed it behind me and merged into the shadow of a rhododendron, getting my outer bearings.

Here the driveway made a wide curve, unprotected by shrubbery. The scud had thinned and the moon was far too bright, but once the loop was crossed, there would be cover from the trees that bordered the road. I walked across the loop and gained the shelter of the trees. I waited a good five minutes, watching. The house remained dark, no lights from any window; no stir nor sound. I set off along the roadway.

I had covered a trifle under my mile when I came to a narrow lane angling to the left. It was fairly straight, what I could see of it in the watery moonlight. It struck in the general direction of the rock, and promised not only a shorter cut but a safer way. I took it. A few score yards and the trees ended. The lane continued, bordered with scrub and bushes just too high for me to look over and far too dense for me to see through.

A half-mile of this, and I had an acutely disagreeable feeling of being followed. It was an extraordinarily unpleasant feeling—as though what followed me was peculiarly loathsome. And suddenly it was at my back —reaching out to me. I wheeled, snatching the gun from the holster.

There was nothing behind me. The lane stretched dimly, and empty.

My heart was pumping as though I had been running; my hands and my forehead were wet with sweat and I felt a stirring of nausea. I fought it down and went on, gun in hand. A dozen steps, and again I felt the stealthy approach—coming closer, closer . . . faster and faster . . . sweeping upon me. I mastered panic impulse to run, and wheeled again—and again saw only empty lane.

I pressed my back against the bushes, and sidled along, watching the path I had traversed——

Now there was furtive movement in the scrub that lined the lane; movement as of things flitting through the bushes to the measure of my steps, watching me, gloating upon me; and there were rustlings and whisperings and thin obscene pipings as though they talked of me as I sidled on and on, legs trembling, nausea growing, and fighting, fighting at every step that panic desire to fling away my gun, cover my eyes with my arms lest I see the things—and run and run.

The lane ended. Step by step I backed away from it

until I could no longer hear the rustlings and the pipings. But still there was movement in the bushes and I knew the things watched me from them. I turned and saw that I was on the edge of the haunted meadow. Sinister enough it had seemed by day, but it had been gay to what it was now, by night, under the scud-veiled, waning moon. It was desolate, unutterably desolate, and the bushes that had seemed like crouching men were now bent souls chained for eternity to desolation, in irrevocable despair.

I could not cross that meadow unless I did it quickly. I could not go back through the piping things. I began to run straight across the meadow, towards the wall.

I was a third over it when I heard the baying of the hounds. It came from the direction of the house, and involuntarily I stopped, listening. It was not like the cry of any pack I had ever heard. It was sustained, wailing, ineffably mournful; with the thin unearthly quality of the obscene pipings. It was the desolation of the meadow given voice.

I stood, throat dry, every hair prickling, unable to move. And nearer drew the baying, and nearer——

The lane spewed shadow shapes. They were black under the moon and they were like the shadows of men, but of men deformed, distorted, changed into abominable grotesques within a workshop in Hell. They were —foul. They spread fanwise from the mouth of the lane and came leaping, skipping, flittering over the meadow; squatting in the crouching bushes, then flinging themselves out again, and as they ran they mewed and squeaked and piped. There was one with bloated body like a monstrous frog that came hopping

242

towards me and leaped croaking over my head. There was another that touched me as it passed—a shadowy thing with long and twisted ape-like arms, dwarfed legs and head the size of an orange set upon a thin and writhing neck. It was not all shadow, for I felt its touch, gossamer as the wing of a moth, thin as mist—yet palpable. It was unclean. A defilement. A horror.

The baying of the dogs was close, and with it a tattoo of hoofs, the drumming of a strong horse, galloping——

Out of the lane burst a great black stallion, neck outstretched, mane flying. Upon his back rode Dahut, ash-gold hair streaming loose in the wind, eyes flaming with the violet witch-fire. She saw me, and raised her whip and screamed, reining in the stallion so that he danced, forefeet high in air. Again she screamed, and pointed to me. From behind the stallion poured a pack of huge dogs, a dozen or more of them, like stag-hounds . . . like the great hounds of the Druids.

They raced down upon me like a black wave, and I saw that they were shadowy, but that in the blackness of their shadows red eyes gleamed with the same hell-fires that were in Dahut's. And behind them thundered the stallion with Dahut—no longer screaming, her mouth twisted into a square of fury and her face no woman's but a fiend's.

They were almost upon me before my paralysis broke. I raised the automatic and shot straight at her. Before I could press trigger again, the shadow pack was on me.

Like the thing that had touched me, they, too, had substance, these shadow hounds of Dahut. Tenuous, misty—but material. I staggered under their onslaught. It was as though I fought against bodies made of black cobwebs, and I saw the moon as though it were shining through a black veil; and Dahut upon the stallion and the desolate meadow were dimmed and blurred as though I looked through black cobwebs. I had dropped my gun and I fought with bare hands. Their touch had not the vileness of the ape-armed thing, but from them came a strange and numbing cold. They tore at me with shadowy fangs; gripped my throat with red eyes burning into mine, and it was as though the cold poured into me through their fangs. I was weakening. It was growing harder to breathe. The numbness of the cold had my arms and hands so that now I could only feebly struggle against the black cobwebs. I dropped to my knees, gasping for breath. . . .

Dahut was down from the stallion and I was free from the hounds. I stared up at her and tried to stagger to my feet. The fury had gone from her face, but in it was no mercy and out of its whiteness the violet flames of her eyes flared. She brought her whip down across my face. '*A brand for your first treachery!*' She lashed me again. '*A brand for your second!*' A third time. '*A brand for this!*'

I wondered, dazedly, why I did not feel the blows. I felt nothing; all my body was numb, as though the cold had condensed within it. Slowly it was creeping into my brain, chilling my mind, freezing my thought.

She said: 'Stand up.'

Slowly, I got up.

She leaped upon the stallion's back. She said: 'Raise your left arm.'

I lifted it, and she noosed the lash of the quirt round my wrist like a fetter.

She said: 'Look. My dogs feed.'

I looked. The shadow hounds were coursing over the meadow and the shadow things were running, hopping from bush to bush, squeaking, piping in terror. The hounds were chasing them, pulling them down, tearing at them.

She said: 'You, too, shall—feed!'

She called to her dogs and they left their kills and came coursing to her.

The cold had crept into my brain. I could not think. I could see, but what I saw had little meaning. I had no will, except hers.

The stallion trotted away, into the lane. I trotted at its side, held by the fetter of Dahut's lash, like a runaway slave. Once I looked behind. At my heels was the shadow pack, red eyes glinting in their bodies' murk. It did not matter.

And the numbness grew until all I knew was that I trotted, trotted——

Then even that last faint fragment of consciousness faded away.

CHAPTER XIX

' CREEP, SHADOW! '

THERE was no feeling in my body, but my mind was awake and alert. It was as though I had no body. The icy venom from the fangs of the shadow hounds still numbed me. But it had cleared from my brain. I could see and I could hear.

All that I could see was a green twilight, as though I lay deep in some ocean abyss looking upward through immense spaces of motionless, crystal-clear green water. I floated deep within this motionless sea, yet I could hear, far above me, its waves whispering and singing.

I began to rise, floating up through the depths towards the whispering, singing waves. Their voices became clearer. They were singing a strange old song, a sea-song old before ever man existed . . . singing it to the measured chime of tiny bells struck slowly far beneath the sea . . . to measured tap, tap, tap on drums of red royal coral deep beneath the sea . . . to chords struck softly on harps of sea-fans, whose strings were mauve and violet and crocus yellow.

Up I floated and up, until song and drum-beat, chimes and sighing harp-chords blended into one——

The voice of Dahut.

She was close to me, and she was singing, but I could not see her. I could see nothing but the green twilight, and that was fast darkening. Sweet was her voice and pitiless . . . and wordless was her song except for its burden. . . .

246

'Creep, Shadow! Thirst, Shadow! Hunger, Shadow! Creep, Shadow—creep!'

I strove to speak and could not; strove to move and could not. And still her song went on . . . only its burden plain. . . .

'Creep, Shadow! Hunger, Shadow . . . feed only where and when I bid you! Thirst, Shadow . . . drink only where and when I bid you! *Creep, Shadow . . . creep!'*

Suddenly I felt my body. First as a tingling, and then as a leaden weight, and then as a wrenching agony. I was out of my body. It lay upon a wide, low bed in a tapestried room filled with rosy light. The light did not penetrate the space in which *I* was, crouching at my body's feet. On my body's face were three crimson welts, the marks of Dahut's whip; and Dahut stood at my body's head, naked, two thick braids of her pale gold hair crossed between white breasts. I knew that my body was not dead, but Dahut was not looking at it. She was looking at me . . . whatever I was . . . crouched at my body's feet. . . .

'Creep, Shadow . . . creep . . . creep . . . creep, Shadow . . . creep . . .'

The room, my body, and Dahut faded—in that precise order. I was creeping, creeping, through darkness. It was like creeping through a tunnel, for solidity was above and below and on each side of me; and at last, as though reaching a tunnel's end, the blackness before me began to grey. I crept out of the darkness.

I was at the edge of the standing stones, on the threshold of the monoliths. The moon was low, and they stood black against it.

There was an eddy of wind, and like a leaf it blew me

among the monoliths. I thought: *What am I to be blown like a leaf in the wind!* I felt resentment, rage. I thought: *A shadow's rage!*

I was beside one of the standing stones. Dark as it was, a darker shadow leaned against it. It was the shadow of a man, although there was no man's body to cast it. It was the shadow of a man buried to the knees. There were other monoliths near, and against each of them leaned a man's shadow . . . buried to the knees. The shadow closest to me wavered, like the shadow cast by a wind-shaken candle-flame. It bent to me and whispered:

'You have life! Live, Shadow . . . and save us!'

I whispered: 'I am shadow . . . shadow like you . . . how can I save you?'

The shadow against the standing stone swayed and shook.

'You have life . . . kill . . . kill her . . . kill him. . . .'

The shadow on the stone behind me whispered: 'Kill . . . *her* . . . first.'

From all the monoliths rose a whisper: 'Kill . . . kill . . . kill. . . .'

There was a stronger eddy of the wind, and on it I was whirled like a leaf almost to the threshold of the Cairn. The whispering of the shadows fettered to the circling monoliths grew to a locust shrill, beating back the wind that was whirling me into the Cairn . . . shrilling a barrier between the Cairn and me . . . driving me back, out of the field of the monoliths. . . .

The Cairn and the monoliths were gone. The moon was gone and gone was the familiar earth. I was a shadow . . . in a land of shadows. . . .

There were no stars, no moon, no sun. There was only a faintly luminous dusk which shrouded a world all wan and ashen and black. I stood alone, on a wide plain. There were no perspectives, and no horizons. Everywhere it was as though I looked upon vast screens. Yet I knew there were depths and distances in this strange land. I was a shadow, vague and unsubstantial. Yet I could see and hear, feel and taste—I knew that, because I clasped my hands and felt them, and in my mouth and throat was the bitter taste of ashes.

Ahead of me were shadow mountains, stacked against each other like gigantic slices of black jade; lamellar; distinguishable from each other only by their varying darknesses. It seemed that I could reach out a hand and touch them, yet I knew they were far and far away. My eyes—my sight—whatever it was that functioned as sight in this shadow that was I—sharpened. I was ankle deep in sombre, shadowy grass starred by small flowers that should have been gay blue instead of mournful grey. And shadowy livid lilies that should have been golden and scarlet swayed in a wind I could not feel.

I heard above me a thin trilling, plaintively sweet. Shadowy birds were winging over me towards the distant mountains. They passed . . . but the trilling lingered . . . shaped itself into words . . . into the voice of Dahut.

'. . . *Creep, Shadow! Hunger . . . Thirst!*'

My way was towards the mountains—the shadowy birds had pointed it. I had a swift moment of rebellion. I thought: *I will not take it. This is illusion. Here I stay. . . .*

The voice of Dahut, pitiless: ' *Creep, Shadow!* *Learn whether it is not real!* '

I began to walk, through the sombre grass, towards the black mountains.

There was a muted beat of hoofs behind me. I turned. A shadowy horse was driving down upon me, a great grey destrier; armoured. The shadow who rode it was armoured; the shadow of a big man, wide of shoulder and thick of body; unvisored, but chain-mailed from neck to feet; in his belt a battle-axe and across his shoulders a long two-edged sword. The destrier was close, yet the sound of its hoofs was faint, like distant thunder. And I saw that far behind the armoured man raced other shadowy horsemen, leaning forward over the necks of small steeds. The armoured man drew up his horse beside me; looked down at me with faint glint of brown eyes in shadowy face.

' A stranger! Now by Our Lady I leave no straggler in the path of the wolves I draw! Up, Shadow . . . up! '

He swung an arm and lifted me; threw me astride the destrier behind him.

' Hold fast! ' he cried, and gave the grey horse the spur. Swiftly it raced, and ever more swiftly. Soon the slices of the black mountains were close. A defile opened. At its mouth he stopped, and looked back, made gesture of derision and laughed: ' They cannot catch us now. . . .'

He muttered: ' Still, I do not know why my horse should be so weary.'

He stared at me from shadowy face. ' I do know . . . you have too much life, Shadow. He who casts you is not . . . dead. Then what do you here? '

250

He twisted, and lifted me from the horse, and set me on the ground gently.

'See!'—he pointed to my breast.

There was a filament of glistening silver, fine as the finest cobweb, floating from it . . . stretching towards the ravine as though pointing the way I must take . . . as though it came from my heart . . . as though it were unwinding from my heart. . . .

'You are not dead!' Shadowy pity was in his regard. 'Therefore you must hunger . . . therefore you must thirst . . . until you feed and drink where the thread leads you. Half-Shadow—it was a witch who sent me here, Berenice de Azlais, of Languedoc. But my body has long been dust and I have long been content to feed on shadow fare. Long dust, I say and so suppose . . . but here one knows no time. My year was 1346 of Our Lord. What year was yours?'

'Nigh six centuries after,' I said.

'So long . . . so long,' he whispered. 'Who sent you here?'

'Dahut of Ys.'

'Queen of Shadows! Well, she has sent us many. I am sorry, Half-Shadow, but I can carry you no farther.'

Suddenly he slapped his sides, and shook with laughter. 'Six hundred years, and still I have my lemans. Shadowy, 'tis true—but then so am I. And still I can fight. Berenice—to you my thanks. St. Francis . . . let Berenice hereafter toast less hotly in Hell, where without doubt she is.'

He leaned and clapped me on the shoulder. 'But kill your witch, Half-brother—if you can!'

251

He rode into the ravine. I followed in his wake, walking. Soon he was out of sight. How long I walked I did not know. It was true that there was no time in this land. I passed out of the ravine.

The black jade mountains were palisades circling a garden filled with pallid lilies. In its centre was a deep black pool in which floated other lilies, black and silver and rusty-black. The pool was walled with jet. . . .

It was there that I felt the first bite of the dreadful hunger, the first pang of the dreadful thirst. . . .

Upon the wide jet wall lay seven girls, dull silver shadows . . . and exquisite. Naked shadows . . . one lay with chin cupped in misty hands, a glint of deepest sapphire blue eyes in her shadowy face . . . another sat, dipping slender feet in the black of the pool, and her hair was blacker than its waters, black spume of blacker waves, and as fine . . . and out of the black mist of her hair eyes green as emeralds but soft with promise glanced at me. . . .

They arose, the seven, and drifted towards me.

One said: 'He has too much of life.'

Another said: 'Too much . . . yet not enough.'

A third said: 'He must feed and drink . . . then return, and we shall see.'

The girl whose eyes were sapphire blue asked: 'Who sent you here, Shadow?'

I said: 'Dahut the White. Dahut of Ys.'

They shrank from me. 'Dahut sent you? Shadow —you are not for us. Shadow—pass on.'

'*Creep, Shadow!* . . .'

I said: 'I am weary. Let me rest here for a while.'

252

The green-eyed girl said: 'You have too much of life. If you had none you would not be weary. Only life grows weary——'

The blue-eyed girl whispered: 'And life is only weariness.'

'Nevertheless, I would rest. Also I am hungry, and I thirst.'

'Shadow with too much of life . . . there is nothing here that you can eat . . . nothing here that you can drink.'

I pointed to the pool. 'I drink of that.'

They laughed: 'Try—Shadow.'

I dropped upon my belly and thrust my face towards the black water. The surface of the pool receded as I bent. It drew back from my lips . . . it was but the shadow of water . . . and I could not drink. . . .

'. . . *Thirst, Shadow . . . drink only when and where I bid. . . .*'

The voice of Dahut!

I said to the girls: 'Let me rest.'

They answered: 'Rest.'

I crouched upon the rim of jet. The silver girls drew away from me, clustered, shadowy arms entwined, whispering. It was good to rest, although I felt no desire to sleep. I sat, hands clasping knees, head on breast. Loneliness fell upon me like a garment; loneliness rained upon me. The girl whose eyes were blue slipped to my side. She threw an arm around my shoulders, leaned against me.

'When you have fed . . . when you have drunk . . . come back to me.'

I do not know how long I lay upon the rim of jet

around the black pool. But when at last I rose, the
girls of tarnished silver were not there. The armoured
man had said there was no time in this land. I had
liked the armoured man. I wished that his horse had
been strong enough to carry me wherever he had been
going. My hunger had grown and so had my thirst.
Again I dropped and tried to sip of the pool . . . the
shadow waters were not for me. . . .

Something was tugging at me, drawing me on. It
was the silver filament, and it was shining like a thread
of living light. I walked out of the garden, following
the thread. . . .

The mountains were behind me. I was threading
my way through a vast marsh. Spectral rushes
bordered a perilous path, and in them lurked shadow
shapes, unseen but hideous. They watched me as I
went, and I knew that I must go carefully lest a mis-
step give me to them. A mist hung over the marsh,
a grey and dead mist that darkened when the hidden
things furtively raised themselves . . . or fled ahead to
crouch beside the path and await my coming. I felt
their eyes upon me—cold, dead, malignant.

There was a ridge feathered with ghostly ferns,
behind which other shadowy shapes lurked, pushing
and crowding against each other, following me as I
threaded my way through the spectral rushes. And at
every step more woeful became my loneliness, more
torturing my hunger and my thirst.

I passed the marsh and came out upon a dim path
that quickly widened into a broad highway which,
wavering, stretched across an illimitable and cloudy
plain. There were other shadow shapes upon this

highway . . . shapes of men and women, old and young, shapes of children and of animals . . . but no shape inhuman or unearthly. They were like shapes formed of heavy fog . . . of frozen fog. They flitted and loitered, ran or stood forlorn . . . singly, in groups, in companies. And as they went by, or overtook me, or I overtook them, I felt their gaze upon me. They seemed of all times and of all races, these shadow folk. There was a lean Egyptian priest upon whose shoulder sat a shadowy cat that arched its back and spat soundlessly at me . . . three Roman legionaries whose round, close-fitting helmets were darker stains upon their heads and who raised shadowy arms in the ancient salute as they strode past . . . there were Greek warriors with helms from which shadow plumes streamed, and shadowy women in litters carried by shadow slaves . . . and once a company of little men went by on shaggy silent ponies, spectral bows at backs, slanting shadowy eyes glinting at me . . . and there was the shadow of a child that turned and trotted beside me for a space, reaching up its hands to the slender filament that was leading me . . . dragging me . . . where?

The road went on and on. It became ever more thronged with the shadow people, and I saw that many more were going my way than against me. Then at my right, out upon the vaporous plain, a wan light began to glow . . . phosphorescent, funereal . . . like the glimmer of the corposants, the lights of the dead . . . among the monoliths. . . .

It became a half-moon that rested upon the plain like a gigantic gateway. It sent a path of ashen light across the plain, and from the high road into that path, the shadow people began to stream. Not all—one that tarried paused beside me; gross of body; with plumed and conical hat and cloak that streamed and wavered in a wind I could not feel, as though by it his gross body were being whipped in tatters.

He whispered: 'The Eater of Shadows eats from a full board.'

I echoed, thinly: 'The Eater of Shadows?'

I felt his gaze upon me, intent. He tittered in a voice like the rustling of rotting, poisonous leaves: 'Heh-heh-heh . . . a virgin! New-born into this delectable world! You know nothing of the Eater of Shadows? Heh-heh-heh . . . but he is our only form of Death in this world, and many who weary of it go to him. This you do not yet fully perceive, since he has not made himself manifest. They are fools,' he whispered, viciously. 'They should learn, as I have learned, to take their food in the world from which they came. No shadow-food . . . no, no, no . . . good flesh and body and soul . . . *soul*, heh-heh-heh!'

A shadowy hand snatched at the shining filament, and recoiled, twisting as though seared . . . the gross shadow cringed and writhed as though in agony. The rustling voice became a vile high whining.

'You are going to your marriage feast . . . going to your marriage bed. You will have your own table . . . a fair table of flesh and blood and soul . . . of life. Take me with you, bridegroom . . . take me with you. I can teach you so much! And my price is only a few crumbs from your table . . . only the smallest share in your bride. . . .'

Something was gathering in the doorway of the half-

moon; something forming upon its glimmering surface . . . fathomless black shadows were grouping
themselves into a gigantic, featureless face. No, it was
not featureless, for there were two apertures like eyes
through which the wan phosphorescence shone. And
there was a shapeless mouth which gaped while a
writhing ribbon of the dead light streamed out of it
like a tongue. The tongue licked among the shadows
and drew them into the mouth, and the lips closed on
them . . . then opened again, and again the tongue
licked out. . . .

'Oh, my hunger! Oh, my thirst and hunger! Take
me with you, bridegroom . . . to your bride. There is
so much I can teach you . . . for such a little price. . . .'

I struck at that gibbering shadow and fled from its
dreadful whispering; fled with shadowy arms covering
my eyes to shut out the vision of that vague and dreadful face. . . .

'. . . Hunger, Shadow . . . feed only where and when
I bid. Thirst, Shadow . . . drink only where and when
I bid! . . .'

And now I knew. I knew where the silver filament
was dragging me, and I tore at it with shadowy hands,
but could not break it. I tried to run back, against it,
and it swung me round, dragging me inexorably on.

I knew now what the evil, tittering shadow had
known . . . that I was on my way to food and drink
. . . to my marriage feast . . . to my bride——

Helen!

It was on her body and blood and life my hunger
was to be appeased, my thirst slaked.

Upon—Helen!

257

The shadow-land lightened. It became crystalline. Heavier, blacker shadows thrust themselves within it. These steadied, and the land of shadows vanished.

I was in an old room. Helen was there, and Bill and McCann, and a man I did not know; a lean and dark man with thin, ascetic face and snow-white hair. But wait . . . that must be Ricori. . . .

How long had I been in shadow-land?

Their voices came to me as a low humming, their words an unintelligible drone. I did not care what they were talking about. My whole being was focused upon Helen. I was starving for her, famishing for her. . . . I must eat and drink of her. . . .

I thought: *If I do . . . she must die!*

I thought: *Let her die . . . I must eat and drink. . . .*

She raised her head sharply. I knew that she was aware of me. She turned and looked straight at me. She saw me . . . I knew that she saw me. Her face whitened . . . then grew pitiful. The amber-gold of her eyes darkened with a wrath in which was complete comprehension . . . then became tender. Her little rounded chin hardened; her red mouth with its touch of the archaic became inscrutable. She got up and said something to the others. I saw them rise, staring at her incredulously—then search the room with their eyes. Except Ricori, who looked straight at her, stern face softened. And now words shaped themselves from the low humming of their voices. I heard Helen say:

' I fight Dahut. Give me an hour. I know what I am doing '—a wave of colour spread over her face— ' believe me, I know.'

I saw Ricori bend and kiss her hand; he raised his

head and there was iron assurance in the look he gave her. . . .

'And *I* know—win, Madonna . . . or if you lose, be sure that you shall be avenged.'

She walked from the room. The shadow that was I crept after her.

She walked upstairs, and into another room. She turned on lights, hesitated, then locked the door behind her. She went to the windows and drew down the curtains. She held her arms out to me.

'Can you hear me, Alan? I can see you . . . faintly still, but more plainly than below. Can you hear me? Then come to me.'

I quivered with desire for her . . . to eat and drink of her. But the voice of Dahut was in my ears, not to be disobeyed—'Eat and drink . . . *when* I bid you.'

I knew that the hunger must grow stronger, the thirst more consuming, before I could be loosed from that command. This so that only all the life of Helen could appease the hunger and slake the thirst. So that feeding, drinking . . . I killed her.

I whispered: 'I hear you.'

'I hear you, darling. Come to me.'

'I cannot come to you—not yet. My thirst and hunger for you must grow greater . . . so that when I come to you—you die.'

She dimmed the lights; raised her arms and loosed her hair so that it fell in shining red-gold ringlets almost to her waist. She asked:

'What keeps you from me? From me who loves you . . . from me whom you love?'

'Dahut . . . you know that.'

'Beloved—I do not know that. It is not true. None can keep you from me if I truly love you and if you truly love me. Both are true . . . and I say to you come to me, beloved . . . take me.'

I made no answer; I could not. Nor could I go to her. And more ravenous grew the hunger, more maddening the thirst.

She said: 'Alan, think only that. Think only that we love. That none can keep us from each other. Think only that. Do you understand me?'

I whispered: 'Yes.' And tried to think only that while the hunger and the thirst for her . . . for the life of her . . . were two starved hounds straining at the leash.

She said: 'Darling, can you see me? See me clearly?'

I whispered: 'Yes.'

She said: 'Then look . . . and come to me.'

She raised her arms again, and slipped from her dress; drew off slippers and stockings. She let fall from her the silken sheath that remained. She stood facing me, all lovely, all desirable, wholly human. She threw back her hair uncovering her white breasts . . . her eyes were golden pools of love that held no shame. . . .

'Take me, beloved! Eat and drink of me!'

I strained against the fetters that held me; strained against them as a soul led up from Hell to the gates of Paradise would strain to break its bonds and enter.

'She has no power over you. None can keep us apart . . . come to me, beloved.'

The fetters broke . . . I was in her arms. . . .

Shadow that I was, I could feel her soft arms around

me . . . feel the warmth of her breast pressing me closer, closer . . . feel her kisses on my shadowy lips. I merged with her. I ate and drank of her . . . of her life . . . and felt her life streaming through me . . . melting the icy venom of the shadow hounds. . . .

Releasing me from the shadow bondage. . . .

Releasing me from Dahut!

I stood beside the bed looking down on Helen. She lay, white and drained of life, half covered by her red-gold hair . . . and was she dead? Had Dahut conquered?

I bent shadowy head to her heart and listened and could hear no beat. Love and tenderness such as I had never known throbbed from me and covered her. And I thought: *This love must surely be stronger than death . . . must give back to her the life I have taken. . . .*

And still I could not hear her heart. . . .

Then despair followed the pulse of that love. And on its wake a hate colder than the venom of the shadow hounds.

Hate against Dahut.

Hate against the warlock who called himself her father.

Hate implacable, relentless, remorseless against both.

That hate grew. It merged with the life I had stolen from Helen. It lifted me. Upon its wings I was rushed away . . . away from Helen . . . back through the shadow-land. . . .

And awakened . . . shadow no more.

CHAPTER XX

THE LAST SACRIFICE

I LAY upon a wide, low bed in a tapestried room where an ancient lamp burned with a dim rose light. It was Dahut's room from which she had sent me forth as a shadow. My hands were crossed upon my breast, and something bound my wrists. I raised them and saw twined tight round them the witch-fetters—a twisted thread of pale-gold hair, the hair of Dahut. I broke them. My ankles were crossed and bound with the same fetters, and these I broke. I swung from the bed. Around me was a robe of the soft white cotton, a robe like that I had worn to the sacrifices. I tore it from me with loathing. There was a mirror over the dressing-table—on my face were the three marks of Dahut's whip-branding, no longer crimson but livid.

How long had I been in the shadowy land? Long enough to allow Ricori to return—but how much longer? More important, what time had elapsed since—Helen? A clock showed close to eleven. But was this still the same night? It might not be—shadow time and shadow space were alien. I had seemed to cover immense distances, and yet I had found Helen just outside de Keradel's gates. For I was sure that that old room had been in the house McCann had taken.

And clearly, this return of mine had not been expected by Dahut—at least not so soon. I reflected grimly that I always seemed to be a little ahead of

schedule so far as Dahut and her father were concerned.
. . . I reflected much more grimly that it had never
benefited me greatly. Nevertheless, it must mean
that her dark wisdom had its limits—that there had
been no shadowy spies to whisper to her my escape . . .
that she believed me still under her sorceries; still
obedient to her will; still held back by her command
until my lust for Helen had grown strong enough to
kill when loosed. . . .

Might that not also mean her purpose had failed . . .
that loosed too soon I had not killed . . . that Helen
was—alive?

The thought was like strong wine. I walked to the
door and saw that the heavy inside bars were down.
How could they have been dropped, since only I was
in the room? Of course . . . I was Dahut's prisoner,
and she wanted no tampering with my body when she
was not beside it. She had barred the door and made
use of the secret opening into my room to come and go.
Quite evidently she had considered the bars safe from
my helpless hands. I lifted them cautiously, and tried
the door. It was unlocked. I opened it as cautiously,
slowly, and stood peering out into the hall, listening.

It was then I first felt the unease, the trouble, the—
fear, of the old house. It was filled with fear. And
with wrath. It came to me not only from the shadowed
hall, but from all of the house. And suddenly it
seemed to be aware of me, and to focus itself upon me,
frantically . . . as though it were trying to tell me why
it was troubled and raging and afraid.

So sharp was the impression that I closed the door,
let one of the bars fall, and stood with my back to it.

The room was unhaunted, unafraid and shadowless, the faint rose light penetrating to every corner. . . .

The house invaded the room, striving to make articulate to me what it was that troubled it. It was as though the ghosts of all those who had lived and loved and died there were in revolt . . . appalled by something about to happen . . . something execrable, abhorrent . . . an evil something that had been conceived in the old house while its ghosts had watched, impotent to prevent . . . and now were appealing to me to avert it.

The house trembled. It was a tremor that began far beneath it and throbbed up through every timber and stone. Instantly that which had feared and had appealed to me withdrew; sweeping down to the source of the trembling—or so it seemed to me. Again the house trembled. Trembled in actuality, for the door at my back quivered. The trembling increased and became a shuddering under which the solid old hand-hewn joists creaked and groaned. There followed a distant, rhythmic thudding.

It ceased, and the old house quivered, then seemed to settle, and again the joists cracked and groaned. Then a stunned silence . . . and again the ghosts of the old house were around me, outrage in their wrath, panic in their fear, crying, crying to me to hear them . . . to understand them.

I could not understand them. . . . I walked to the window, and crouched there, peering out. It was a dark night, sultry and oppressive. There was a flashing of lightning from far beneath the horizon and faint distant rumbling of thunder. I went quickly about the room looking for some weapon, but could find none. My intention was to get into my room, clothe myself and then hunt down Dahut and de Keradel. Precisely what I was going to do after I found them I did not know—except to end their sorceries. All confusion as to whether these were sorceries or super-illusions was gone. They were evil realities belonging to a dark wisdom evilly used . . . none should be allowed to live to wield this evil power . . . and they were swiftly mounting to some atrocious, dreadful climax which must be thwarted at any cost. . . .

The ghosts of the old house were silent—I had got their message at last. They were silent, but they had lost none of their fear, and they were watching me. I went to the door. Some obscure impulse made me pick up the white robe and throw it round me. I stepped out into the hall. It was filled with shadows but I gave them no heed. Why should I, who myself had been a shadow? As I passed they clustered and crept behind me. And now I knew that the shadows too were afraid, like the old house . . . were cringing before some imminent and dreadful doom . . . like the ghosts, were beseeching me to avert it. . . .

From below came the murmur of voices, then that of de Keradel raised in anger, and following it, the laughter of Dahut—taunting, mocking, brittle with menace. I slipped to the head of the stairs. The lower hall was but dimly lighted. The voices came from the big living-room, and that the two were quarrelling was evident, but their words were inaudible. I crept down the stairs and flattened myself beside the edge of one of the heavy curtains which covered the doorway.

I heard de Keradel say, voice now level and controlled: 'I tell you that it is finished. There remains only the last sacrifice . . . which I perform to-night. I do not need you for that, my daughter. Nor after it is done shall I ever need you more. And there is nothing you can do to stop me. The end towards which I have been working all my life has been reached. He . . . has told me. Now . . . He . . . will become wholly manifest and ascend His throne. And I '—all de Keradel's egotism was in his voice, colossal, blasphemous—'and I shall sit beside Him. He . . . has promised me. The dark power which men in all ages and in all lands have sought—the power which Atlantis almost attained and that Ys drew but thinly from the Cairn—the power for which the medieval world so feebly groped—that power will be mine. In all its fullness. In all its unconquerable might. There was a rite none knew, and . . . He . . . has taught me it. No, I need you no longer, Dahut. Yet I am loth to lose you. And . . . He . . . is inclined to you. But you would have a price to pay.'

There was a little silence, and then Dahut's voice, very still: 'And that price, my father? '

'The blood of your lover.'

He waited for her answer—as did I, but she made none, and he said: 'I do not need it. I have pressed the paupers and have enough and to spare. But his would enrich it, and it would be acceptable to Him. He . . . has told me so. It would strengthen His draught. And . . . He . . . has asked for it.'

She asked, slowly: 'And if I refuse? '

'It will not save him, my daughter.'

266

Again he waited for her to speak, then said with simulated and malicious wonder:

' What—a Dahut of Ys to hesitate between her father and her lover! This man has a debt to pay, my daughter. An ancient one—since it was for one who bore his name that an ancestress of yours betrayed her father. Or was it you—Dahut? It is my duty to cancel that ancient wrong . . . lest, perchance, it should recur.'

She asked, quietly: ' And if I refuse—what of me? '

He laughed: ' How can I tell? Now, I am swayed by my fatherly impulses. But when I sit beside Him . . . what you may mean to me I cannot know. Perhaps—nothing.'

She asked: ' What shape will He assume? '

' Any or all. There is no shape He cannot take. Be assured that it will not be the inchoatic blackness which the dull minds of those who evoked Him . . . by the rites of the Cairn, forced upon Him. No, no—He . . . might even take the shape of your lover, Dahut. Why not? He . . . is inclined to you, my daughter.'

Now at this my skin grew cold, and the hatred I felt for him was like a band of hot iron around my temples, and I gathered myself to leap through the curtains and lock my hands round his throat. But the shadows held me back and whispered, and the ghosts of the old house whispered with them—' Not yet! Not yet! '

He said: ' Be wise, my daughter. Always this man has betrayed you. What are you with your shadows? What was Helene with her dolls? Children. Children playing with toys. With shadows and dolls! Pass from childhood, my daughter—give me the blood of your lover.'

She answered, surprisingly: 'A child! I had forgotten that I had ever been a child. I wish I was the child I was in Brittany—not what you have made of me.'

He made no reply to that. She seemed to wait for one; then said, tranquilly:

'So you ask for the blood of my lover? Well—you shall not have it.' She added, contemptuously: 'Evoke your Demon—without it.'

There was the crash of an overthrown chair. I drew the curtain a hair's breadth aside and peered in. De Keradel stood at the head of the table glaring at Dahut. But it was not the face or the body of the de Keradel I had known. His eyes were no longer pale blue . . . they were black, and his silvery hair seemed black and his body had grown . . . and long arms reached towards Dahut and long taloned fingers clutched at her.

She threw something down upon the table between her and him. I could not see what it was, but it sped like a small racing and shining wave straight at him. And he threw himself back from it, and stood trembling, eyes again blue but suffused with blood, and body shrunken.

'Beware, my father! Not yet do you sit on the throne with . . . Him. And I am still of the sea, my father. So beware!'

There was a shuffle of feet behind me. The blank-eyed butler was at my side. He started to kneel—and then the vagueness went from his eyes. He sprang at me, mouth opening to cry alarm. Before he could make a sound, my hands were around his throat, thumbs crushing into his larynx, my knee in his groin. With a strength I had never before known, I lifted him by his neck and held him up from the floor. His legs wrapped round me and I thrust my head under his chin and drew it sharply up. There was a faint snap and his body went limp. I carried it back along the hall and set it noiselessly on the floor. The whole brief struggle had been soundless. His eyes, blank enough now, stared up at me. I searched him. In his belt was a sheath, and in that a long, curved and razor-sharp knife.

Now I had a weapon. I rolled the body under a deep settle, stole back to the living-room and peeped through the curtains. It was empty, Dahut and de Keradel gone.

I stepped back for a moment into the cover of the curtains. I knew now what it was the ghosts of the old house had feared. Knew the meaning of the trembling and rhythmic thudding. The cavern of the sacrifices had been destroyed. It had served its purpose. How had de Keradel put it? . . . he had ' pressed the paupers ' and had enough and more than enough blood for the last sacrifice. Incongruously, a line came into my mind—' He is trampling out the winepress where the grapes of wrath are stored. . . .' Not so incongruous . . . I thought: *De Keradel has trampled out another winepress for the Gatherer's drink.* My blood was to have been mixed with it, but Dahut had refused to let it be!

I felt no gratitude towards her for that. She was a spider who thought her fly securely in her web, and

269

was resisting another spider's attempt to take it from her. That was all. But the fly was no longer in her web nor did it owe her for its release. If I felt increase of hatred for de Keradel, I felt no decrease of it for Dahut.

Nevertheless, what I had heard had changed the vague pattern of my vengeance. The design clarified. The shadows were wrong. Dahut must not die before her father. I had a better plan . . . it came to me from the Lord of Carnac whom Dahut thought had died in her arms . . . and he counselled me as he had counselled himself, long and long and long ago in ancient Ys.

I walked up the stairs. The door to my room was open. I switched on the lights, boldly.

Dahut was standing there, between me and the bed. She smiled—but her eyes did not. She walked towards me. I thrust the point of the long knife towards her. She stopped and laughed—but her eyes did not laugh. She said:

'You are so elusive, my beloved. You have such a gift for disappearance.'

'You have told me that before, Dahut. And '—I touched my cheek—'have even emphasized it.'

Her eyes misted, welled, and tears were on her cheeks.

'You have much to forgive—but so have I, Alan.'

Well, that was true enough.

'. . . Beware . . . beware Dahut. . . .'

'Where did you get your knife, Alan?'

A practical question that steadied me; I answered it as practically: 'From one of your men whom I killed.'

'And would you kill me with it—if I came close?'

270

'Why not, Dahut? You sent me as a shadow into the shadowy land and I have learned its lesson.'

'What was that lesson, Alan?'

'To be merciless.'

'But I am not merciless, Alan—else you would not be here.'

'Now I know you lie, Dahut. It was not you who released me from that bondage.'

She said: 'I did not mean that . . . nor do I lie . . . and I am tempted to try you, Alan. . . .'

She came towards me, slowly. I held the point of the knife in readiness against her coming. She said:

'Kill me if you want to. I have not much love for life. You are all that I love. If you will not love me— kill me.'

She was close; so close that the point of the knife touched her breast. She said:

'Thrust—and end it.'

My hand dropped.

'I cannot kill you, Dahut!'

Her eyes softened, her face grew tender—but triumph lurked under the tenderness. She rested her hands on my shoulders; then kissed the whip-welts one by one, saying:

'By this kiss I forgive . . . and by this I forgive . . . and by this I forgive. . . .' She held her lips up to me. 'Now kiss me, Alan—and with that kiss say that you forgive me.'

I kissed her, but I did not say that I forgave, nor did I let fall the knife. She trembled in my arms and clung to me and whispered:

'Say it . . . say it. . . .'

I pushed her away from me and laughed.

'Why are you so eager for forgiveness, Dahut? What do you fear that makes my forgiveness so desirable before your father kills me?'

She asked: 'How did you know he means to kill you?'

'I heard him say so when he was making that pleasant little demand for my blood not long ago. Bargaining with you for me. Promising you a substitute who would be far more satisfactory.' Again I laughed. 'Is my forgiveness a necessary part of that incarnation?'

She said, breathlessly: 'If you heard that, you must also know that I would not give you to him.'

I lied: 'I do not. Just then your servant forced me to kill him. When I was free to resume my eavesdropping—returned, in fact, to cut your father's throat before he could cut mine—you and he had gone. I supposed the bargain closed. Father and daughter reunited and of one purpose—setting forth to prepare the funeral meats—myself, Dahut—to set out the marriage tables. Thrift, thrift, Dahut!'

She winced under my mockery; whitened. She said, strangled: 'I made no bargain. I would not let him have you.'

'Why not?'

She said: 'Because I love you.'

'But why this insistence upon my forgiveness?'

'Because I love you. Because I want to wipe away the past. Begin afresh, beloved. . . .'

For a moment I had the queer feeling of double memory; that I had acted this scene before in minutest detail, had heard the same lines; and realized I had in that dream of ancient Ys, if dream it had been. And now, as then, she whispered piteously, despairingly:

'You do not believe me . . . beloved, what can I do to make you believe?'

I answered: 'Choose between your father—and me.'

She said: 'But I have chosen, beloved. I have told you . . .' Again she whispered: 'How can I make him believe?'

I answered: 'End his—sorceries.'

She said, contemptuously: 'I do not fear him. And I no longer fear that which he evokes.'

I said: 'But I do. End his—sorceries.'

She caught the pause this time, and its significance. Her eyes dilated, and for seconds she was silent, studying me. She said, slowly:

'There is but one way to end them.'

I made no comment on that.

She came to me and drew my head down to her and looked deep into my eyes.

'If I do this . . . you will forgive me? You will love me? Never leave me . . . as once before you did . . . long and long and long ago, in Ys . . . when once before I chose between my father and you. . . ?'

'I will forgive you, Dahut. I will never leave you as long as you have life.'

That was true enough, but I closed every window of my mind so she might not glimpse the determination that was its source. And again, as it had been in Ys, I took her in my arms . . . and the lure of her lips and her body shook me and I felt my resolution weaken . . . but the life within me that had come from Helen was implacable, inexorable . . . hating Dahut as only one woman who loves a man can hate another who loves him. . . .

273

She loosed my arms from round her. 'Dress, and
wait for me here.' She passed through the door.

I dressed, but I kept the long knife close.

The tapestry that concealed the secret panel wavered,
and she was in the room. She wore an archaic robe of
green; her sandals were green; her girdle was not golden
but of clear green stones that held the shifting gleam of
waves, and a wreath of green sea flowers bound her hair.
Upon her wrist was the silver bracelet set with the black
stone that bore in crimson the trident symbol which was
the summoning name of the sea-god. She looked like a
sea-god's daughter . . . maybe she was. . . .

I felt my resolution weakening again until she came
close and I could see clearly her face. It was unsmiling,
and the mouth was cruel, and the hell sparks were
beginning their dance in her eyes.

She lifted her arms and touched my eyes with her
fingers, closing them. The touch of her fingers was like
that of cold sea-spray.

'Come!' she said.

The ghosts of the old house were whispering: '*Go
with her . . . but beware!* . . .'

The shadows were whispering: '*Go with her . . . but
beware!* . . .'

. . . *Beware Dahut.* . . . My hand tightened on the
knife-hilt as I followed her.

We went out of the old house. It was strange how
plainly I could see. The sky was heavy with clouds,
the air murky. I knew the night must be dark indeed,
yet every stone and bush and tree stood out plain, as
though by some light of its own. Dahut led me by a

dozen paces, nor could I lessen that distance, try as I might. She moved like a wave, and around her played a faint nimbus of palest golden-green like the phosphorescence that sometimes clothes a wave moving through darkness.

The shadows fluttered and swayed around us, interlacing, flowing in and out of each other, like shadows cast by some great tree fretted by a fitful wind. The shadows followed us, and flanked us, and swayed before us—but they shrank from Dahut, and never was there one between her and me.

There was a glow beyond the oaks where were the standing stones. It was not the wan gleam of the corposants. It was a steady, ruddy glow as from still fires. I heard no chanting.

She did not go towards the oaks. She took a way that led upward to the ridge of rocks hiding the standing stones from the water. Soon the path topped the ridge, and the open sea lay before me. It was a sullen sea and dark, with long, slow swells breaking sluggishly on the ledges.

The path climbed steeply over a cliff which lifted above the waves a full two hundred feet. And suddenly Dahut was on its crest, poised on its verge, arms outstretched to the sea. From her lips came a call, low and inhumanly sweet; in it the plaintiveness of the gull's cry, the singing of waves over unfathomable, unspoiled deeps, the chant of deep-sea winds. It was a voice of the sea transmuted goldenly in a woman's throat, but losing no inhuman quality and taking on no human one.

It seemed to me that the surges stopped as though listening while that cry went forth.

Again she sent the call . . . and once again. And after that she cupped her hands to mouth and cried a word . . . a name.

From far out at sea there came a roaring answer. A long white line of foam sped from the darkness, a great comber whose top was the tossing manes of hundreds of white horses. It raced shouting against the ridge and broke.

A column of spume swept up and touched her outstretched hands. It seemed to me that something passed to it from her hands, and that as the spume fell something within it glittered silver with a glint of scarlet.

I climbed up to her. There was no hint of tenderness now in her eyes or face. Only triumph . . . and her eyes were violet flames. She lifted a fold of her dress, veiling eyes and face from me.

The bracelet of Ys was gone from her arm!

She beckoned, and I followed her. We skirted the ridge, and ever the ruddy glow grew brighter. I saw that the surges were no longer sullen, but that great waves marched with us, clamouring; white banners of foam streaming; white manes of the sea-horses tossing.

The path ran now below the crest of the ridge. Ahead, on the landward side, was another upthrust of rock; and here again she waited for me. She stood with face averted, still covered by the fold. She pointed to the rock. She said:

'Climb—and see.' Once more the spray-cold fingers touched my eyes. 'And hear'—they touched my ears.

She was gone.

I climbed the rock. I scrambled over its top——

Strong hands caught my arms, pinioning them behind

me, forcing me to my knees. I twisted and looked into the face of McCann. He was bending, his face close to mine, peering as though he found it difficult to see me clearly.

I cried: 'McCann!'

He swore, incredulously; released me. Some one else was on the rock—a lean and dark man with thin, ascetic face and snow-white hair. He, too, was leaning and peering at me as though he found it difficult to see me. That was odd, for I could see them both clearly. I knew him . . . he had been in the old room where my shadow search for Helen had ended . . . Ricori.

McCann was stammering: 'Caranac—Caranac!'

I whispered, steeling myself against any blow: 'Helen?'

'She lives.' It was Ricori who answered.

My whole body went weak with reaction so that I would have fallen had he not caught me. A new fear took me.

'But *will* she live?'

He said: 'She has had a—strange experience. When we left her she was fully conscious. Steadily growing stronger. Her brother is with her. You are all she needs. We are here to take you back to her.'

I said: 'No. Not until——'

Gale blast that closed my mouth as though a hand had struck it. Crash of wave against the ridge, shaking it. I felt the spray of it on my face, and it was like the whip of Dahut and it was like the cold fingers of her on my eyes. . . .

And suddenly McCann and Ricori seemed unreal and shadowy. And suddenly I seemed to see the shining body of Dahut swaying onward upon the path between the sea and the ridge . . . and I heard a voice in my heart—the Lord of Carnac's voice—and mine: *How can I kill her, evil as I know her to be.* . . .

Ricori's voice . . . how long had he been talking? . . . 'and so when last night you did not appear, I used, as you had suggested—my judgment. After we were assured of her safety, we set out. We persuaded the guardians of the gates to let us enter. They will guard no more gates. We saw the lights, and we thought that where they were you would most likely be. We distributed our men, and McCann and I came by chance upon this excellent place for observation. We saw neither you nor the Demoiselle Dahut . . .'

. . . *Dahut!* . . . another wave broke upon the rock, and shook it, then surged back shouting . . . shouting —*Dahut!* Another gust roared over the rock . . . roaring—*Dahut!*

Ricori was saying: 'They are down there, awaiting our signal——'

I interrupted, attention abruptly centred: 'Signal for what?'

He said: 'To stop what is going on down there.'

He pointed towards the inward edge of the rock, and I saw that its edge was outlined black against the depth of the ruddy light. I walked to the edge and looked down——

The Cairn was plain before me. I thought: *How strangely close it seems . . . how stark the monoliths stand out!*

It was as though the Cairn were but a few yards away . . . de Keradel so close that I could reach out my hand

and touch him. I knew that there were many of the standing stones between me and the Cairn, and that it must be a full thousand feet away. Yet not only could I see the Cairn as though I were beside it, I could see within it as well.

Strange, too, although the wind was roaring overhead and whipping us on the rock, that the fires before the Cairn burned steadily; flickering only when those who fed them sprinkled them from the black ewers they carried . . . and that although the wind came from the sea, the smoke of the fires streamed straight against it.

And strange how silent it was down there among the monoliths when steadily grew the shouting and the clamour of the sea . . . nor did the flashing of the lightning marching ever higher dim the fires, nor did the rumbling thunder invade the silence of the plain more than did the clamour of the combers. . . .

Those who fed the fires were not now in white but in red. And de Keradel was clothed in a robe of red instead of the white robe of the sacrifices. He wore the black belt and the cincture, but the shifting symbols on them glittered scarlet . . . not silver. . . .

There were ten of the fires, in a semicircle between the three altars and the monoliths which faced the threshold of the Cairn. Each was a little more than a man's height, and they burned with a cone-shaped, still flame. From the peak of each arose a column of smoke. They were as thick as the arm of a man, these columns, and having risen twice the height of the fires they curved, and then streamed straight towards the threshold of the Cairn. They were like ten black arteries of which the ten fires were the hearts, and they were threaded with crimson filaments, like little fiery veins.

The blackened hollowed stone was hidden by a greater fire which burned not only red but black. Nor was this, like the others, a still flame. It pulsed with slow and rhythmic beat—as though in truth it were a heart. Between it and the great slab of granite, upon which he had beaten in the breasts of the sacrifices, stood de Keradel.

There was something lying upon the stone of sacrifice, covering it. At first I thought it a man, a giant, lying there. Then I saw that it was an immense vessel, strangely shaped, and hollow.

A vat.

I could look into this vat. It was half-filled with a clotted, reddish-black fluid over the surface of which ran tiny flames. Not pale and dead like the corposants, but crimson and filled with evil life. It was to this vat that the blank-eyed men who fed the fires came to have their ewers refilled. And it was from it that de Keradel took that which he sprinkled upon the pulsing fire . . . and his hands and his arms were red with it.

On the threshold of the Cairn was another vessel, a huge bowl like a shallow baptismal font. It was filled, and over its surface ran the crimson flames.

The smoke from the lesser fires, the ten crimson-threaded arteries, met in the thicker column that arose from the throbbing fire, mingled with it, and streamed as one into the Cairn.

The silence of the plain was broken by a whimpering, a faint wailing, and up from the bases of the monoliths shadows began to rise. They lifted, as I had first seen them, to their knees . . . and then they were wrenched from the earth, and whimpering, wailing, were sucked into the Cairn . . . beating about it . . . fighting to escape.

Within the Cairn was the Gatherer . . . the Blackness.

From the first I had known It was there. It was no longer shapeless, nebulous—part of an infinitely greater Something that dwelt in space and beyond space. The Gatherer was breaking loose . . . taking form. The small crimson flames were running through It . . . like corpuscles of evil blood. It was condensing, steadily becoming material.

The font on the threshold of the Cairn was empty.

De Keradel filled it from the vat . . . and again . . . and again.

The Gatherer drank from the font and fed upon the shadows, and upon the smoke of the fires which were fed by blood. And steadily It assumed shape.

I stepped back, covering my eyes.

Ricori said: 'What do you see? All I see are men in red, far away, who feed fires—and another who stands before the house of stones . . . what do you see, Caranac?'

I said: 'I see Hell opening.'

I forced myself to look again at that which was being spawned from the Cairn's stone womb . . . and stood, unable now to look away. . . . I heard a voice, my own voice, screaming:

'*Dahut . . . Dahut . . .* before it is too late!'

As though in answer, there was a lull in the clamour of the sea. Upon the ridge at our left appeared a point of brilliant green light . . . whether far away or near I could not tell with that strange witch-sight Dahut had given me. It became an oval of brilliant emerald. . . .

It became—Dahut!

Dahut . . . clothed with pale green sea-fires, her eyes like violet sea-pools and wide—so wide that they were ringed with white; her slim black brows a bar above them; her face white as foam and cruel and mocking; her hair like spindrift of silver. Far away or not, she seemed as close to me as did de Keradel. It was as if she stood just above the Cairn . . . could reach out, as I, and touch de Keradel. To me that night, as in the shadowy land, there was no such thing as distance.

I caught Ricori's wrist, pointed and whispered: 'Dahut!'

He said: 'I saw far away and dimly a shining figure. I thought it a woman. With your hand upon me, I seem to see her more plainly. What do *you* see, Caranac?'

I said: 'I see Dahut. She is laughing. Her eyes are the eyes of no woman . . . nor is her face. She is laughing, I say . . . can't you hear her, Ricori? She calls to de Keradel . . . how sweet her voice and how merciless . . . like the sea! She calls—"My father, I am here!" He sees her . . . the Thing in the Cairn is aware of her . . . de Keradel cries to her—"Too late, my daughter!" He is mocking, contemptuous . . . but the Thing in the Cairn is not. It strains . . . towards completion. Dahut calls again—"Is my bride-groom born? Is the labour done? Your midwifery successful? My bed-fellow delivered . . ." Can't you hear, Ricori? It is as though she stood beside me. . . .'

He said: 'I hear nothing.'

I said: 'I do not like this jesting, Ricori. It is— dreadful. The Thing in the Cairn does not like it . . . although de Keradel laughs . . . It reaches out from the Cairn . . . to the vat on the stone of sacrifice . . . It drinks . . . It grows . . . God! . . . *Dahut! . . . Dahut!*'

The shining figure raised hand as though she heard . . . and bent towards me . . . and I felt the touch of her fingers on eyes and ears . . . her lips on mine. . . .

She faced the sea and threw wide her arms. She cried the Name, softly—and the sea-winds stilled . . . again, like one who summons as of right—and the shouting of the combers waned . . . a third time, jubilantly.

Shouting of the combers, thunder of the surges, roaring of the winds, all the clamour of sea and air, arose in a mighty diapason. It melted into chaotic uproar, elemental bellowing. And suddenly all the sea was covered with the tossing manes of the white sea-horses . . . armies of the white horses of the sea . . . the white horses of Poseidon . . . line upon endless line racing out of the darkness of ocean and charging against the shore.

Beyond the lower line of the ridge between that high rock on which stood Dahut and this high rock on which stood I, arose a mountain of water . . . lifting, lifting swiftly, yet deliberately. Changing shape as it lifted ever higher . . . gathering power as it lifted. Up it lifted and up; a hundred feet, two hundred feet above the ridge. It paused, and its top flattened. Its top became a gigantic hammer. . . .

And beyond it I seemed to see a vast and misty shape towering to the clouds, its head wreathed with the clouds and crowned with the lightnings. . . .

The hammer swung down . . . down upon the Thing in the Cairn . . . down upon de Keradel and the red-clad, blank-eyed men . . . down upon the monoliths.

The Cairn and the monoliths were covered with waters, boiling, spouting, smashing at the standing stones. Uprooting, overturning them.

For an instant I saw the evil fires glare through the waters. Then they were gone.

For an instant I heard an unearthly shrilling from the stone womb of the Cairn, and saw a Blackness veined with crimson flames writhing under the hammer stroke of the waters, struggling in the myriad arms of the waters. Then it, too, was gone.

The waters rushed back. They licked up at us as they passed, and a wave swirled round us knee-high. It dropped . . . chuckling.

Again the mountain arose, hammer-topped. Again it swept over the ridge and smote the Cairn and the standing stones. And this time the waters rushed on so that the oaks fell before them . . . and once more they retreated . . . and once more they lifted and struck and swept on . . . and now I knew that the old house with all its ghosts was gone. . . .

Through all, the sea-fire shape of Dahut had remained unmoved, untouched. I had heard her merciless laughter above the bellowing of the sea and the crashing of the hammer strokes.

Back rushed the last waters. Dahut held her arms out to me, calling: 'Alain . . . come to me, Alain! '

Clearly could I see the path between her and me. It was as though she were close—close. But I knew she was not and that it was the witch-sight she had given me that made it seem so. I said:

'Good luck, McCann. Good luck, Ricori.'

'. . . Alain . . . come to me, Alain. . . .'

My hand dropped on the hilt of the long knife. I shouted: 'Coming—Dahut! '

McCann gripped me. Ricori struck down at his hands. He said: 'Let him go.'

'. . . Alain . . . come to me. . . .'

I stopped at the edge of the rock. The waters were rushing back, over the ridge. A swirl swept out. It coiled around Dahut to the waist. It lifted her . . . high and high. . . .

And instantly from over her and from every side of her a cloud of shadows swept upon her . . . striking at her with shadowy hands . . . thrusting at her, hurling themselves at her, pushing her back and down . . . into the sea.

I saw incredulity flood her face; then outraged revolt; then terror—and then despair.

The wave crashed back into the sea, and with it went Dahut, the shadows pouring after her. . . .

I heard myself crying: 'Dahut . . . Dahut! '

There was a prolonged flaring of the lightning. By it I saw Dahut . . . face upturned, hair floating around her like a silver net, her eyes wide and horror-filled and . . . dying.

The shadows were all around her and over her . . . pushing her down . . . down. . . .

The witch-sight was fading from my eyes, the witch-hearing stilling in my ears. Before that sight went, I saw de Keradel lying on the threshold of the Cairn, crushed beneath one of its great stones. The stone had pulped breast and heart of de Keradel as he had pulped the breasts and hearts of the sacrifices. There was only his head and his arms . . . his face upturned, dead eyes wide and filled with hate . . . dead hands held high in imprecation and in—appeal. . . .

The Cairn was flat, and of the standing stones not one was erect. . . .

Witch-sight and witch-hearing were gone. The land was dark save for the glare of the lightning. The sea was dark save for the foaming tops of the waves. Their shouting was the voice of waves—and nothing more. The roaring of the wind was the voice of the wind—and nothing more.

Dahut was dead. . . .

I asked Ricori: 'What did you see?'

'Three waves. They destroyed all that was below. They killed my men——'

'I saw much more than that, Ricori. Dahut is dead. It is ended, Ricori. Dahut is dead and her witchcraft ended. We must wait here till morning. Then we can go back . . . back to Helen. . . .'

Dahut was dead. . . .

She was dead as of old, long and long and long ago in Ys . . . by her shadows and by her wickednesses . . . by the sea . . . and by me.

286

Would I have killed her with the long knife if I had reached her before the wave? . . .

The cycle had been reborn . . . and it had ended as it had of old, long and long and long ago . . . in Ys.

The sea had cleansed this place of her sorceries as it had cleansed Ys of them in that long and long and long ago.

Had there been a Helen in Carnac when I set forth from Carnac to Ys to slay Dahut?

Had she cleansed me of the memories of Dahut when I returned to her?

Could—Helen?

TOM STACEY REPRINTS

This series makes available again some of the best books by the best authors of our time, priced at £1.80 each except where otherwise stated. Already published are:

Michael Arlen
  THESE CHARMING PEOPLE

H. C. Bailey
  THE SULLEN SKY MYSTERY
  DEAD MAN'S SHOES

Francis Beeding
  THE LEAGUE OF DISCONTENT
  THE BIG FISH

Hilaire Belloc
  THE FOUR MEN
  DANTON (£2.50)

Earl Derr Biggers
  CHARLIE CHAN CARRIES ON
  THE CHINESE PARROT

Max Brand
  SILVERTIP
  SILVERTIP'S TRAP

Edgar Rice Burroughs
  AT THE EARTH'S CORE
  PELLUCIDAR
  THE MOON MAID
  TARZAN'S QUEST
  THE LAND THAT TIME FORGOT

John Dickson Carr
  BELOW SUSPICION

Robert W. Chambers
  THE SLAYER OF SOULS

Richard Dalby
  THE SORCERESS IN STAINED GLASS (£2.00)

Clemence Dane & Helen Simpson
  ENTER SIR JOHN

Carter Dickson
  THE JUDAS WINDOW
  MURDER IN THE SUBMARINE ZONE
  THE TEN TEACUPS
  THE UNICORN MURDERS

Lord Dunsany
  THE KING OF ELFLAND'S DAUGHTER

John Meade Falkner
  THE LOST STRADIVARIUS

Edna Ferber
  CIMARRON
  SHOW BOAT

Peter Fleming
  THE SIEGE AT PEKING

Erle Stanley Gardner
  THE CASE OF THE VELVET CLAWS

Francis Gérard
  FATAL FRIDAY
  SECRET SCEPTRE

David Graeme
  MONSIEUR BLACKSHIRT
  THE VENGEANCE OF MONSIEUR
    BLACKSHIRT

H. Rider Haggard
  THE ANCIENT ALLAN
  THE GHOST KINGS
  MORNING STAR
  RED EVE

Michael Harrison
  MURDER IN THE RUE ROYALE (£2.00)

Macdonald Hastings
  CORK IN BOTTLE
  CORK ON THE WATER

Christopher Hollis
  DEATH OF A GENTLEMAN

Anthony Hope
  THE HEART OF PRINCESS OSRA

Ronald Kirkbride
  THE KING OF THE VIA VENETO
  STILL THE HEART SINGS

John Lambourne
  THE KINGDOM THAT WAS

C. A. Lejeune
  THANK YOU FOR HAVING ME

Alan Le May
  GUNSIGHT TRAIL

Denis Mackail
  GREENERY STREET

Helen McCloy
  TWO-THIRDS OF A GHOST

John P. Marquand
  STOPOVER: TOKYO
  LAST LAUGH, MR MOTO

A. E. W. Mason
  CLEMENTINA
  FIRE OVER ENGLAND

A. Merritt
  CREEP SHADOW CREEP
  BURN WITCH BURN

Gladys Mitchell
  THE RISING OF THE MOON
  ST. PETER'S FINGER

Clarence E. Mulford
  BAR-20
  THE COMING OF CASSIDY
  HOPALONG CASSIDY
  JOHNNY NELSON

Talbot Mundy
  KING, OF THE KHYBER RIFLES

Frank L. Packard
  THE ADVENTURES OF JIMMIE DALE (£2.00)

Stuart Palmer
  THE PUZZLE OF THE BRIAR PIPE

Melville Davisson Post
  UNCLE ABNER

Clayton Rawson
  DEATH FROM A TOP HAT
  NO COFFIN FOR THE CORPSE

Sax Rohmer
  BROOD OF THE WITCH-QUEEN
  THE GOLDEN SCORPION
  THE YELLOW CLAW
  THE MYSTERY OF DR. FU-MANCHU

R. C. Sherriff
  THE FORTNIGHT IN SEPTEMBER

Lady Eleanor Smith
  THE MAN IN GREY

G. B. Stern
   THE YOUNG MATRIARCH (£2.50)
Phil Stong
   STATE FAIR
Rex Stout
   CRIME ON HER HANDS
   RED THREADS
   SOME BURIED CAESAR
   WHERE THERE'S A WILL
Angela Thirkell
   THE HEADMISTRESS
   THE OLD BANK HOUSE (£2.00)
S. S. Van Dine
   THE BENSON MURDER CASE
Daniele Varè
   THE MAKER OF HEAVENLY TROUSERS

Edgar Wallace
   LIEUTENANT BONES
   SANDI THE KING-MAKER
Alec Waugh
   JILL SOMERSET (£2.00)
P. C. Wren
   ACTION AND PASSION (£2.25)
   FORT IN THE JUNGLE
S. Fowler Wright
   THE SIEGE OF MALTA (£3.50)
Dornford Yates
   SHE PAINTED HER FACE
Philip Yordan
   MAN OF THE WEST

CHILDREN'S BOOKS

John Bennett
   MASTER SKYLARK (£1.80)
Frances Hodgson Burnett
   RACKETTY-PACKETTY HOUSE (£1.30)
   THE COZY LION (£1.30)
Thornton W. Burgess
   OLD MOTHER WEST WIND (£1.70)
   MOTHER WEST WIND'S CHILDREN (£1.70)
Austin Clare
   THE CARVED CARTOON (£1.80)
Mrs. Molesworth
   THE TAPESTRY ROOM (£1.50)

Howard Pyle
   THE MERRY ADVENTURES OF ROBIN
   HOOD (£2.25)
E. M. Silvanus
   THE PELICAN AND THE KANGAROO (£1.80)
G. B. Stern
   THE UGLY DACHSHUND (£1.20)
Phil Stong
   THE HIRED MAN'S ELEPHANT (£1.40)
Charlotte M. Yonge
   UNKNOWN TO HISTORY (£2.20)

Tom Stacey Reprints Ltd
28–29 Maiden Lane, London WC2E 7JP